DO NOT [barcode: D0561628]
SON OF PARADISE!

Her voice froze Eric's brain, her words thundered in his skull. At the bottom of the darkness she sat on an onyx throne and laughed. Strands of ebony hair swirled languidly up from her head and snaked about his tumbling body.

Poor fool. You know a secret you must not share.

Her black tresses slid over his body, binding him, arousing him in a strange and frightening way. She laughed again, voluptuously evil, sexual and deadly.

You are a warrior, my warrior.

"Who are you?" Eric shouted, writhing in the weblike strands that held him.

I will remake you in my image, and you will take the place of the creature you helped to kill.

He saw it then, the small horn that curled upward from her forehead. She smiled and parted her lips, revealing tiny fangs.

Eric screamed. It was not his blood she wanted. It was his soul. . . .

ROC (0451)

ENCHANTING REALMS

☐ **THE EYE OF THE HUNTER by Dennis L. McKiernan.** From the best-selling author of *The Iron Tower* triology and *The Silver Call* duology—a new epic of Mithgar. The comet known as the Eye of the Hunter is riding through Mithgar's skies again, bringing with it destruction and the much dreaded master, Baron Stoke. (452682—$5.99)

☐ **MOONRUNNER: GATHERING DARKNESS by Jane Toombs.** His family was cursed by the power of the beast—could he protect them from their own dark magic and the stalkers who sought their lives? (452372—$4.99)

☐ **A SWORD FOR A DRAGON by Christopher Rowley.** The most loyal bunch of dragon warriors and human attendants ever to march on campaign had just been re-formed when Bazil Broketail and his human boy, Relkin, returned from a search for Bazil's beloved green dragoness. But when the Goddess of Death marks them both as her chosen victims for capture and sacrifice, they must face unexpected danger.

(452356—$5.99)

☐ **THE ARCHITECTURE OF DESIRE by Mary Gentle.** Discover a time and a place ruled by the Hermetic magic of the Renaissance, by secret, almost forgotten Masonic rites, a land divided between the royalists loyal to Queen Carola and the soldiers who follow the Protector-General Olivia in this magnificent sequel to *Rats and Gargoyles*. (452348—$19.00)

Prices slightly higher in Canada.

Buy them at your local bookstore or use this convenient coupon for ordering.

NEW AMERICAN LIBRARY
P.O. Box 999 – Dept. #17109
Bergenfield, New Jersey 07621

Please send me the books I have checked above.
I am enclosing $_____ (please add $2.00 to cover postage and handling).
Send check or money order (no cash or C.O.D.'s) or charge by Mastercard or VISA (with a $15.00 minimum). Prices and numbers are subject to change without notice.

Card #_____ Exp. Date _____
Signature_____
Name_____
Address_____
City _____ State _____ Zip Code _____

For faster service when ordering by credit card call **1-800-253-6476**

Allow a minimum of 4-6 weeks for delivery. This offer is subject to change without notice.

BROTHERS
OF THE
DRAGON

by

Robin Wayne Bailey

A ROC BOOK

ROC
Published by the Penguin Group
Penguin Books USA Inc., 375 Hudson Street,
New York, New York 10014, U.S.A.
Penguin Books Ltd, 27 Wrights Lane,
London W8 5TZ, England
Penguin Books Australia Ltd, Ringwood,
Victoria, Australia
Penguin Books Canada Ltd, 10 Alcorn Avenue,
Toronto, Ontario, Canada M4V 3B2
Penguin Books (N.Z.) Ltd, 182–190 Wairau Road,
Auckland 10, New Zealand

Penguin Books Ltd, Registered Offices:
Harmondsworth, Middlesex, England

First published by Roc, an imprint of New American Library,
a division of Penguin Books USA Inc.

First Printing, June, 1993
10 9 8 7 6 5 4 3 2 1

Copyright © Byron Preiss Visual Publications, Inc., 1993
Cover art copyright © Louis Harrison, 1993
All rights reserved

 REGISTERED TRADEMARK—MARCA REGISTRADA

Printed in the United States of America

Without limiting the rights under copyright reserved above, no part of
this publication may be reproduced, stored in or introduced into a
retrieval system, or transmitted, in any form, or by any means (elec-
tronic, mechanical, photocopying, recording, or otherwise), without the
prior written permission of both the copyright owner and the above publisher of this book.

BOOKS ARE AVAILABLE AT QUANTITY DISCOUNTS WHEN USED TO PROMOTE
PRODUCTS OR SERVICES. FOR INFORMATION PLEASE WRITE TO PREMIUM
MARKETING DIVISION, PENGUIN BOOKS USA INC., 375 HUDSON STREET, NEW
YORK, NEW YORK 10014.

If you purchased this book without a cover you should be aware that this
book is stolen property. It was reported as "unsold and destroyed" to the
publisher and neither the author nor the publisher has received any
payment for this "stripped book."

For Marlys Davis and Cory Mills;
For all the gang in Kindred Spirits;
For Jerry Miller;
For Bobby behind the bar;
and for Diana,
who counted forty-six shooting stars

Chapter One

THE wind sighed down out of the dark mountains and whispered through the pines and tall maples that filled the Catskill wilderness. Leaves and needles rustled softly, creating a susserant music that rose for a brief moment over the constant sound of the thin waterfall at the far end of the narrow, gloomy clove and over the trickling of the black stream that cut through its lush heart.

Towering sandstone walls rose on either side of the gorgelike clove. High above, tenuous gray clouds, like vaporous angels, raced across the ribbon of night sky that could be seen from the clove's deep bottom. Directly overhead, the summer triangle shone, bright Vega and Deneb and Altair. The swelling light of a full moon, though only half visible above the eastern rim, overwhelmed the paler stars.

Eric Podlowsky sat quietly on a tiny camp stool by the side of the stream, admiring the sky and listening to the songs of the night. He had not enjoyed a moment like this for some time. He opened his red plaid shirt and enjoyed the feel of the wind on his skin. It was unseasonably warm for Green County in May, but that only made the nights, which otherwise would have been cool in the mountains, more comfortable.

The wind blew a bit more forcefully for a moment, then settled again to a soft breeze. The nylon-taffeta tent, big enough for two, fluttered cheerily but settled down once the wind died. Eric reached down and flipped the off switch on his battery-powered Coleman lantern and drew out a second can of Budweiser from the small cooler at his left side. A soft hiss sounded as he popped the top.

The stars overhead shone a little clearer without the lantern, but Eric paid them little attention. He scanned the eastern rim of the clove for some sign of his crazy brother. It was Robert's fault that they'd gotten lost; he was the one who had insisted that they veer off the marked trail. Eric didn't really care about that. They'd find their way again when it was daylight. Meanwhile, they had discovered this totally isolated clove. Such narrow gorges were common in the Catskills, favorite spots for campers and hikers. They were fun to explore.

But, there was no indication at all that anyone else had ever been here. There were no trails, no old campsites, no refuse. It was as if he'd found a totally virgin world. He felt privately glad that his brother had gotten them lost.

He glanced around for Robert, then remembered that he was alone. Robert was always getting up and taking off unexpectedly. One moment they were enjoying a prepackaged dinner together while they soaked their feet in the stream. The next minute Robert was up and grabbing for his shoes.

"Let's climb it," he'd said, staring at the eastern rock face as he tied the laces.

Eric had looked up as he put the trash from their meal back into a knapsack. "In the dark?" he'd answered. "Are you crazy?"

He should have known better than to ask. Rock climbing was a passion with Robert. One of many passions. His brother only winked at him before he melted into the night. *Melted* was the word for it, too. They both had grown up wandering the Catskill wilderness, and Robert could move more quietly through the woods than any man Eric had ever met.

Eric sat down on his camp stool again, feeling old, wishing he'd gone with his brother to climb the side of the clove. He was only thirty, five years Robert's senior, yet he'd had trouble keeping up with Robert on the trail. His feet and legs ached from the day's trek, and that annoyed him. He'd always figured his job as a mail carrier would keep him in shape.

He lifted the Budweiser, took a slow draft, and frowned at himself as he looked at the can. *Too damn much of this stuff,* he told himself. He poured the remainder out and crushed the can before stuffing it in the knapsack.

Eric sighed. In all, though, it had been a great day. He and Robert had been so close once, and he'd missed that closeness. The drive up from Manhattan along Highway 87 and the time they'd spent on the trail had given them the chance to regain that. Robert's late-night call to come pick him up at his Chelsea apartment and—even more—his suggestion that they take this hiking trip had surprised Eric. Fortunately, Eric had plenty of leave time from his postal job stored up.

He glanced toward the eastern rim again and

spied his brother. He shook his head with a mixture of awe, amusement, and worry. Little brother had always had such a flare for the dramatic.

Robert stood framed against the full moon, a black silhouette on an achingly pure white background. Slowly, with fluid grace, he balanced on his right foot and extended his left leg in a controlled side-kick. Simultaneously, he extended his left hand in a classic forefist strike.

Eric watched transfixed as Robert executed the forty-two movements of the Gankaku kata and then began them all over again. He had not seen his brother do kata in a long time. Once they had studied karate together, and judo too, but that seemed such a long time ago.

Eric rose languidly to his feet, never taking his eyes off Robert. When Robert reached the end of Gankaku and began the exercise yet again, Eric moved with him, tentatively at first, as he remembered the movements, then with greater surety. Crossed-forearms block, left middle level punch, right punch, pivot. His hiking boots tore at the thick grass. With a skill almost equaling his brother's, he executed the *nidan-geri* double kick, another crossed-forearms block, and another pivot.

It felt good to move out here in the darkness and the night air. With one eye on Robert, he matched his brother's movements and drew a deep, satisfied breath. From atop the clove's rim he heard the echo of his brother's *ki* shout. Eric, though, respected the clove's templelike silence and did his best to move without making any sound at all.

At the twenty-fifth movement of the kata, however, balanced on his left leg with his right foot tucked firmly behind his left knee, Eric froze.

Abruptly, he grinned. The grin widened as he abandoned his form and stared at his brother. He chuckled to himself, watching Robert continue flawlessly through the pattern.

Gankaku, Eric thought to himself. His brother still had the same bizarre sense of humor he'd always had. *Gankaku. Crane on a Rock.* That was the kata's name and its translation. He shook his head again, still grinning, as Robert, balanced on the clove's rim, flowed through the classic crane stance and into the next movement.

Eric sighed and sat down. He'd spent too much time teaching little kids and beginner housewives at the Dowdsville community center. His basics were still good, but his advanced skills had deteriorated. Robert, on the other hand, had continued to study, gotten so caught up in it that he'd eventually dropped out of his graduate program at New York University to spend a year touring the Orient. It was plain to see, even with only a silhouette to judge by, that his little brother had far surpassed him.

He wiped a bead of sweat from his forehead and reached into the cooler for another Budweiser. As he opened it, beer and foam gushed upward, and a frothy stream ran down the side of the can and over his hand to spill onto the grass between his feet. Eric barely noticed. He took a sip and watched his brother and the refulgent moon that climbed ever higher.

I should be jealous of you, Eric thought, as he stared at the silhouette that never seemed to be still. *I'm not, though. I just wish I'd done things differently.* He glanced up at the sky, finding the star formation called the summer triangle. The three corner stars shone beautifully.

He could have been somebody, like his brother. He'd gone to New York University too. Taken a degree in geology. But all the time there he'd felt smothered by the concrete and the filth and the sheer mass of humanity. It had been easy to flee back to the Catskills at the end of it, and in the Catskills he'd stayed. Hiding. That was the word, and he knew it now. He'd hidden from the world in these hills and mountains.

Seeing Robert brought all that home to him. Eric didn't think of himself as a failure—his self-pity didn't go that far—but he wasn't exactly a success either. He just felt like he was spinning his wheels, biding time while he delivered people's mail.

Robert, on the other hand, hadn't wasted any opportunity. He'd finished his degree and stayed in New York. He was an author now, with five books on the stands. He'd traveled to the far side of the world too. To Okinawa and Thailand and China and other magical places that Eric had only dreamed about.

Eric gazed upward again. He had a little trouble this time finding the summer triangle, but slowly it came into focus. He craned his neck back to see better and teetered off the camp stool onto his rump.

"Jesus!" someone exclaimed. Bewildered, Eric twisted toward the voice as Robert bent down to help him up. He pointed to the cans piled on the ground by the overturned stool. "That's a whole six-pack!" Robert said, proving to Eric that he had made good use of his degree and could count. "Just since I left! You're drunk, big brother!"

"Not drunk," Eric answered quietly. He stared at the pile of cans. He didn't remember drinking that many. He hadn't seen Robert climb down, either. He blinked. "Just wobbly," he continued as he righted the camp stool and sat down again. "I was looking at the stars and overbalanced, that's all."

"Uh-huh," Robert said dubiously as he unbuttoned his blue chambray shirt, slipped it off, and wiped his face with it. Sweat glistened on his chest and shoulders, and ran down his legs from the hems of his khaki shorts. Strands of curly blond hair stuck to his forehead. He switched on the Coleman light and sat down on the bank of the stream to wash his feet.

Eric leaned over and switched it off again. "Save the batteries," he muttered. Then, more brightly, "Hey, I read your new book!"

Robert pulled one foot out of the water, crossed it over the other knee, and began to massage it. "*A Pale Knock?*" he asked with the barest hint of disdain.

"Scared my socks off," Eric commented proudly. "Nothing like a good ghost story. Your readers will eat this one up."

Robert didn't answer. He continued to massage the foot. The sound of a small sigh escaped his lips, however.

"Mom liked it too," Eric continued and popped open yet another beer. "Even better than that last one, *Grave Misgivings.*"

Robert gave a snort and a short chuckle. "Oh, yeah, big brother," he said with mirthful sarcasm. "I'll just bet she loved that one." He made an exaggerated face. "Boy meets ghoul, ghoul eats boy, and not in a nice way." He gave another snort and returned to his foot massage. "She's got all my novels on display atop the television set, but she's never read one of them. We both know that."

"Well, horror's not her cup of tea," Eric answered with patient resignation. "She's still proud of you and tells everybody when you have a new book out. She brags about you all the time."

"And what about Dad?" Robert asked, again with that hint of sarcasm. There was no mirth in it this time, though. "He brag about me too?"

A brief silence filled the clove, broken only by the gentlest rustle of the leaves and a sigh of the wind.

"I've never understood what it is between you two," Eric confessed finally. He stood up from the stool and began to pace behind Robert. He took a sip of beer as he watched his brother's bare back. "I can't believe he's so pissed because you used a pseudonym on your books. Lots of writers do that, don't they?" He took another drink and swallowed. "Why's he so pigheaded?"

Robert didn't answer. He put one foot back in the water, lifted the other, and began to rub it. "Just drop it, okay?" he said softly.

Eric was only half-listening though. "It's like he thinks you besmirched the family honor or something by shortening Podlowsky to Polo. But, hell, how do you get Podlowsky on a book cover? And would you buy a horror novel from someone called Podlowsky?"

"He's a good Catholic," Robert muttered sarcastically, as if it had any relevance to the discussion. "Leave him alone."

Eric stopped his pacing. Even drunk he didn't

mistake his brother's tone. "Why don't you come into Dowdsville tomorrow and see them?" he asked hopefully. It had been almost two years since Robert and his father had seen each other. And it was such a silly damn quarrel too, over a name.

"No," Robert whispered, with a shake of his head.

"But you've come all this way!" Eric pushed.

"Forget it!" Robert snapped. He got up suddenly, obviously irritated, and put his shirt back on without bothering to button it. He bent, seized the zipper that held the tent flaps closed, and jerked it downward. The sound of the metal scrape was loud and alien in the quiet clove. His anger was almost palpable as he slipped inside.

A few moments later, he emerged and faced his brother. "Look," he said, his manner apologetic, "I called you because—because I had to get out of Manhattan for a while. I just had to. All right?"

"Why?" Eric persisted, waving the can of beer he held, sloshing its contents. "All the way up the highway you barely said a word. Then we hit the trail, and you're all smiles and jokes again." He leaned forward, glaring at his younger brother. "I'm drunk, Bobby," he said, "but I'm sure as shit not blind. I don't see you for a year, and suddenly I get a call in the middle of the night." He raised the thumb and forefinger of his free hand and mimed speaking into a phone receiver. He made a fair imitation of his brother's voice too. " 'Hi, I'm at Chelsea and Seventh Avenue, can you pick me up?' Hey, I know when something's bothering you, little brother. I always did. And right now you're hiding a chunk of pain the size of God's ego." He forced a grin and winked, changing his tone. "What's her name?"

Robert frowned. He grabbed the Budweiser from his brother's hand and took a swig, which in itself was surprising. Robert never used to touch alcohol.

"It's not a woman," Robert said with barely controlled calm. "I'm just under some pressure. I've got a manuscript overdue, and the ending's giving me trouble. You try writing two books a year. I needed to get out of the city for a while, okay?"

Eric stared at his brother, not fooled by the lie. But he knew better than to press the matter. Robert was a private person, and no amount of shaking could get from him what he didn't want to give.

He snatched back his beer and swallowed a mouthful, all the while holding Robert's gaze over the can's rim. Finally he lowered the can, swallowed, and forced a loud belch. "So," he said at last. "We'll make it a quiet weekend in the woods then."

Robert allowed a tight smile, and the tension visibly left his shoulders. "The quieter, the better," he answered tartly. "So shut up for a while. I want to get some sleep." He turned, ducked low, and disappeared back inside the tent. A long metallic zip sounded from within as Robert opened his sleeping bag.

Eric returned to his camp stool. "I saw you on the ridge," he called toward the tent.

The bottom of the tent flap lifted, and Robert poked his head out. "You could see me from down here?" he answered with surprise.

"Gankaku," Eric replied, as if naming the kata would remove any doubt. "Even from a distance your form looked great. How was Okinawa?"

Robert raised up on his elbows with just his head, shoulders, and arms poking outside the tent. He threw the flap and the inner insect net back over the top of the tent. Then, settled again, he rested his chin in his hands and looked thoughtful.

"Magic," he said at last. "China was best, though. We stopped there for a month on the way back."

"Stopped there for a month," Eric interrupted with mock scorn. "Who's *we*?"

Robert chewed the corner of his lip before he answered. "Another student," he said. "A fighter I met when I visited the Cuong Nu Dojo in Gainesville, Florida. His name was Scott Silver, and he was really into full-contact sport. We traveled together and shared expenses. Met some really great instructors."

"Florida?" Eric said, raising an eyebrow as he lifted the Budweiser to his mouth again. "I didn't hear about that trip either."

"It was basically a stop on a promotional tour for *Grave Misgivings*," Robert answered with a shrug. "No big deal. But when I visit a city for one of those things I try to check out the local martial arts scene. The Cuong Nu school really impressed me."

"And you just happened to mention to this guy you were going to Okinawa?"

"Yeah," Robert said. "Scott had wanted to do the same thing for some time, but he couldn't afford it alone. So we got to talking and figured out that by sharing the costs we could both take a longer vacation than either of us could have on our own. And we'd each have someone to work out with regularly on the trip."

The wind blew across the clove again. The tent flap and insect screen blew down over Robert's face. He pushed it back. The moon shimmered for a moment in his blond hair and on his pale skin before a passing cloud darkened the entire clove. "I wish you could have come," he said to his brother, as he glanced upward.

"I wish you'd asked me," Eric answered, setting his beer aside. He followed his brother's gaze. The brilliant night sky was no longer clear. Unexpectedly, clouds raced from west to east, like desperate spirits, from one rim to the other. He turned his attention back to his brother. "I might have gone."

"You?" Robert scoffed good-naturedly. "Leave Dowdsville? For a whole year?"

"Hey!" Eric countered defensively. "I went to college."

Robert gave a knowing chuckle. "Yeah, and came home almost every weekend you got the chance. You were the only student in the whole school with a car that got driven more than once a month. You paid more for a parking space than you did for tuition."

Eric squinted one eye shut and glared sideways at his brother. Slyly covering the hole in the top of the Budweiser with his thumb, he gave the can a shake. "How would you know, pip-squeak?" he challenged. "You didn't even start at NYU until a year after I graduated."

"Yeah, well, you're still a legend there," Robert told him. Then he made a grab for the tent flap and tried to pull it down as his brother leaned forward suddenly. "Oh, no! Eric! Don't!"

Beer spewed from the can. Laughing, Eric gave it another shake, drenching his brother before Robert could withdraw, splattering the tent flap and the forward edges of both their sleeping bags. Heedless of their equipment, Eric crawled in after his brother.

Wide-eyed, Robert made a grab for the can. His reflexes were lightning-fast, yet Eric intercepted him. His fingers closed on Robert's wrist before Robert ever touched the beer. He gave it another shake, and more of the contents shot out, spraying them both.

"I'm not that old or that slow yet, little Bobby," Eric laughed, tightening his grip on his brother's wrist.

"Nope," Robert agreed, "but you are that stiff!" Before Eric could react, Robert slipped his older brother's grip with a simple aikido escape. Then, grasping Eric around the neck, he brought his left foot suddenly upward and planted it in Eric's stomach. *"Tomoe-Nage!"* he cried gleefully as he sank backward and executed the classic judo throw.

Eric gave a groan as he went upward and over inside the small tent. The seams of the nylon fabric gave a loud rip. Stakes snapped off in the ground. The whole thing came down around the two brothers like a balloon suddenly punctured. For a brief time the fabric writhed as the pair struggled within. Then two heads poked up through the ruined flap. The echoes of gasping and giggling slowly faded.

"That always was my favorite throw," Robert confessed to his brother.

Eric looked out over the rippling blue puddle that had recently been his tent. "Well," he said with a sigh, "I'd been intending to buy one of those new lightweight frame jobs anyway." He crawled outside again and stood up.

Robert followed him. "I think we can salvage it."

He bent to pull one of the broken stakes from the ground and examined the loop of the attached guy rope. "But once we get it up again, we'll still have to spend the night in beer-soaked sleeping bags."

Eric crawled out from under the fallen tent and stood up. His shirt and the front of his shorts were soaked. "Let's drag 'em outside," he suggested. "They'll dry faster."

Robert bent down to turn on the lantern, then hesitated. "Look," he said softly as he stared into the darkness. "Down at the far end of the clove." He straightened and took a few steps away from the camp, then stopped again.

Eric dropped the end of the sleeping bag he'd managed to fish out of the collapsed tent and went to his brother's side. "That's the waterfall," he exclaimed in a disbelieving whisper. "It's glowing!"

Shoulder to shoulder, the two brothers gazed at the strange phenomenon. The sound of the fall was a muted rush. When the wind blew and the leaves rustled, they could barely hear it at all. Yet they could see the water shimmering, falling, glowing with a dull greenish light.

"You're the geologist," Robert murmured without looking at his brother. "Some kind of lichen?"

"In your dreams," Eric retorted. He'd majored in geology, but he certainly didn't consider himself a scientist. He knew of nothing that could explain what he was seeing. "You're the horror writer. This is more your province."

Robert's hand settled on his brother's shoulder. It was an unconscious gesture that established an immediate connection between them, a bond and a small expression of the closeness that Eric had missed for so long. He wondered if Robert could feel his goose bumps.

Before either could speak again, the glow faded. The waterfall could still be heard in the darkness of the clove, but that was all. Eric drew a deep breath and held it as he glanced at his brother. Then he did the very first thing that came into his mind. He dived for the light and flipped it on.

"What the hell was that?" he demanded, his flushed face appearing even more pale in the sudden brightness.

But Robert was gone. So were his boots. Damn him! Eric felt a cold chill that had nothing to do with the breeze. He snatched up the lantern and plunged headlong into the thick undergrowth, following the bank of the stream toward the waterfall. Brambles scratched his bare legs. Roots and dead limbs lying unseen on the spongy earth tried to trip him. Low branches whipped at his face. He crashed onward, racing, half-stumbling sometimes, knowing with an angry, fearful certainty, goddamn it, that Robert was ahead somewhere.

"Robert!" he called out. "Robert!" The light of the Coleman lantern swung back and forth like a machete's blade as he searched the darkness. "Answer me, damn you!"

Then he was at the waterfall. It wasn't much of a fall—a bare curtain of water maybe four feet wide. The Catskills were full of such. It made a small roar now as it cascaded down the sandstone wall of the clove from the rim sixty or seventy feet above. A thin mist hung in the air and quickly dampened Eric's face.

"Robert!" he cried again, his heart thundering as he spun about, shining his light all around.

"Over here," Robert answered.

Eric flashed the lantern toward the sound of his brother's voice. "Where?" he called.

Robert touched him on the shoulder. Eric nearly jumped out of his skin.

"Shit, Bobby! Don't do that! Make some fucking noise when you move!" Eric wiped a hand over his face and pretended to swat at a mosquito as he stared at the narrow, noisy plunge and the wetly gleaming stone wall behind it. "It was just a fucking trick of moonlight that made it glow." His breathing was short and ragged as his thoughts raced to find a rational explanation. "That's it! The full moon hit the water just right. That's all we saw, damn it!"

"No," Robert said quietly, hugging himself and peering at the water. "I saw someone."

"You're crazy," Eric scoffed as he shone the light into all the thick bushes that grew around the stream and near the fall. "You couldn't see anybody way down here. Too many trees!"

"Not down here," Robert answered strangely. He turned slowly and stared into the darkness, searching. "Near the tent. He was ..." He stopped and shook his head. "It couldn't have been."

"Couldn't have been what?" Eric snapped irritably. When Robert didn't answer right away, Eric grabbed his arm. His brother was trembling.

"Scott," Robert finally said, his voice barely a whisper. "I thought I saw Scott."

Eric was sarcastic. "You've been sneaking my beers. There's nobody out here in this hellangone wilderness but us."

Robert turned slowly. The Coleman uplit his face, turning his eyes into deep black sockets, lending him an almost demonic visage. "Then one of us must be about a quart low," he said, bending down. He pointed at the ground. The blades of grass were splattered with a black, sticky fluid.

Eric bit his lip as he reached out and collected some on the tip of his index finger. He rolled it between the finger and the ball of his thumb and sniffed. "Blood," he announced uneasily, stating what his brother had already surmised. He shone the light on the earth ahead of them. "There's a trail of it."

"Leading to the waterfall," Robert added, rising.

"Where the hell did it come from?" Eric muttered as he wiped his fingers in the grass, then on his shorts. "Your friend Scott couldn't have followed us here."

"No," Robert said, his voice hard-edged as he stared at the fall again. "He certainly couldn't have." Robert moved a few paces ahead, eyeing the ground, following the blood trail. Eric hurried after him with the light. "Look," Robert said abruptly. He stopped, bent down once more, and lifted a small silver medallion on a thin chain.

The ornament was no bigger than an old-fashioned, double-sided razor blade. It fairly sparkled in the Coleman's light. One side had been polished to a mirror brilliance. The opposite side was silvery and covered with a series of tiny glyphs and a line of writing in some foreign language. When Robert moved it under the light, the lettering caught the Coleman's glow and shot back reflected rays of silver edged impossibly with flashes of emerald.

"You understand any of that?" Eric asked, examining the odd medallion. The chain, though it appeared delicate, proved deceptively strong. He handed it back to his brother.

Robert held it up by the chain and twirled it before the Coleman. Lances of radiance shot in all directions. Suddenly he reached out and flipped off the light, plunging the clove into darkness. When his eyes adjusted, he looked at his brother and shook his head. "Did you notice?" he asked as he wiped his fingers on his shirt. "This thing's wet. There's still water between the chain's links."

Eric peered warily into the gloom. "Dew?" he suggested.

Robert ran his hand over the grass and held up the palm. "No dew." Again he turned toward the waterfall.

"Look," Eric said reasonably, scratching his head. "That thing could have been lying there for days, maybe longer."

Robert gave him a disdainful look. "It's too shiny. No tarnish. No dirt in the links. Just water."

Eric swallowed. Abruptly, every shadow became a hiding place, every breath of the wind a whisper. Clouds swept wildly across the moon, causing its milky light to flicker and fade. He scanned the rim of the clove for movement. When a sudden gust shook the raspy leaves, he jumped again. The night, he decided, was getting to him.

"Your friend Scott," Eric said. "Could it be him? Playing a joke maybe?"

Robert barely glanced at Eric, then turned away. "No," he answered. But there was a startling intensity in Robert's eyes and a hard set to his jaw. His hand clenched and unclenched around that silver medallion. For a paralyzing instant Eric thought he glimpsed something that he had never seen in his brother before.

"Bobby?" he said hesitantly.

"Let's go," was all that Robert said. He rose and took the Coleman lantern from Eric, flipped it on, and began to follow the blood spoor. It was a short trail. A smear on a leaf, a dark splotch on a dead log.

It took them straight to the waterfall.

Eric and Robert stood side by side. The thin curtain of water gleamed in the lantern's light. The rush of the fall drowned the lapping of the small pool and the stream that flowed away through the clove's heart. Robert knelt again. The stone shelf on the pool's edge was splashed with blood.

Eric waved an arm in annoyance at a small cloud of insects. The blood had attracted them. "So much for your nice quiet weekend," he commented disgustedly.

Robert held up the medallion by the ends of the broken chain and twirled it again in the lantern's light. It sparkled with a liquid shimmer, as if he held a piece of the waterfall in his hand. All around, the clove seemed to hold its breath. "Wait here," he told his brother.

"No damn way," Eric answered, grabbing his younger brother's arm and snatching the lantern. "If we're gonna do this, we're gonna do it together."

With Eric leading, they moved around the bank of the pool toward the narrow waterfall. The lantern's light bounced back off the water. If there was a small cave behind it, as they both suspected, it wasn't obvious. Eric knew it was possible, though. The entire Catskill range was riddled with cloves and caves. Glaciers and streams, erosion and weathering, had made the place a geological wonder.

"This all strikes me like something out of one of your books," he muttered to his brother as he leaned as far out as he could and tried to peer behind the fall. Water cascaded over his face and down the neck of his shirt, icy cold. He squeezed his eyes shut and reached out with one hand. The fall wasn't wide. If there was an opening, he should be able to find it.

"Damn!" he gasped, straightening. He drew a deep breath and shook water from his ears. "There *is* a cave!"

Robert didn't hesitate. He squeezed past his brother and leaned under the fall, reaching out to feel for himself. Then suddenly, he was through the fall and out of sight.

"Goddamn it!" Eric raged, slapping the Coleman lantern with enough force to jar the batteries inside it. The light flickered for a moment, then steadied. "I'm gonna kick your reckless butt!"

Eric leaned under the fall again, found the edge of the cave mouth, and pulled himself through. Sharp stone scraped his shoulders. His left sleeve ripped loose at the seam. The floor was slippery underfoot and sloped upward. He nearly fell, but Robert shot out a hand and caught him.

Eric cursed as he caught his balance and knocked Robert's hand away. He glared angrily at his brother, shivering and soaked to the bone. "You idiot!" he shouted. "You tell me the next time you're gonna do something stupid!" He glanced back toward the mouth of the cave. It was barely a foot and a half wide at the entrance, high and narrow. Not so much a cave as a crack in the clove wall.

"Shut off the light," Robert told him, his voice barely audible over the roar. The waterfall was small, but the sound of it was greatly magnified in the cave's tight confines.

Eric wore a look of disbelief. "Are you crazy?" He demanded.

"Shut off the light," Robert repeated in a deadly calm voice.

Eric gave a low, disgusted growl and shook his head. But he raised the Coleman, found the switch, and flipped it off. To his instant surprise, they were not plunged into the darkness he'd expected.

A dull greenish radiance flowed from Robert's upraised fist, penetrating between his fingers, revealing his bones through the very skin. Suddenly Robert relaxed his grip. The medallion slipped free to spin and swing on the end of its chain. It shimmered like an emerald star, and the walls of the cave seemed to respond with a matching glow. Just beyond the entrance, the curtain of water sheened and sparkled. In the other direction, the cave seemed to widen. Neither brother could see a back wall or any end to the cave. Instead, an aching white light throbbed, far away, like a fire at the heart of a vast green jewel.

Eric let his breath out slowly as he pressed himself against the wall. "I don't think I'm ready for this, Bobby," he said. "I'm a small-town postman. I lead a quiet life."

Then Robert shouted, "Eric!"

Too late Eric realized that the white light was rushing toward them. There wasn't time to dive back through the opening. He made a grab for Robert and flung his arms protectively around his brother as the light struck them. Someone screamed.

A cold fire seared Eric. Every nerve in his body shrieked with its own high-pitched voice. One long, seemingly endless wail ripped from his throat. With all his might he clung to his little brother.

It ended abruptly, as if a switch had been thrown to turn off the pain. Eric opened his eyes and gazed around. The green glow was gone. He lifted a hand cautiously and touched his face, expecting to find all his flesh melted away. He was undamaged.

But he knew at once that they were in trouble.

The sky beyond the mouth of the cave burned like a thing on fire. Oranges and reds, yellows, streaks of purple. There was no sign of the waterfall. Outside the cave entrance thick grass made a rich green carpet that stretched toward a forest on the far side of an expanse.

Eric felt Robert's breath on his face. "I never knew you could hit such a note," Robert muttered as he freed himself from Eric's embrace. "Fay Wray would be proud." He turned toward the entrance.

Uncertainly, Eric followed his brother. Side by side, they leaned out of the cave into the warmth of a hot evening breeze. There was no trace of a waterfall, a pool, or a stream. No sign of their tent or equipment. The woods that grew on the far side of the meadow were not the familiar woods where they had made their camp. There was no sign of the clove or of Eric's beloved mountains.

"I don't know what's happened," said Robert, staring at the last traces of the sun as it set behind the forest. A bright, red-glowing orb, it seemed to set fire to every leaf and limb, to every blade of grass.

He held up the silver medallion. It spun on its broken chain, flashing in the weird sunlight, almost mocking them. "But this sure isn't the Catskills."

Eric's heart gave a lurch. "Well," he commented, trying to hide his fear with a little sarcasm, "it sure as hell isn't Kansas either."

Chapter Two

ROBERT looked out across the meadow, his heart hammering. The sky blazed with wild sunset colors. Two hundred yards away the forest closed about, forming an uneven ring. Beyond the trees to the east, a spectacular mountain vista soared. The air was still hot. The sweet smell of pine and heather and juniper wafted on the softly blowing breeze.

Robert paid little attention. He gazed warily at the forest on the far side of the meadow, noting the shivering of the leaves, the subtle stirring of the black limbs and branches. He measured the shadows between the great old trunks and searched for any sign of movement.

At his feet, heavy drops of blood splotched the grass and the cave floor. A bloody handprint marred the stone near his shoulder. Robert struggled to hold himself together. It wasn't Scott he'd seen in the shadows near the tent, he told himself. It couldn't have been Scott.

Yet he'd seen him as plainly as he could see Eric now.

He gazed surreptitiously at his brother, who was feeling along the cave's rear wall, pounding on it with his fist, probing at the rock, finally giving it a kick.

"Damn it!" Eric barked. "It's solid stone!"

Robert tried to hide his trembling. All the fist-beating in the world wasn't going to reveal a door in the back of the cave. They hadn't come here by any normal means. He stared at the bloody hand-print again. He didn't think Eric had noticed it yet. *Whose blood?* he asked himself. Not Scott's.

He loved his brother, but there was so much he didn't know how to tell him. He felt shamed by that admission, as if he were violating the trust they shared. Eric's first impulse in the face of danger had been to grab and protect him. And now, protecting Eric was Robert's impulse. He should get Eric home. He wondered, though, if they could get home. He held the medallion up to the swiftly fading light and studied the writing on it. He gazed at the handprint again.

"We were led here, big brother," he announced. "Deliberately."

"Hell with that," Eric said caustically as he continued his search for a hidden door in the cave wall. But then he relented a little. "Led by who?"

Robert thought back. He was sure it was Scott's face he'd seen beyond the tent in the shadows among the trees. His lip trembled as he started to mouth the name and then stopped. So great had been his shock at seeing his friend that he hadn't been able to cry out, and when Scott turned and ran back into the darkness, all he could do was follow, plunge into the bushes without even a word to Eric in a mad attempt to overtake . . . nothing.

"I don't know," Robert lied. He stared toward the distant mountain range that loomed in the east.

The peaks were streaked with mysterious purples, somber blacks, and morose blues, as if some really depressed painter had been turned loose on a gigantic canvas. "I don't understand it," he continued, "but something or someone brought us here. I mean, think of it. First I see . . ." he hesitated, reluctant to name Scott again, ". . . someone in the shadows. He disappears, but I find the blood trail. Then we find the medallion. Then the cave. And here we are. You'd have to be blind or a fool not to see a plan in it."

"I'm not blind," Eric snapped, giving up his search and coming to join his brother at the entrance. "And I don't think I'm a fool. But all I've got right now is a whole lot of questions." He stepped cautiously out of the cave and into the open. Bracing his hands on his hips, he turned his gaze from left to right and toward the forest on the far side of the clearing. "I want some answers."

Robert thrust the medallion into the left front pocket of his shorts and followed his brother a few steps across the grass. The breeze brushed over him; though it was warm, it chilled him in his wet clothes. "You're awfully accepting of all this," Robert noted with a calm he didn't really feel. A sense of dread nearly overcame him. His guts crawled. There was a terrible sensation, some dark déjà vu about this place, that almost sent him running for the cave again. Yet nothing looked familiar.

"I've lived with you and read your books," Eric quipped with a shrug. "I'm fluent in strangeness." Robert didn't miss the tension in his brother's voice. Eric was just as frightened as he was.

After they'd gone a few paces, Eric stopped, turned, and glanced back toward the cave. He touched Robert's arm and pointed. The cave was part of a steep cliff. That was not what had caught Eric's attention, however. On a wide ledge above the mouth, someone had built a small cabin. It leaned at a crazy angle, as if it had been slapped together with great haste. A good stiff wind could have easily blown it over the edge.

"How'd you know that was there?" Robert asked quietly.

"I didn't," Eric answered. "We left the Coleman in the cave. I was going back for it. Then I saw that. Think anyone's home?"

"Only way to find out is to knock," Robert said with a grim shake of his head. He began to button his blue chambray shirt. The fabric was still soaked and clung to him, but the wind and the warm air promised to dry it quickly. "Let's see if there's a way up."

Eric ran back into the cave for the light while Robert searched for a means of ascending to the cabin. About twenty paces east of the cave he found a crudely cut stairway chiseled in the soft stone. He waved a hand as his brother emerged with the lantern. They were going to need it, he figured, glancing at the sun. It squatted just behind the treetops in the west, casting long, splintery shadows across the meadowland.

Robert reached the top of the ledge first and waited for Eric to join him. The cabin commanded a splendid view. To the west, staring into the fiery glow of the sun, he could just make out the meandering rim of a lake. He blinked and rubbed his eyes, unable to bear the sun's brilliance.

"It's like some kind of sentry post," Eric said,

coming to his side. "You can see the whole area from up here."

The cabin door leaned at an awkward angle, supported on a single twisted hinge that rust had scarred and nearly eaten through. Robert pushed it open gingerly, half expecting it to fall off at his touch. It gave a stubborn squeak as it dragged on the floor. Robert pushed harder, forcing it back.

The place was home to nothing but dust and cobwebs. The window shutters were closed and barred. The last rays of sunset lanced through the gaps between the inexpertly assembled logs of the walls. Robert crept to the center of the single room, the floorboards creaking under his weight.

Eric switched on the Coleman. A narrow rope bed stood in one corner. The down mattress on the cording had long since rotted away, leaving only a mass of ruined fabric and a scattering of feathers that stirred lazily at the slightest draft. In another corner was a crudely built wooden table, roughly square, with a pair of rickety chairs. A cracked ceramic plate sat on the table, along with a cup and the half-melted stump of a candle.

Eric went to a barrel near the bed and lifted the wooden lid. "Water," he announced. But the Coleman's light gleamed on the brackish scum that floated on the surface. He licked his lips and lowered the lid back into place. "Not fit to drink, though." He paced around the room, shining his light everywhere. Near the mantel of the long-dead fireplace, he found a slender pole. "Looks like a bo-staff," he said appraisingly. He set the light up on the shelf and took the weapon in both hands. "Odd wood," he commented. "Really flexible." He picked up the light again, keeping his find.

Robert unshuttered one of the two windows. The breeze swirled in, stirring dust and feathers. The lighting improved only a little, but the smell of fresh air was a welcome change from the cabin's dust. He went to the bed. If they unlashed the rope from the frame they might be able to use it. But when he tested the cord it crumbled at his touch. So much for that idea. He moved toward the table.

The floor creaked and groaned as Eric stole across the room to Robert's side. "Let's go, Bobby," his brother said. "Nobody's been here for years."

"Then who put that there?" Robert asked nervously. All the moisture had gone out of his throat, and he felt cold all over. He extended one finger and pointed at the table.

Eric swept the Coleman around. On the table's surface, written in the thick dust in plain letters, he read the word *Polo*.

Robert swept a hand across the table, erasing his name. He rushed from the cabin into the warm, clean air and filled his lungs with it. His heart triphammered. His pulse roared in his ears. *Polo*. Scott had always called him Polo!

Eric hurried after his brother, giving the door a kick to force it wider. The wood shivered, and the hinge squealed. Eric emerged with the lantern and his staff. "What the hell was it, Bobby?" he cried. "What happened? All I saw was your big hand swipe!"

A loud groan made them both whirl. From somewhere inside the cabin came a cracking and popping. The cabin leaned even further toward the rim of the ledge, then gave a lurch as timbers and struts gave way. The walls strained at an impossible angle. The roof crashed down, and it all collapsed with a terrible grace, like a house made of playing cards.

"So much for spending the night," Eric sighed as he surveyed the wreckage. He glanced toward the sky, which had taken on the bruised color of twilight. "There's not much sun left."

"There's enough," Robert declared sharply, heading for the steps. "And we've got the Coleman. I want to look around down below."

"For what?" Eric demanded in a strained voice.

"I don't know!" Robert snapped, reaching the stone steps. "Just leave me alone!" He flung up his arms and made a face. "Something!"

He descended the smoothly worn steps at a dangerous speed, chiding himself for shouting at his brother. He wasn't mad at Eric. He was frightened. And he didn't like being frightened, particularly in front of his big brother.

He didn't dwell on that now, though. He reached the bottom, moved back toward the cave, and stared at the ground, seeking footprints, more blood, anything that might give him a clue.

Someone had lured his brother and him into that cave, he felt sure. Finding his name written in the dust of the cabin only confirmed it. But where did they go? What direction would they take?

He scanned the rim of the forest. The shadows were deep and black there. Beneath the thick leaves and branches it was already night. He moved out further into the meadow, watching the ground, searching the skyline.

Eric walked along wordlessly beside him, and after a while Robert began to feel a vague sense of guilt. "Let's go back to the cave," he suggested.

"Tomorrow we can try to figure out where we are and how to get home."

Eric regarded him for what seemed like a long time, and Robert stared back. The breeze fluttered the black curls of Eric's hair, and the failing sun gleamed in his eyes. They had the same green eyes, emerald-pure and penetrating. Robert always hated it when Eric turned that scrutinizing gaze on him. Then his brother's features softened. Wearing a wry, troubled grin, he shook his head, tucked the lantern under one arm, and clapped Robert on the shoulder. That was it. He turned and started back toward the cave.

A loud crashing sounded in the forest off to their right. Both brothers froze in midstep. An unearthly cry, some kind of animal noise, ripped through the gathering darkness.

A chill ran up Robert's spine. He'd never in his life heard such a sound. He gave his brother a sidewise glance. Eric hugged the Coleman and his staff. Lines of tension radiated across his forehead as he peered intently at the nearest line of trees.

A great black beast charged into the clearing and made straight for them. Streamers of fire poured from its eyes. Its black hide shimmered. Its form was horselike, but from its brow sprouted a gleaming ebony spike as long as a man's arm.

"Tell me I'm still drunk!" Eric shouted.

Robert didn't waste the time. "Run for the cave!" he cried, giving Eric a rough shove in the appropriate direction.

Eric didn't need to be told twice. He flung down both the lantern and the staff and ran as hard as he could. Robert followed, pumping arms and legs with all his might, but he kept one eye on the beast.

It moved with amazing speed. There was no way they would reach the safety of the cave in time. Without a word to Eric, Robert stopped. He watched his brother's back only long enough to make sure Eric kept going. Then he turned toward the beast and flung up his arms.

"Yah!" he shouted, drawing its attention. "Here, you ugly son of a bitch!"

The unicorn charged straight for him. Robert listened to the sound of its hooves as they beat the earth. He drew a deep breath, centering himself, putting away all his fear as he watched the monster come on. The tip of that deadly horn flashed, dipped, and leveled toward his chest.

Barely in time, he flung himself away, curving through the air in a graceful arc, and executing a rolling breakfall as he struck the earth. He continued to his feet and spun around, ready to meet another attack.

The beast screamed in frustration and reeled about. Robert's heart thundered. If it was a unicorn, it was nothing like those fairy tale animals. Its skin was snakelike, glittering with oily black scales. Its tail, too, was serpentine; it lashed the air with a writhing fury. But those eyes! Those eyes burned with fire. Real flame poured upward out of those horrible sockets.

It was a terrible and deadly beauty.

The beast charged him again. This time Robert turned and ran toward the forest, hoping to lure it still farther from Eric. Without looking back he felt the monster overtaking him, bearing down on him. Its breath blew hot against his back.

Again he flung himself sideways and rolled to his feet. Frantically he looked around. Eric had seen him. Robert heard his name called. His brother was running across the meadow to help. Damn him! Why didn't he stay in the cave? With barely a moment to spare, Robert spied the staff his brother had dropped. He ran for it.

The unicorn screamed a challenge. Robert calculated the remaining distance to the weapon and doubted his chances. Still he ran. The power of those fatal black hooves shook the ground under him. Desperately he leaped and rolled, and his hands closed on the staff.

In one motion he rose, spun, and swung with everything he had. The strange wood struck the monster across its mouth, but the blow, delivered with all Robert's might, hardly fazed it. The staff broke in two with a loud crack. Too late, Robert tried to dodge. Though he escaped the horn, a huge shoulder smashed him backward. He hit the ground stunned, unable to draw breath, his head ringing.

The monster bellowed triumphantly and wheeled about to finish him. Robert gasped for air, trying to will his body to move. The ground shivered under his spine as the beast charged. He saw those eyes, those hooves, the spike lowered.

Suddenly Eric appeared between Robert and the unicorn. He gave a shout and flung his arms wildly in an effort to divert the monster. Instead, it charged on. Eric gave a grunt and caught the horn with both hands. The impact knocked him into the air, but still he clung, not daring to let go.

Robert found his strength barely in time to roll aside. Horrified, he struggled to his knees as the monster tossed Eric through the air with a powerful snap of its neck. Eric landed badly and his cry of pain stung Robert's ears. The unicorn reared up, intent on trampling Eric.

Without thinking, Robert ran at the creature and leaped onto its back. With all his desperation he slammed the knife edge of his stiffened left hand down on the unicorn's neck and skull. The monster bellowed its rage. On the ground, Eric dragged himself out of the way. A loud growl issued from Robert's throat. He squeezed with his knees and dug the fingers of his right hand under the beast's scales, finding purchase. With an almost hysterical anger, he rained blows upon the unicorn's neck and head.

It bucked him off with ridiculous ease, and Robert found himself flying helplessly through the air. He twisted and managed to roll as he hit the ground. A flash of searing pain shot through his right hand. He looked down and found his palm full of blood. The scales had cut him!

But a greater dread drove away any thought of pain. Eric had recovered and found his feet. The unicorn whirled and prepared to charge. But Eric showed no sign of running. Instead, he drew a deep breath, clenched his fists before his chest and forced them slowly downward as he exhaled and drew in a fresh deep breath. His eyes narrowed to concentrated slits. He turned one shoulder to the beast.

"Eric!" Robert cried.

But Eric paid him no attention. The unicorn rushed at him, head lowered, horn glittering. Eric held his ground. His right hand drew upward in a high arc. Like a bullfighter at the moment of truth, he waited. All Robert heard was the pounding of those hooves and his own high-pitched scream.

With an almost serene calm, Eric sidestepped the charge. His raised right hand slashed downward in one perfect stroke. The sound of his *kiai* was matched by a loud crack.

Hornless, the unicorn reared and screamed in anguish. It spun about, and its tail whipped the air. It screamed again. A dark ichor streamed down its face from the ravaged stump that marked the place on its brow where the horn had been.

Then its cry took on a vengeful note. It stared at Eric. The fire in its eyes crackled and smoked. Bellowing, it rushed him. Eric tried to leap aside, but this time, with uncanny intelligence, the creature snapped its head sideways, catching him in midleap, batting him out of the air like a fly.

Eric gave a groan as he struck the earth. The monster reared over him and smashed downward with its hooves. Eric rolled frantically out of the way, but the monster reared again. Again Eric barely avoided death. There was no chance to get to his feet. Again the beast reared.

Robert heard his brother's panic-filled scream and the sickening thud of those hooves. With a shout born of the despair that filled his heart, he ran at the unicorn. At the same time, he saw the black spike that had been the beast's horn where it lay in the grass. He swept it up and plunged it deep into the monster's neck. A thick fluid shot into the air, fountaining, drenching him as he withdrew the spike and plunged it in again, this time straight into the unicorn's broad breast. With all his enraged strength he leaned on the weapon, shoving the point in deeper.

The unicorn screamed with pain and smashed him aside. Bright stars exploded in Robert's head as he hit the ground. An unnatural, knifing pain flared behind his right shoulder. Still he managed to raise up on one elbow.

The unicorn staggered backward. Then its right front leg buckled and it fell over on its side. Agonized screams filled the clearing as it thrashed on the ground. The horn jutted, gleaming wetly, deeply embedded, while blood splashed from the wound in the monster's neck. Its great chest heaved laboriously as it gasped for air. For a moment, it lay still. Then, it raised its head again and made one final, stubborn effort to get up. Its last cry was no more than a pitiful whimper. Finally, it died.

Robert turned on his side and stared at his unmoving brother. "Eric!" he called, then again, "Eric!" His brother didn't answer. Robert threw back his head and gave a cry of anguish that surpassed even the unicorn's.

He slumped back onto the ground, exhausted by grief and pain. His senses reeled, and for a time the world seemed to swim around him. Slowly it righted itself.

He crawled to Eric's side and gathered his brother in the crook of one arm. Eric's face was a red mess of blood, and blood ran back into the tangled, sweat-drenched mass of black hair. A deep laceration stretched from his hairline almost to his right eyebrow. Already the flesh around the gash was swelling and turning black. His heart near to bursting, Robert rocked his brother back and forth.

When Eric gave a tiny moan, Robert's heart missed a beat. Suddenly his eyes misted over, and he pressed his cheek to his brother's. Eric's head turned a little and nestled into Robert's shoulder, and Robert held him that way, gently, while the night deepened around them. There was no place to take him, no easy way to move him, nothing to do but sit there and hold him and hope.

One by one, stars began to pepper the velvet sky. Eric would have known them by name and called them off as they winked into being. Eric had spent a lot of nights when they were kids trying to teach his little brother the constellations. But Robert had never learned.

He looked down and brushed a lock of hair back from Eric's face as a soft wind blew out of the forest. The leaves in the trees rustled. A pair of birds, the first Robert had seen in that strange sky, gyred upward from the woods and climbed into the night. Crickets began to play their sawing music.

Robert waited, wondering what to do. Eric would have known what to do. He always knew. But Eric couldn't help now. Eric needed help. Robert stared down at his brother, afraid to move him. Except for those two small sounds Eric hadn't stirred. Robert turned his gaze toward the ruined cabin on the ledge above the cave mouth. That was no longer an option. There was only the cave.

His own pain began to come home to him. His shoulder ached fearfully where he'd fallen on it. The cut on his right hand stung like fire, and his legs and arms were scraped in a score of places. He ran his tongue over dry lips, suddenly aware of a powerful thirst.

In the darkness he could barely see the bulk of the dead beast that was the cause of his grief. He gazed up at the sky again and tried to recall the names of some of the stars, as if that might somehow wake his brother. But nothing looked even vaguely familiar. "Rigel," he guessed, pointing to

one bright star with his free hand. "Rigel," he repeated, more loudly, encouraging Eric to open his
eyes, sneer, and offer a correction. But Eric didn't
move.

The darkening flesh around the gash above Eric's
right temple where the unicorn's hoof had struck
him was beginning to swell to frightening size.
Robert felt his panic grow as he looked closer at it
and touched it with his thumb. He used his shirt-
tail to wipe away some of the encrusted blood and
glanced toward the cave again, convincing himself
that he had to get his brother to shelter. He needed
light, though, and remembered the Coleman lantern. Eric had dropped it somewhere close by. As
gently as he could, he slipped his arm from around
Eric and laid his brother's head softly on the grass.
"I'll be back," he whispered as he rose.

But before he took another step a rush of wind
swept over him. An instant later, a great, marvelous creature soared over the edge of the cliff above
the cave, past the clearing and out over the tops of
the forest trees. Immense wings, glowing palely
with some strange bioluminescence, gracefully pin-
ioned the air.

The creature made a sweeping turn. Robert
stared openmouthed at the sensuous neck, the un-
dulating length of slender tail. He had an impression of small, powerfully clawed feet curled up
against the belly as the creature approached again.
The glow of its wings washed the earth beneath it
with a yellowish light.

It was fantastic, beyond any beauty he had ever
seen. But that thought was like cold water in Robert's face. He had thought the same of the unicorn.

Here was another monster, and Eric was already down!

He stared around grimly for a weapon. In the dark there was no sign of the broken staff. It had been next to useless anyway. He ran to the carcass of the unicorn and wrapped his hands around the horn embedded in its heart. Gritting his teeth, planting a foot on its scaled shoulder, he ripped the horn free and turned to face the new menace.

High in the air, the monster raised its wings to a nearly vertical position, and with the grace of a shimmering leaf, it floated to the earth, settling in the middle of the meadow. When it touched the ground the wings slowly folded. Pools of soft radiance spread upon the grass beneath them. Robert seemed to feel, as well as see, the glittering, diamondlike eyes, full of an almost mesmeric fire, that turned his way. As with the unicorn, there was some intelligence there!

Something moved near the creature's left wing. A small black shadow darted across the amber glow and melted into the general darkness. Robert clutched the horn and crept closer to Eric. Crouching low, every sense alert, he waited.

Several yards away, a figure emerged from the darkness. It strode briskly forward, arms swinging. Robert rose suddenly from his crouch, ready to fight. The figure stopped abruptly, as if startled, and stared at him. A silhouetted hand went to the waist.

Robert moved instinctively, vacating the spot where he'd stood a moment before. A soft *thooop* sounded, and something hissed by his ear. Another *thooop*. He felt a sharp sting just below his left collarbone.

A dart! Almost immediately a cold numbness began to spread from the tiny wound. He snatched at it, yanked it free. A splinter of wood, no more than a needle with a puff of feathering. Already his vision began to blur, so swiftly did the poison work. Heart thundering, he glanced down at his brother, then at his half-seen assailant. The world was spinning crazily.

All he could think of was Eric. He had to protect his brother, and the only way he could do that was to take this stranger down quickly while he still was able.

He closed the distance between them in three swift strides, feeling the bite of another dart in the center of his chest. He ignored it, though. The figure retreated, but not swiftly enough. He threw his best high roundhouse kick and made a solid connection to the head. His foe went down hard without so much as a groan. Mercilessly, Robert raised his foot and prepared to smash his heel into an unprotected face.

But the darts had done their work well. As he balanced briefly on one leg, summoning his strength for the finishing blow, the world tilted under him. Meadow and forest, sky and stars, all became a swirling vortex that sucked him down. He felt the earth under him as he toppled over, felt the sharp edges of the grass pressed against his cheek, a single cool blade that tickled his open eye. A dreadful cold spread all through his veins, chilling him from the inside. He tried to move, but his limbs wouldn't obey. He tried to scream, but a rasping gurgle was all he managed. A moment more, and even that was beyond him.

A shadow fell over his face. Someone knelt down.

A black cascade of hair slipped over a silhouetted shoulder and brushed against his face. A woman! In the faint starlight he could barely make out her features as she rolled him onto his back. In one hand she clutched a short blowtube, in the other a dart ready to load.

Though his body was paralyzed, his mind was not. He studied his enemy as best he could. She wore clothes of a rough black leather. Her thick gloves were of the same leather. A band of white cloth was tied around her head to keep her hair back.

Something more caught Robert's eye. Around her neck hung a close-fitting silver chain. From that chain depended a smaller version of the same silver medallion he carried in his pocket.

Bending over him, the woman said something in a language Robert couldn't understand. She rubbed the side of her head where his kick had landed as she spoke, and the look she gave him was not particularly forgiving. She left him and moved toward Eric. Robert could do nothing to stop her as she moved out of his narrow range of sight.

Then she was beside him again. She spared him a brief frown before she cupped her hands to her mouth, threw back her head, and sang a high, sharp note. The sound flowed with crystal purity through the night, and she pushed it three more notes up the scale and held the last one with a quavering vibrato until she had no more breath.

Though Robert couldn't move, he still could hear the beat of massive pinions. From the corner of his eye he watched the gigantic flying creature at the far side of the field rise gracefully, almost delicately, into the night, its wings pulsing with a soft amber radiance. But it did not fly away. Instead, it circled high over the area like a fantastic, never-blinking firefly, playing on the currents of wind that swept over the edge of the cliff.

The woman bent down beside Robert again and plucked the second dart from his chest. She wiped the point carefully on a piece of his shirt before she returned it to a small holster sewn into the back of her right glove. Robert paid little attention, though, as he watched the sky.

Two more creatures, as fabulous as the first, sailed side by side out of the darkness above the cliff. But while the first one's wings burned with a greenish-amber glow, one of the new ones shimmered with the colors of a living fire opal and the other simply appeared to be a thing on fire!

Once again the woman rose and sang her four-note song. All three creatures floated down to the earth, much nearer this time. The wind generated by their wings rushed over Robert and rippled the grass as if it were water. Now the clearing was filled with strange, shifting colors as the beasts stretched and flexed and fanned themselves.

Robert heard voices calling excitedly, and the woman beside him waved and answered. Two figures, one a dark-haired man about Eric's age, the other a young boy of maybe fourteen, rushed up with blowpipes in their hands, darts at the ready. Quickly, though, they sheathed the darts, thrust the pipes back into their belts, and bent down to examine Robert. He felt their hands on him, probing him roughly in embarrassing places, but he was helpless to resist.

The man exclaimed in surprise when he extracted the silver medallion from Robert's pocket.

He held it up by its chain for the others to see and muttered something to the boy.

But the woman interrupted. She held up the unicorn horn and pointed to the dead monster nearby. Both her companions gaped, and all three fell silent as they looked from the beast to Robert, then to Eric, and to the beast again.

The woman barked some instructions. The man and boy nodded. The boy lifted Robert's feet while his older companion grasped him under the arms. Together, they carried him toward one of the waiting beasts. He could do nothing to protest, so he tried to calm himself by observing everything carefully.

The creatures, he realized, were mounts. Just in front of those powerful wings, saddles and packs were securely strapped in place, but Robert saw nothing to serve as reins. He was bound across the saddle of the amber-winged beast. The bonds were surprisingly gentle, however; they passed mostly around his waist and chest, leaving his hands free. A moment later, the woman climbed up into the saddle with him. With a thong from one of her packs she slung the unicorn's horn across her back. Then, settling herself, she ran a hand lightly along Robert's spine.

She leaned forward and spoke softly into his ear. He could understand nothing of her speech, but it had a sweet, lilting quality.

From his awkward position, he watched as the man and boy bore his unconscious brother toward the creature with the fire opal wings. Thankfully, they did not bind Eric. With the greatest care, as if concerned for his injuries, they lifted him into the creature's saddle. Then the boy climbed up behind him, wrapped his arms around Eric, and held him tightly. Eric's head rolled back into the boy's shoulder.

The fear lifted from Robert's heart. Whoever these people were, they apparently intended no further harm. He listened to the muted speech of the dark-haired man and boy and watched until the man turned and walked out of his limited field of vision. All the while, the woman stroked and rubbed his back and murmured to him. He found an odd reassurance in her voice. Or perhaps, he reasoned, it was mild, delayed shock.

Robert was unsure how much time passed. Finally, their dark-haired companion reappeared. He held the battery-powered Coleman lantern up to show the woman. It was turned off and shed no light. They exchanged a few remarks, regarded it curiously without discovering the toggle, then stowed it in the woman's packs.

The woman waited for her comrade to move away. When he was out of Robert's sight, she opened her mouth and sang a single note in an achingly pure soprano. She held it for a moment, then slid three notes up the scale. At the same time, two more voices, strong tenors, rang out.

Robert's stomach gave a lurch as he felt the creature under him start to rise. The earth fell swiftly away, and in only a few heartbeats the clearing and the cave were gone from sight. The wind rushed by, sharp as a whip on Robert's bare face.

Another wonder revealed itself as they soared higher still. A moon nearly twice as large as the one he knew hung in pale refulgence on the forested rim of this new world. Nor was it the only marvel that graced the night. A powdery ring, bluish in color but dotted here and there with diamond-bright fragments, arced across the firmament.

The woman's hand pressed firmly but gently upon his back. She sang again, a series of beautiful, perfect notes. Her mount dipped its right wing and wheeled in a new direction. The moon and the ring passed from Robert's field of vision, but the other pair of creatures came up beside them, and he saw his brother in apparent sleep in the youngest rider's arms. When one of the dragons veered suddenly away, Robert followed its fire-winged flight as long as he could.

He gave over worry. This was all some dream anyway, he told himself. He had crossed the edge of madness, crossed it perhaps even before he had called Eric and begun this trip.

The world and the stars and the blackness of night all shifted and coalesced around him, but their forms were unfamiliar, their patterns without meaning. He could feel the soft hide and the powerful muscles of the beast on which he rode, feel the shivering pulse of its mighty wings. He could feel the wind, smell the sweet scent of the woman next to him, hear her clear voice as she sang.

It was a dream. Or it was madness. Maybe it was both.

In the far distance, the mountains rose against the star-speckled night. Sweeping, wind-blistered mountains, weathered and ancient, full of mystery, they might have been the Catskills. That high, shining peak might have been Mount Doubletop, and that one next to it, Slide Mountain, where giants were said to play at ninepins on stormy nights.

Robert laughed inwardly. *Fool,* he told himself.

Those are not Eric's beloved Catskills. He knew it, too, for a fact. It might be a dream, and it might be madness, but whatever it was, wherever, he knew this:

He was far, far from home.

Chapter Three

SEVERAL times the sharp edge of the wind caused Eric to awaken. Each time he stirred a bit, then slipped back into a restless slumber. In those brief waking periods, though, images flashed before his eyes like fragments of dreams. Mountains rose before him, ominous and old, and the world raced by as if he were flying!

His skull throbbed. Pain lanced through his right side. His vision wouldn't focus. He tried to sit forward, but someone held him firmly. He leaned his head back on a soft shoulder and slipped into unconsciousness.

Again the wind forced him awake. His eyes fluttered. A weak smile teased the corners of his lips. What a nice dream! A beautiful dragon, its wings burning with a queer amber fire that shimmered against the black night, flew beside him. A young woman with streaming black hair rode upon the beast's neck. In her lap, she cradled his brother's blond head and stroked him. An amber glow played over their faces as those massive wings rose and fell.

It troubled him only a little that he knew his eyes were open. Dreams were like that, strange and unpredictable. Maybe he shouldn't have his eyes open. Oh, what the hell, then. He patted the arms that held him, wondering only vaguely whose arms they were, and once more let go of consciousness.

He woke yet again, this time with a sudden start. A chill raced up and down his spine. Something had touched his face. It was the most tenuous of sensations, like walking through a single, unseen strand of a spider's web. He blinked hard, trying to focus. A face floated out there in the night. A woman. Her hair drifted like a mist about her face. Cold eyes shone like stars, and her lips were the color of a rose with bloody thorns. She regarded him with icy hatred.

So you can see me, Son of Paradane, a voice that might have been the wind whispered in his ears. The tone was full of surprise. Then the voice turned grim. *You will remember me only as part of your delirium, but I am coming for you.* The voice and the image melted back into the fabric of darkness, leaving a taste of evil in Eric's fevered mind. He cried out, but words would not take form in his mouth. The arms that held him tightened.

The range of mountains loomed, blacker than the night. Eric squinted, forcing his eyes to focus despite the throbbing that filled his head. He rode a dragon too. He realized that now. Just like the beast that flew beside him. Only his had prettier wings.

He had been only dimly aware of the soft singing behind him until it changed suddenly. Before, it had been almost a lullaby, soothing and easing his pain. The melody changed now, and the singer dropped his pitch. Eric's dragon turned away from the amber-winged creature that carried his brother. It skimmed low over the mountain peaks, so low that Eric could see the tall cresting trees swaying in the wind, the rippling of the leaves in silvery moonlight.

He listened to the song, unable to understand any of the words. Maybe it didn't have words; he couldn't be sure. A young tenor voice flowed flawlessly up the scale and down again, and the dragon, as if guided somehow by the song, banked in a slow arc to the left, sinking even closer to the tops of the mountains. Eric peered down at the shivering trees, into the black recesses and canyons, into narrow cloves. Far away, some river threaded a course through the mountains like an argent ribbon, black water gleaming where the moonlight touched it.

The singer changed his song again, and the dragon banked to the right. Eric tried his best to think, to remember who it was that held him. Where was he? What was he doing on this awesome beast? Who was the woman with the eyes of ice? Some memories seemed so sharp. But it was so hard to think. Pain beat a drum on the inside of his skull, and his side ached.

A covey of honking geese scattered suddenly to get out of the dragon's way. Eric languidly raised one hand to protect his face. From behind him came a low, youthful chuckle. Who? Before Eric could say or do anything the dragon dipped again. The last of the mountains flashed past. The silver river pulsed with moonlight and with the reflected colors of his dragon's wings as they sailed above it straight into the heart of a sprawling valley. Eric spied the dark silhouette of a town.

The second dragon reappeared, suddenly wingtip to wingtip with his own. He looked over to see his brother and the woman who rode the beast. Through his pain he suddenly saw that Robert was not in her lap at all but bound awkwardly to her saddle!

Again the singer changed his song. From the high scales to the lower, his voice dropped, sure and rich as brandy. Side by side the dragons swept above the darkened town. The glow of their wings lit the streets and rooftops. But if the town was dark, the people were not long asleep. Windows flew back, and pale faces stared skyward. Doors opened, and men and women spilled out, clamoring in excitement. Just past the far edge of town the dragons gyred suddenly. Three swift, dizzying revolutions and Eric's beast touched the ground, close enough to the last buildings that it laid its head down on the end of the main street.

The townspeople surged around the dragon, seeking a chance to touch it, calling up to the riders, but the voice behind Eric sang a sudden, sharp note.

The crowd fell silent and backed away to give the dragon and its passengers space. But there was still the light of wonder in their eyes, an eagerness in their expressions and movements as they whispered among themselves and pointed. One man raised his small daughter onto his shoulders to give her a better view. She grinned and gurgled and clapped her tiny hands.

They showed no fear of the monster in their midst. The light from the dragon's wings played beautifully upon their faces. Three men separated themselves from the others and came forward to help Eric down. For an uncertain instant, he slid downward over scaly flesh, but the men caught him. His feet touched solid ground for a second as two of them supported him with his arms around their shoulders. His legs gave way.

The tenor voice shouted something. A burly, bearded man with arms the size of tree trunks, who wore a blacksmith's leather apron, pushed through the throng. Snarling and barking orders in a language Eric didn't understand, he forced everyone back. Then he scowled at the pair who held Eric. A moment later he lifted Eric in his two arms as if he were the most precious of dolls.

Still, a jolt of pain shot through Eric's head and side, and he nearly cried out. He held it back though, toughing it out in the presence of so many strangers. As the giant turned and strode through the crowd, Eric shot a glance back at the dragon. A young boy of no more than fourteen, rail thin and dark-haired, stood on the dragon's saddle. For an instant their gazes met. Then the dragon rider jumped lithely down to the ground, and the crowd closed in around him.

Eric wondered about his brother. The second dragon had landed just a little farther away, in the field beyond town. Some men had run out to meet it as well. So far they hadn't returned.

The big blacksmith carried him toward a building, kicked open a door with one booted foot, and went inside. Immediately, a dog began to bark within. The crowd followed them as far as the threshold but stopped there. The blacksmith pushed the door shut with his heel. A few oil lamps hung from the low ceiling. Tables and chairs were arranged all around. An old hound, tethered in one corner, stood on shaky, sticklike legs and stared at him, tongue lolling. It gave another sharp bark and scratched at the floor with its nails until an old woman rushed in from another room and smacked it between the ears.

The place was some kind of tavern, to judge by the stale odor of alcohol and the mugs and cups that sat abandoned upon the tables. Eric licked his lips at the thought of beer, realizing how thirsty he was.

"Put me down," he instructed in a weak voice.

The big man looked at him and answered in his own incomprehensible language. Rather than letting Eric down, he strode toward a wooden staircase at one side of the room, and ascended it. Eric's feet banged on the railing. The old woman gave a howl and rushed forward with her apron to polish away any mark. Her sharp voice followed the blacksmith up the stairs.

Eric found himself in a dimly lit corridor on the upper floor. One candle burned in a sconce mounted on a wall. A waxy smoke had long since stained the space above it. "Can't you speak English, man?" he snapped at the blacksmith. His head pounded. He was in no mood for games, and he was worried about Robert.

The blacksmith looked at him with a sympathetic expression and shook his head as he carried him down the narrow corridor. The floor creaked under every step. There were several doors. His bearer chose one and kicked it open with the same disdain he had demonstrated at the front entrance. At the same time, Eric heard rapid footsteps, creaking, and a new voice on the stairs. A much smaller, thinner man hurried up behind them, carrying a fat stub of a candle in one hand and a sloshing basin of water in the other. His tiny, waspish face was screwed up in nervous excitement, and he jabbered breathlessly. Eric could understand nothing that he said.

The giant carried him inside a dark room and placed him on a small, wood-frame bed with a thick feather mattress. The sheets smelled of scented herbs. The smaller man set the candle on a side table, and the room brightened a little. Eric gave a groan as he settled his head into a soft pillow. Both of his hosts froze at the sound and stared worriedly at him.

Abruptly, the small man gave the blacksmith a scolding and pushed him out of the way. He then went to the basin of water, which he had placed on the table with the candle, and lifted out a sopping cloth. He wrung it gently, brought it to the bedside, and dabbed at Eric's forehead. Eric gave another groan at the contact and knocked the hand away. A wave of pain surged through him. He tried to sit up. The blacksmith rushed to his side, put a restraining hand on his shoulder and gave him a stern look.

The small man spoke in a rush of words as he folded the damp cloth and placed it on Eric's brow. Eric forced himself to lie still, but watched the two of them from the corners of his eyes. The blacksmith went to stand beside the door. The small man rose from the bedside, went to the table, and lifted another cloth from the water. He came back with the fresh cloth and exchanged it for the first one.

A third person, the old woman from downstairs, entered the room. She wore a tangled knot of gray hair atop her head, but strands and wisps stuck out in all directions, framing her prune-wrinkled face. Her dress was of old brown homespun with a big, faded-blue apron over it. In one hand she held a little ceramic bowl. She muttered something to the small man and glared briefly at the blacksmith. The small man snapped a response. The old woman stuck out her tongue. Then she went to the table.

She set her bowl down by the candle. From the big pocket of her apron she extracted a handful of tiny wood chips. She dropped them into the clay vessel, all except for one. That she held in the candle flame until it began to glow and smoke. When it was burning to her satisfaction, she placed it back in the bowl with the rest. A fine white smoke curled slowly up, and a pungent fragrance seeped throughout the room.

The blacksmith scowled and muttered to the small man, who just shook his head tolerantly as he changed the cloth on Eric's forehead again.

From a second pocket the old woman pulled a handful of leaves. She began to hum some kind of tune. Facing the doorway, she shook the leaves like dice, and scattered them upon the threshold. For good measure, she threw a second handful over the rest of the floor. Finally, she turned back to the small man, jabbered something, and stuck out her tongue at the blacksmith again before she departed.

"That stuff stinks," Eric murmured as the smell of the incense in the ceramic bowl grew stronger. He wrinkled his nose and pointed.

The small man turned around, stared briefly at the bowl and nodded. He said something to the blacksmith, who apparently agreed. The big man picked up the smoking vessel gingerly. It was obviously hot. He opened the door quickly and disappeared, trailing fumes.

Though they treated him with kindness and concern, Eric's thoughts turned to his brother. Robert was a prisoner somewhere, bound with ropes.

Eric's skull still throbbed as he tried to think. What did he know of these people? These strangers? For all he knew, his brother could be suffering tortures while he lay here in this bed.

He had to find Robert. That single imperative began to ring in his head like the pounding of a huge bell. *Find Robert. Find Robert.*

He raised up on one elbow and gave a soft moan. The small man was all that stood between Eric and the hallway door. Eric's vision blurred as he sat up a little more, and another wave of pain swept over him. The little man bent over him, trying to push him gently back on the bed.

Eric knocked the man's hands away and swung his feet over the side. Again, the little man tried to force him back to bed. Eric's anger swelled as he gave him a rough push. "My brother!" he mumbled, the words slurring. He rose shakily to his feet, fighting back an unexpected nausea. The little man blocked his way, daring to put a hand on Eric's chest in an effort to thwart him. With a cry of rage, Eric grabbed his attacker and slammed him against the wall. The little man's head cracked like an egg. He slumped in the corner, trailing a thick red smear down the length of the wooden wall.

Eric reached for the door, his senses swimming. The handle wouldn't quite hold still. Finally he seized it with both hands and jerked the door open. With one hand on the wall, he groped his way into the corridor. He lurched and caught himself, and tried to shake the haze from his brain as he straightened and started forward again.

One of the side doors opened, and the blacksmith stepped suddenly out to bar his path. Spying Eric, his eyes widened with surprise. Eric didn't give him any chance to sound an alarm. He slammed a roundhouse kick into the giant's stomach. The man doubled over with a *whoof*. Eric closed in and smashed his right elbow against the back of the blacksmith's head, following instantly with a vicious knife-hand to the upper neck. He felt the vertebrae crack. The entire floor shook as the giant fell.

For a moment, Eric sagged back against the wall, clutching his head, fighting vertigo. Two men dead, and the pain screamed behind his eyeballs. He couldn't let it stop him, though. Nothing would stop him. He had to find Robert! Had to stop them before they hurt his brother!

The stairs were ahead, just beyond the flickering candle in the sconce. The flame tormented him, tried to confuse him with its dizzy dancing and guttering. He smashed it with the back of his fist, extinguishing its treacherous light, oblivious to the hot wax that splashed his hand. He thought only of the stairs and Robert.

Halfway down, a red film flooded his vision. He clutched at the banister for support and stumbled, half-slipped down the rest of the stairs. At the bottom, he nearly tripped over a chair. With an angry growl, he flung it out of his way and watched it shatter against the far wall. The dog, still tethered in its corner began to bark furiously. Eric leaned on the nearest table and peered around to find the door. His vision slipped out of focus again. He squeezed his eyes shut and pinched the bridge of his nose.

A noise and a sharp intake of breath made him whirl. It was only the old gray-haired woman. She stared at him, wide-eyed, trembling, her gnarled hands wrapped in the folds of her worn blue apron. Eric pushed the table aside and ran for the door. Seizing the iron handle, he wrenched it open and rushed outside.

"Robert!" he screamed as he stumbled into the street. "Robert!"

The pain was one long rushing roar that filled his head and pressed against the backs of his eyes. He could barely see, hardly think. In a dull corner of his mind he realized he couldn't help his brother. Still he ran, because the pain drove him.

"Robert!" he screamed again. But now it was a cry for help.

The dragons were gone, but a few people still lingered in the unlit streets. They glared at him with evil eyes. Why hadn't he seen before? They were monsters. Clawed hands reached out to seize him. He batted them away, screamed, struck wildly at a few, and stumbled toward the center of the town square.

The doors of the houses and shops opened. From all directions the monsters came toward him, shambling, groping for him, hollow-eyed and hungry.

Eric felt something at his back. The low rock wall of the town well. Frantically, he looked around. There was nowhere to run, no chance to escape! The monsters closed in. He put one hand to his throbbing head and it came away bloodied. *Robert!* he cried silently, despairing. *Robert!* Why couldn't he think?

Dozens of vile, lipless faces swam before him. Hands ripped his clothing. Eric whirled and stared down into the well's black depths and thought of falling. The thought was as good as the deed. He fell, and fell and fell. . . .

But it was not escape. She was there. The woman with the eyes of ice. At the bottom of the darkness she sat on an onyx throne and laughed, laughter that was the sound of ice breaking on a lake. Strands of ebony hair swirled languidly up from her head and snaked about his tumbling body. The walls of the well disappeared. He hung in a void, caught in a web.

Do not struggle, Son of Paradane! Her voice was a freezing burn inside his brain, her words thunder in his skull. *Poor fool. You know a secret you must not share.*

Her black tresses slid over his body, binding him, arousing him in a strange and frightening way. She laughed again, voluptuous evil, sexual and deadly. Tendrils of silky hair drew him closer to her. He saw her lips, red as rubies, and the small red tongue she passed over them, her face pale as the snows of winter.

You want me, Eric Podlowsky, she whispered seductively. *You killed those meddling fools to come to me, to please me. How easy it was for you, taking their lives with your hands. You are a warrior, my warrior.*

"Who are you?" Eric shouted as he writhed in the weblike strands that held him.

But his questions didn't matter to her. She sat on her throne, radiating dark power as she toyed with him. He could sense that he had but a moment of her attention. For him, perhaps a fatal moment.

I will remake you in my image, she announced, *and you will take the place of the creature you helped to kill. Is that not a fitting reward, Son of Paradane?*

He saw it then, the small horn that curled upward from her forehead, nearly hidden in the impossible swirls and coils of raven hair. She smiled and parted her lips, revealing tiny thornlike fangs.

Eric screamed. It was not his blood she wanted. She began to suck out his soul. "No!" he cried uselessly. Her gaze froze him. He could not even struggle as she laughed and laughed. Like a leech she drew the vitality and warmth out of him, and more, some inner, unexplainable piece of himself. He resisted, tried to force her out of his mind, clinging desperately to that spark. Still, he felt it going, going . . .

A hand closed suddenly around his, and someone gave his arm a tug.

This time it was the darkness that screamed. Eric felt the coils of hair tighten about him, choking. Still, he managed to twist his head around to see who it was that had his hand. At first he thought it was Robert. But the blond hair was too straight, and the eyes were blue fire.

The young stranger didn't look at him at all, but strained and pulled until the coils of hair began to loosen and yield to his strength. Darkness screamed again, and the sound of her fury was fearful. The strands that held him snapped.

Eric clung to the stranger's hand, suspended and swinging in the void. The woman was gone. So was the greater part of the pain in his head. A dull ache remained, but that was all. He craned his neck, trying to get a better look at his savior. Blond hair, Robert's age, thin and muscular, shining eyes . . . !

Eric made a guess. "Scott?"

The hand that held his let go. Eric gave a long wail and fell, fell . . .

He came to, not at the bottom of a well but in bed, stripped naked, covered by a single thin sheet.

He reached up slowly and explored the bandage that someone had wound around his head. The candle still burned on the side table, but the basin was gone.

The old gray-haired woman sat in a chair on the far, shadowed side of the room, completely asleep, her hands folded in her lap, jaw slightly agape, head rolled forward. She had changed her shapeless brown dress for a shapeless white one. In the dim candlelight she looked like a picture of everyone's grandmother.

Eric gathered the sheet about his waist and swung his feet over the side of the bed. He hesitated, but this time the expected nausea did not come. Biting his lip, he turned a guilty eye toward the bloodstain he knew should be on the wall near the door. Someone had washed it clean. He drew a slow breath and let it out. The wooden floor proved cool against his bare soles as he rose. His toe brushed against something. A dry leaf. The floor was littered with them.

The old woman's eyes snapped open. Rising from her chair, she gave an insistent shriek and gestured toward the bed.

Eric had done enough fighting. "I'm thirsty," he said simply. Realizing she didn't understand, he touched his throat and tried to think of an appropriate hand gesture.

The door opened, and a shadow loomed on the threshold. The blacksmith stared at him. Eric regarded the big man with stunned surprise. He was alive! Not even bruised!

The grizzled giant came forward and helped Eric into the chair where the old woman had sat moments earlier. Then he said something to her over his shoulder as he bent and tugged the sheet higher up around Eric's bare chest. The old woman scurried out of the room, returning moments later with a steaming cup of hot broth. The blacksmith took it from her and passed it into Eric's hands while she watched with approving eyes.

"Thanks," Eric said gratefully. He took a sip of the stout, bitter beverage, unable to take his eyes from the blacksmith, ashamed of his actions and at the same time vastly relieved.

The blacksmith reached out a huge hand and patted Eric's shoulder. Then he turned and left the room. The old woman hesitated a moment longer, her half-crazed gaze lingering on Eric until he took another drink from his cup. Then she smiled, showing a mouthful of gaps and broken teeth, and followed the blacksmith.

Alone, Eric leaned back in the chair and watched the flickering candle flame. He regarded the wall in the corner where he'd cracked the smaller man's head, and a wave of depression washed over him. He was glad he hadn't hurt the blacksmith, but there was no such hope for his first victim. They might have cleaned away the blood, but he couldn't forget the image or the sound the little man's skull had made as it struck.

He took another sip of the hot broth and considered what his next move should be. His head was full of dim images, flashes of memories. A woman with eyes of ice. He still felt the power of that gaze upon him, chilling.

Drawing the sheet closer for warmth, he touched his wound gingerly as he tried to remember. The skin felt swollen, drawn too tightly over his cheekbone and brow. He wasn't quite sure how much had really happened and how much was part of some delirium nightmare.

With a gentle creaking of the hinges, the door swung back. Eric looked up expectantly. By the shadow on the floor, he knew who it was. His brother grinned at him as he entered.

"Robert!" Eric said, leaning forward in his chair.

"Don't get up," Robert told him as he came into the room. "That's a nasty cut and bump on your head." He crouched in front of Eric and laid one hand on his older brother's arm. "How's your vision?" he asked, peering closely into Eric's eyes.

"Good enough to see your ugly face," Eric answered, regarding Robert with a pleased grin. "It was a bit blurry before, but it's better now."

Robert squeezed Eric's hand and stood up. "You had quite a concussion," he said, pacing the center of the small room. "You've been out for two days."

"Two days?" Eric exclaimed. He winced suddenly and clutched at the side of his head.

"Take it easy," Robert warned him. "Pietka did a good job stitching up the cut, but you're going to hurt for a day or two yet." Robert sat down on the side of the bed. The quaint wooden frame gave a little squeak.

"What happened to your hand?" Eric asked, noting the white bandage that encircled his brother's right hand.

Robert raised the hand a bit, flexed the fingers, and gave a shrug. "I sliced my palm on that damn monster's scales. No major damage."

Eric gave a deep sigh, and his face clouded over. "It wasn't a nightmare then. At least, not all of it."

"Not in the sense you mean," Robert answered. Eric brought the cup of broth to his lips and drank. The steam crept up his nostrils, and he rubbed a finger over the tip of his nose as he silently regarded his brother. Robert was dressed strangely, in pants of loose black leather. His shirt was also thin leather. It laced up the front in an archaic style. He'd traded his hiking boots, too, for new black ones that reached halfway up his calf.

"Where the hell are we, Bobby?" Eric asked quietly. The room was warm, but he drew the sheet up around his chest and held it there with one hand while he clutched the mug of broth with the other. He couldn't seem to rid himself of some strange chill.

"Palenoc," Robert answered and leaned forward with his elbows on his knees. There was an intense gleam in Robert's eyes. Eric knew his brother had not been idle.

"Pale knock?" he repeated, frowning.

Robert nodded and looked away, trying to hide a troubled look. "That's what the locals call this place." He gestured toward a shuttered window near the foot of the bed. "You mind if I open that?"

Eric shook his head and took another sip of broth. "Be careful what you let in," he advised after a quick swallow.

Robert got up from the bed, unlatched the shutters and pushed them back. A warm night wind blew into the room, causing the candle flame to flutter and pop. For a moment, shadows swirled about the walls and floor.

Someone leaned into the room and peered at both brothers. Eric stared at the small, wasp-faced man who had cleaned his wound. He, too, was alive, just like the blacksmith. The wall hadn't been washed. There had never been a bloodstain. Eric wondered if he had gotten out of the bed at all. "I think I've had one hell of a dream," he said, half to himself.

The little man said something to Robert and looked at Eric. A big grin spread over his face and he left them alone again.

"That's Pietka," Robert explained as he settled down on the edge of the bed again. "He owns this place. He's also the closest thing to a physician they have in these parts. That's why the *sekournen* brought you here."

"*Sekournen?*" Eric repeated, his frown returning. "What's that? Can you understand that guy?"

"Not very well," Robert admitted, "but I'm picking up a few words here and there. *Sekournen,*" he said again. "They're the dragonriders."

Eric gave a little moan and rubbed his temple. "I don't think I want to hear this," he muttered. "Let's just get out of here and get home."

Robert looked away again. His brows pinched together, and his lips curled into a frown. He got up, went to the window, and leaned against the wall while he stared into the night. The silhouettes of the nearest rooftops stood out starkly against the starlit sky. Robert drew a deep breath and let it go. "I can't leave, Eric," he said finally.

"Are we prisoners?" Eric asked, his grip tightening on the mug.

"Of course not," Robert replied. "Everyone treats us well. Especially me. Something about my hair and eyes." He paused and rubbed a hand over his chin. "But there's another reason."

"The writer seeking out new experiences?" Eric interrupted harshly. "This place is crazy, Bobby! It isn't real! We're both having some kind of hallucination!"

"Real enough," Robert shot back, "to nearly crack your skull open." He turned back to the window. "If you're scared, I'll tell them you want to go home. We got here. There must be a way back."

"That silver medallion," Eric remembered, ignoring the affront to his courage. "Maybe it's a clue. It can get us home!"

"They took it from me," Robert said. "The thing is special for some reason to the *Sekournen*. They each wear similar medallions."

"These *Sekournen*?" Eric pressed. "How many are there?"

"I've met three so far," Robert told him. "A woman, a man, and a boy. The three who found us. I get the impression there are more."

Fatigue washed over Eric. He looked around for some place to set his empty cup, but the only table was on the other side of the room by the door. Robert was being his usual tight-lipped self, never volunteering information. Sometimes his little brother could be so irritating.

"I don't suppose you could just sit the fuck down and tell me what's going on?" he asked wearily. He raised a hand and massaged his left temple. The contact hurt, but like playing with a sore tooth, he couldn't resist.

Robert turned back to face him again. The candlelight played on his brother's pale, chiseled features and gleamed dully in his blond hair. Still, he seemed to wrap himself in the shadows as he stood with his back to the night. There was an almost spectral quality to Robert that Eric had never noticed before, a strangeness that sent a sudden shiver through him.

"Think, Eric," Robert paced in sudden agitation

across the floor and quietly pushed the door to the corridor closed. When he spoke again, he kept his voice low. "What was the title of my last book? *A Pale Knock.* And the name of this place? *Palenoc.*" His pacing took him back and forth through the room. The boards creaked at every step. He wrung his hands, curled them into fists, flexed his fingers. "I can't explain it. There's a weird familiarity about things. I look up at the moon here and that blue ring across the sky, and they spark something inside me. Something dreadful that I can't quite put a finger on."

Robert sat down briefly on the bed and put his head in his hands. He rose just as suddenly and went to the window, his back to his brother. Eric had the feeling there was more his brother wanted to tell him, and so he kept quiet, waiting for Robert to fight the war inside himself.

When Robert finally spoke, his voice was little more than a grim, fearful whisper. "Scott's here." He stopped, still fighting some private battle. His words came out like muffled rifle bursts. "It's impossible," Robert continued. "But he's here. I feel it. I can't leave till I find him."

Eric had never seen his brother so intense. Or, he thought, so afraid. Bobby never feared anything. He was the daredevil, the gung ho kid who climbed rocks and traveled the world and generally kicked ass. But something had hold of him.

"Who is Scott, Bobby?" Eric asked quietly as he turned his empty mug nervously between his hands. A vague flash of his nightmare came back to him. Somebody catching him, pulling him away from danger. "More than just a traveling companion."

Robert chewed his lip and sat down on the bed

again. "We skipped over into China for a while," he said, speaking of his Orient trip. "I wanted to climb Hengshan Mountain in Zhejian Province. There's a Buddhist monastery at the top. Scott had never done any rock climbing before, and it rained nearly the entire week we were there." He shrugged, then leaned forward and forced a wan smile. "You know me. A little rain never could stand in my way."

"You climbed it anyway?" Eric interrupted. He knew his brother could be reckless. "And Scott had no experience?"

Robert nodded. "None."

Eric frowned. "He fell?"

"I fell," Robert corrected. "We were more than halfway up the slope when I slipped." He got up again and went back to the window to stare outside. Eric had the feeling it was not the rooftops and shadows of Palenoc he was seeing, however. "I only fell about twenty feet," Robert went on sullenly, "but I sprained the hell out of my left ankle and knee. Scott wouldn't leave me and go for help. He carried me back down." He drew a deep breath and turned slowly to face his brother again. Even in the candlelight his face was as white as the sheet Eric wore.

"Now he's here," Robert continued uneasily. "And I have to find out how, because I know it's not possible."

Robert was holding something back. Eric knew his brother too well not to realize that. "There's more to it, Bobby," he pressed. "Give."

But Robert shook his head. "That's it," he answered stubbornly. "Scott Silver is here somewhere, and I've got to find him." He moved away from the window and stopped by the side of the chair. His hand fell lightly on Eric's arm. "We can talk more later. I see I've tired you. I'll come back after you've rested."

He took the cup away from Eric and set it on the table by the candle. Then he returned and helped Eric back to his bed. Eric had to admit it felt better to lie down again, with the soft pillow cradling his head and the feather mattress cocooning around him.

Robert fluffed the sheet over him. "You get some more sleep," he said. "I'll tell Frona to bring you some food when you wake up."

"Let me guess," Eric said, folding one arm under the pillow and settling himself. "The crazy old woman. I thought you couldn't understand them?"

"Pietka's mother," Robert informed him as he backed toward the door. "We manage to make ourselves understood on the simple things."

"You're not telling me everything, Bobby," Eric stated evenly. "What are you holding back?"

A shadow fell across Robert's face, and he hesitated on the threshold, one hand still on the handle of the door before he drew it closed. "You get some rest," Robert answered after a pause. "We'll talk more later."

Eric felt that same strange chill again as he listened to his brother's receding footsteps. They seemed to echo in the narrow hallway far longer than they should have. The wind swept in through the window near the foot of his bed and swirled about the room. With a sputter, the candle snuffed out. The smell of tallow diffused into the air. Somewhere out in the corridor another candle or lamp burned. Its dim and distant glow, alone, crept around the edges of the door and kept away total darkness.

"There's no place like home," Eric muttered to himself as he stared about in the gloom. "There's no place like home." *Damn it, anyway,* he thought. There was never a good witch around when you needed one.

From somewhere beyond the window came the hoot of an owl, as lonely a sound as Eric had ever heard. He listened to it for a while, unable to sleep. Finally, he got up and wrapped the sheet about his waist as he had before. He went to the window and looked out. The town was dark, not a lamp in a single window. Black rooftops and chimneys reared against the velvet night. No one moved in the streets.

It must be the wee hours of morning, he decided. He leaned out a bit and tilted his head back to study the sky. Nothing looked familiar, not one constellation, not one star. He folded his arms around himself and repressed a shiver, vaguely recalled a vision of a half-glimpsed moon and a planetary ring.

After a time, he dragged the chair over to the window and sat down. The wind played in his hair and over his bare chest. It was summer warm, full of the fragrances of the mountains beyond the town. He couldn't see those mountains in the darkness. His window faced the wrong way. But he could feel them out there, like a ponderous shadow on the whole town.

Somewhere a dog began to bark.

From the corner of his eye he detected movement. Someone walked in the street below, a lone figure. A young man. Perhaps Robert's age. He stopped, slowly turned, and stared upward. Their gazes met. But the man turned and passed on without so much as a nod of acknowledgment. Eric continued to watch. But when he blinked the figure was gone! As if the night had swallowed him.

The dog stopped barking.

Eric half rose out of his chair and leaned on the sill. Then he settled back again. He stared thoughtfully up at the sky and ran a fingertip lightly over his lips.

"Palenoc," he whispered, trying on the name of this strange world in which he found himself. He rapped his knuckles on the wooden arms of his chair. *"Pale Knock."* He repeated the title of his brother's book. Was that a coincidence? He rapped on the chair again.

Outside the window, secure in its unseen perch, the owl kept him company.

Chapter Four

ROBERT left his brother's room, closing the door softly behind him. For a moment his lips drew into a thin, taut line, and he stared at the bandage on his hand. The cut on his palm stung, but he told himself it was nothing and forced away any awareness of the pain.

He walked softly down the corridor, past his own room, and down the stairs. Three old men sat around a table, drinking from mugs and muttering among themselves. Pietka sat with them, his old hound leashed to the table leg near his feet. All talking stopped. The old men gazed at Robert with an air of expectancy. Everyone looked at him that way. It made him uncomfortable. Pietka started to get up, but Robert shook his head and gave a slight wave. The innkeeper sat down again. Robert went to the door, opened it, and stepped outside.

The quiet was almost unnerving. He was used to the incessant roar of Manhattan—the rumble of subway trains, the noise of automobiles, constant voices. He stepped off the inn's low stoop and started down the street. The smell of the river wafted through the air. Fresh pine from the mountains, too. The soft, fine dust puffed up around his boots as he walked. Most of the town slept, undis-

turbed by his rambling. A few windows were open
here and there to let in the breeze, but no candles
or lamps glimmered in them, and no one stirred.

He had no particular direction in mind, but he
found himself at the edge of the village, staring up
at the darkly looming mountains. Above the peaks,
the stars burned like cold jewels. Robert walked
past the last outbuilding, past a pen where silent
sheep huddled together, past a cultivated garden
patch. Just beyond the town, the ground started to
rise. He wandered up a hill overlooking the dark
little houses and shops and barns, and when he
came to an outcropping of rock, he climbed onto the
highest spot and sat down, his chin in his hands, to
wait for the moon and that strange, beautiful ring
to take their places in the Palenoc sky.

His left shoulder ached dully, but he pushed that
pain away too. It was only a mild sprain; it would
pass. It was better already, he told himself. He ro-
tated the joint a bit, testing his mobility, and was
satisfied.

He gazed toward the black silhouette of the town
and beyond. There was no sign of the dragons that
had brought them here. The *Sekournen* woman and
boy slept somewhere below, sheltered in private
homes. Robert couldn't sleep, though. He was a
creature of the night. Back home in his apartment,
with his books and his computer, he always worked
nights and slept away the day. He preferred it that
way. He loved the night.

He allowed himself a faint smile. There was a
strong chance he would be late with his next novel.
His publisher was going to be pissed.

The moon stole over the tops of the mountains
and silvered the rooftops. On the far side of town,

the tranquil river gleamed. Robert gathered his knees close to his chest and hugged himself. His shoulder gave a twinge, but he ignored it. He began to rock gently on his perch, and for a time his mind emptied of all thought or worry. He closed his eyes.

Unbidden, Scott stole into his thoughts. Robert replayed memories of their meeting in Florida, Scott in his crisp white uniform, his technique so flawless, so perfect. In Taiwan they had ridden the rickshaws. In Singapore, the sampans. In Bangkok they shopped their hearts out in the backstreet bazaars and markets. Robert smiled to himself, remembering good times.

But then a darker memory crept in among the good ones. Scott on a New York sidewalk, bleeding, utter shock on his face, begging Robert to help him, his hand clutching Robert's shirt.

With an audible gasp, Robert snapped his eyes open and forced the image away. He pressed a hand to his mouth and blew through his fingers. He trembled. With an act of will he made it stop and locked the memories deep inside some private inner vault. *Be calm,* he told himself. *Calm.*

But from some distant corner of his heart a faint voice called out. *Polo,* it said. *Hey, Polo.* He clapped his hands over his ears, trying to shut it out.

A soft singing rose over that voice. At first it also sounded faint and far away, but it drew closer until Robert realized it was not inside his head at all. It came from somewhere behind him! He turned on his rock and searched the hillside for the singer.

No one was there. The singing, too, had stopped. Only a wind sighed down from the peaks and rustled through the grass.

He turned to face the town again, dismissing the music as a product of his troubled imagination. Perhaps he was going mad. He had plenty of reason to believe that.

But then he heard it once more. That was no wind! He looked sharply around. Higher on the hillside, a small, flickering white light, a candle flame, perhaps, moved against the darkness. He barely glimpsed it before the song stopped and it winked out.

Robert slipped quietly off his rock perch and stared. Nothing moved. He fixed his gaze on the dim silhouette of an old tree near where the light had disappeared. Cautiously he approached the tree and walked around it. No one was there. He peered upward into the branches. The stars shone through the spaces between the broad, shivering leaves, but no one crouched above him. Placing a hand against the rough bark, he leaned against the tree and pursed his lips as he scoured the dark landscape.

> *Sweet as summer flowers, your eyes,*
> *Softer than the velvet rose that dies,*
> *Gentler than the wind, those sighs;*
> *Come now, my love.*

Robert jerked around, his gaze combing the hillside. From left to right he looked, spying nothing, no one. Yet he heard the song clearly. He moved away from the tree and crept a little further up the slope. There he stopped once more.

> *He wanders now some foreign land,*
> *Beyond the moon, beyond the band,*

He dwells upon some starry strand,
My precious love.

Robert spotted the pale light again, way up the hill on open ground. How had he missed it? It swayed slowly back and forth. Maybe it was the flame inside an old-fashioned lantern. But he could see no one in the darkness. The light stilled suddenly and floated in the air. Slowly, it began drifting across the slope. For the briefest instant something shimmered behind that glow. A young woman regarded him, long black hair fluttering about her in the wind, her pale dress billowing. Then he could see her no more, and only that tiny light remained.

"Wait!" he called. "Don't go!"

The light moved across the hillside toward a small copse of trees. Robert pursued, curious to meet the young woman who carried it. He had understood her song; she spoke English! He had to know who she was. The light paused, as if to make sure he still followed, before it disappeared between a pair of large tree trunks.

A soft humming drifted out upon the night, the same tune he had heard before, a wistful, lilting melody. Robert hesitated as he considered his surroundings. The mountains cast ponderous shadows down the hillside, shadows that fell upon the rooftops of the town below. In the sky, the moon crept in its languid course toward zenith. Just behind it, the edge of that strange azure ring made a halo that limned the peaks. Neither moon, nor stars, nor ring shed any light among the trees where his singer had fled.

He drew a deep breath and entered the grove. The wind brushed the leaves. Over that rasping whisper came the young woman's humming. Just ahead, Robert saw her light as it slipped behind another tree. He followed, moving soundlessly. She was not the only one, he told himself, who could play cat and mouse.

Deeper into the grove she led him until the trees were so thick he could no longer see the mountains above, or the town below, or the silver gleam of the river flowing past it. The earth was spongy underfoot, and moss grew heavily on the trees where he leaned his hand. The light appeared and disappeared, always in a new place. Each time that he thought he had lost it for good, Robert heard her tune again, and the light appeared just long enough to entice him further.

> *Beyond the night my lover dances,*
> *In the tender night that so entrances;*
> *Heartfelt sighs and stolen glances*
> *Say he is my love.*

Robert listened to the song with a puzzled frown, unsure if he heard it with his ears. The song was real. Her mouth and throat worked, shaping words. Yet the lyrics seemed to come from inside his head. "That's very pretty," he said in a conversational tone, his voice carrying clear and free through the grove. "What do you call it? Who do you sing it for?" He paused beside a tree, then peeked suddenly around the other side. She wasn't there, nor was the light. He heard a short laugh and whirled.

"Lover," sang the voice inside his head.

She waited for him just a short distance away. Her eyes were filled with mirth, and her milky-white, heart-shaped face crinkled with silent laughter. As the wind blew, her soft white dress fluttered upon her bosom and around her ankles. Her feet were bare. She smiled as she regarded him, and her lips parted slightly. Her arms lifted to him in invitation.

She carried neither lantern nor candle.

"Who are you?" Robert demanded, suddenly wary. Still, he took a step toward her. The world lurched and tilted crazily. He gave a short cry as he felt himself falling.

Two strong hands caught his wrist. Robert kicked and twisted frantically for a moment until he mastered his fear. Dirt filled his mouth. Sputtering, he scrambled with his free hand for some kind of purchase and found the grassy rim of the hole that had nearly claimed him.

He looked up to see who caught him, but more dirt cascaded down from the rim into his eyes. He cursed as someone dragged him up to safety. Half-blinded, Robert scrambled to his feet and rubbed at his eyes.

A familiar voice spoke to him, and a soft hand settled on his shoulder. It was the black-haired *sekournen* woman who had saved him. She pulled him another pace back from the old well, which in the gloom had made such a perfect trap.

Robert glared angrily at the siren who had nearly lured him to his death. "Why . . ." he started.

She only regarded him with sad, empty eyes. Tears began to seep down her pale cheeks. Slowly she hung her head, her dark hair spilling forward, and she covered her face with her hands. A sob broke the stillness, and the sound of weeping echoed in the grove.

The dragonrider let go of Robert's arm and

reached into a small pouch on her belt. Without taking her gaze from the woman on the other side of the pit, she drew out a handful of small dry leaves, crumbled them on her palm and cast the fragments into the air.

A wind blew through the trees. Like a thing of smoke, the siren began to dissipate. Robert's breath caught in his throat as he watched. The sound of weeping grew fainter and fainter, and her body diffused into the night. A small gust scattered wispy pieces of her. Little by little she dissolved away until only the echoes of her grief lingered. Those, too, faded, leaving only stillness.

The hairs on Robert's neck stood on end. "What was that?" He whispered hoarsely to the dragonrider, forgetting she could not understand him. Without asking her permission, he thrust his hand into the pouch on her belt and drew out a handful of crumbling leaves. They looked like the same kind of leaves someone had scattered around his brother's bedroom. He had paid them little attention, assuming that old Frona just kept a sloppy house. He knew better now.

Tossing the leaves aside, he moved carefully around the well and stood on the place where the siren had disappeared. The grass nearly obscured a large, flat stone. Part of an old wall, he discovered with only a little more exploration. A house had stood here once, long ago. Only the roughest foundation remained, barely visible in the weeds and trees.

What had happened to the house? Destroyed? Burned? The grove kept its secret. It seemed possessed now of an air of menace. The darkness felt oppressive.

The dragonrider came to his side. *"Leikkio,"* was all she said as she shook her head. Then she repeated it: *"Leikkio."*

The word sparked a memory in Robert. He uttered it to himself and thought back. Something in his research for *A Pale Knock.* He recalled a note on Finnish ghosts. *Leikkio—the flaming one.* In other lands it was will-o'-the-wisp, jack-o'-lantern, ghost light.

The dragonrider said something to him, her eyes searching his face as her grip tightened gently on his arm. He didn't need to speak her language to know her meaning. "I'm with you, lady," he answered quickly. An icy sweat broke out on his brow. He wiped at it nonchalantly as if it were nothing at all. "Let's get out of here."

Robert let her lead him out of the grove, and she never let go of his arm until they were in the clear again. He looked up toward the mountains, so ominous, then down toward the town. He knew now why no one walked the streets at night, why the villagers shut themselves up safe and secure in their homes and kept mostly to themselves when the sun went down.

He studied the woman at his side. She was a head shorter than he, but tall for a woman. Pretty, too, in a rugged sort of way. Though her hair had been loose the first time he'd seen her, tonight she'd bound it back in severe braids. He guessed her eyes were brown.

He'd seen her only from a distance the past days. While he and Eric had rooms with Pietka, she and the young *sekournen* boy were quartering in a private house. He tapped one finger on his

chest. "Robert," he said. "My name is"—pause—
"Robert."

She understood at once. "Alanna," she said, smiling as she tapped her own chest. She had a beautiful smile.

"Alanna," Robert repeated. He put one hand atop his own head, then put it on hers. Next, he lowered it a few more inches and tilted his head questioningly.

Alanna stared at him for a moment. Her face lit up. "Danyel," she answered, nodding.

So the boy's name was Danyel. Robert was pleased at his progress. It helped him to forget the chill he still felt from the encounter in the grove. He touched Alanna's elbow and walked across the slope toward the outcropping of rock where he had sat earlier.

He leaned against a boulder when they stopped and tapped it with his injured palm. "Rock," he said, attempting to build a vocabulary.

But Alanna wasn't interested. She said something in her own tongue and threw a very clumsy kick at nothing in particular. Then she faced him with a sheepish grin and rubbed her cheek.

"Oh," Robert said. "Sorry about that." He hung his head to indicate his regret.

But Alanna backed off a pace and attempted the kick again. She made a short, staccato speech, and looked up at him expectantly.

Robert cocked an eyebrow and regarded her with new appreciation. She wasn't interested in his apology. She wanted to learn the technique!

"Draw the knee up first," he instructed, demonstrating a simple snap-kick. "Keep your back straight. Don't lean away."

After a few tries Alanna had something that approached a proper kick. She was a quick student. He showed her how to make contact with either the heel or the ball of the foot and watched her face as she applied his teachings. Her concentration was solid. He found himself toying with the idea of actually teaching her.

Now, though, it was he whose concentration wavered. He kept glancing back at the grove and up at the stark outlines of the mountains against the night sky. He felt them like presences at his back. Sometimes he glanced at the moon or the pale blue ring that cut an arc through the firmament.

No matter how he denied it or tried to distract himself, Robert knew the taste of his own fear. When Alanna wasn't looking he peered around and felt his gut tighten just a little bit. He shivered inside. It unnerved him how those mountains resembled his own familiar Catskills. They wore the same eerie, haunted quality.

But that wasn't the only familiarity that puzzled and frightened him. He looked up at the moon, and the word *Thanador* stole into his mind, as if that was its name. But how could he know that?

Alanna touched his arm, and he shook himself, embarrassed that he had allowed his thoughts to drift. She pointed toward the far horizon across the rooftops. A dragon sailed through the darkness, its wings shimmering with the colors of fire. As it drew closer, a second dragon wheeled in from the east. Robert recognized the opal glow of Danyel's mount. Suddenly, a rush of wind pressed against his back, and an amber light bathed him. Alanna's own dragon swooped low out of the mountains, blotting out the moon as it glided past.

Alanna shouted and motioned for him to follow. They ran down the hill as all three dragons landed in the fields at the south end of town. Just as before, sleepy-eyed villagers woke and poured curiously into the streets. Alanna ignored their questions. Through the square she and Robert raced.

A shirtless, bootless Danyel appeared beside them as they reached the edge of town. Across the field, the three dragons fanned their wings impatiently. A pair of figures strode swiftly across the sward. Robert recognized the taller man as the third dragonrider, who had rescued his brother and him.

He tapped Alanna on the shoulder to draw her attention. "Robert," he said, thumping his chest. "Alanna, Danyel," he continued, indicating each of them in turn. He pointed toward their third comrade and gave her a questioning look.

"Valis," she answered at once, grasping his meaning.

The man with Valis was older and smaller. His shoulders were stooped, his breathing labored as he stopped before Alanna. Moonlight glinted off his polished scalp. He wore baggy trousers of a thin white cloth and a loose chemise. A long, sleeveless jacket of dark material hung upon him like a cloak.

Robert found himself taken aback by the piercing look the old man gave him. The acrimony in that gaze! There was a plain sneer on his face, too, as he walked past Robert to speak with Alanna. Robert knew he was the subject of their conversation, but he understood nothing and stood by nervously. From the reactions of the townspeople he could tell that this man was someone of importance. Alanna held up her hands, and the old man touched his palms to hers. They exchanged a few more words, then turned and started up the street together.

Danyel grabbed Robert's hand. The boy gave him a quick smile and led him in Alanna's wake. Valis and the townspeople followed, too, and they all stopped before Pietka's inn. The blacksmith, Brin, waited for them. He held the door back as Alanna and the old man entered. Robert, Danyel, and Valis followed. Politely, but firmly, Brin turned everyone else away and closed the door.

Frona stood nervously in a corner, watching wide-eyed, wiping her hands on a dirty apron. She gave a short burst of chatter, but no one paid her any attention, nor did she make any move to follow them upstairs.

The door to Eric's room opened suddenly, and Pietka leaned out, frowning at the commotion. Then his face lit up with surprise. He gave a big smile and held up his palms as the old man approached, but the man waved Pietka's hands away and instead embraced him warmly.

Inside the room, Eric propped himself up on one elbow in his bed. "What's going on, Bobby?" he asked suspiciously as everyone crowded into the small quarters.

"Got me, brother," Robert answered. "I did finally meet someone who spoke English, but her manners were the pits."

"What?" Eric tried to sit up, but the old man pushed him back down with one hand and settled on the edge of his bed. Pietka went to stand at his side, holding the candle so the light shone brighter over the old man's shoulder. "What is all this?" Eric demanded.

Alanna muttered something to the boy, Danyel,

who left the room, only to return moments later with a long, cloth-wrapped object. Alanna took it from him, untied the cords that were wound around it, and removed the wrapping. The candle-light shone darkly on the smooth unicorn horn as she held it up.

The old man regarded it with a stern and troubled eye, then turned his attention back to Eric. He motioned for Pietka to bend a bit closer with the light as he lifted Eric's right eyelid with the ball of his thumb. Pursing his lips, he lifted the other. "Hold still!" he snapped when Eric winced and jerked away. "I'm trying to help you, *gringo!*" Slowly he began to unwind the dressing on Eric's head.

"You speak English!" Robert exclaimed in surprise.

Pietka muttered something. The old man nodded impatiently. The bandage came away. The gash near Eric's hairline looked red and puffy. Pieces of six tiny thread stitches lay flattened against the skin.

"He's a goddamned doctor," Eric said to Robert.

"My name is Roderigo Diez," the doctor informed them with stiff dignity. He turned and spoke quietly to Pietka, who took a small pair of scissors from a pocket and handed them over.

"Don't you think you should sterilize those?" Robert suggested as the old man leaned toward his brother.

Roderigo Diez straightened and gave Robert a withering look. "You poor little lost Americanos," he said, his voice dripping with sarcasm. "You are so spoiled." He gestured around the room with the scissors. "Have you seen anything that would lead you to believe Pietka sterilized the needle he made the stitches with in the first place?" He leaned toward Eric with the scissors again. "Chalosa is a small fishing and farming town. You won't find any medical universities here."

With a physician's deft skill he snipped the threads that held the gash closed. A fine crusted line of dried blood, perhaps an inch long, showed in the candle's glow. Diez examined it carefully and prodded the swollen flesh around it, evoking another wince from Eric. The smallest drop of blood seeped up.

"That hurt," Eric protested.

The old doctor scoffed. "A hero of your legendary stature can stand a little pain," he said. He raised his hand over the candle, made a fist, passed his other hand over the fist, then uncurled his fingers. A small white stone rested on his palm. Pietka gave a small gasp. Eric raised up a bit to see. Robert and the others bent closer.

The stone was a piece of opaque quartz dotted with dark red spots. Highly polished, it shimmered in the candlelight. The rest of the room seemed to grow darker, almost as if the stone itself somehow drank the light.

"Lucky us," Robert commented drily. He folded his arms across his chest. "He's a magician, too. You get healed and entertained at the same time."

"If you're unimpressed now," the doctor retorted, "wait until you get the bill."

Eric seemed to be barely listening. He stared at the old man's palm, eyes glittering with the candle glow. "That's bloodstone," he said quietly.

Roderigo Diez lifted the stone between thumb and forefinger and turned it in the light. It gleamed. He pressed Eric back onto the bed. Eric cooperated, licking his lips in uncertain anticipation, and Diez touched the gem to the droplet of blood on Eric's brow. For a moment he held it there, then he let go, leaving the stone resting upon the wound.

"What's he doing?" Eric asked his brother nervously, his eyes rolled up in a vain attempt to see the stone on his brow.

Robert shook his head, suddenly intrigued. He had researched the healing properties of crystals and stones as background for his books. He didn't believe, of course, but the material had been interesting. There was no point in trying to explain to his brother, though. "Be calm," he told Eric. "This is not the strangest thing we've seen here."

Yet he wasn't so sure. The stone, which already shone in the candlelight, began to glimmer with a redder energy as the old man hummed over it in a low, nasal tone. Robert leaned closer, but Alanna caught his arm and urged him back. The humming changed pitch, and the stone's color deepened. Roderigo Diez squeezed his eyes shut. Again the humming changed, growing louder, more intense. Robert could almost feel the vibration on his skin. The red glow of the stone rivaled the candle flame. It uplit everyone's faces, lending them strange appearances, casting stranger shadows on the walls and ceiling.

With an abruptness that made Robert jump, Diez stopped. He opened his eyes and bent over Eric, who appeared to be in some kind of trance. Gradually the bloodstone lost its glow. Whereas before it had seemed to shine in the candlelight, it seemed now little more than a common stone. The old man reached out and plucked it from Eric's forehead.

Eric raised a hand and touched the wound experimentally. "The pain's gone," he whispered. He pushed himself up on one elbow and stared in amazement at his brother.

Roderigo Diez spoke to Pietka, who went to the room's small table and lifted a cloth from a fresh basin of water. He wrung the cloth carefully. The doctor took it, folded it into a tight swab and dabbed at Eric's wound. The crusty line of blood washed away.

Except for a thin red scar, there was no trace at all of the gash. Even the swelling around the wound had disappeared.

Pietka murmured in reverent tones. Valis and Alanna conversed excitedly. At the head of the bed, Danyel clapped Eric on the shoulder and grinned a big, boyish grin. Eric glanced around from face to face in bewilderment.

Robert, though, slipped silently from the room into the corridor and leaned against the wall. He pressed his palms together, hooked the thumbs under his chin, and set his forefingers against his lips. He drew a deep breath. His heart thundered in his chest. He shut his eyes briefly, willing himself to be calm. More relaxed, he held up his own bandaged palm, sensing the cut beneath. His lips drew into a taut line as he folded his arms once more and put his hands out of sight.

When he had himself under control, he went back inside. His brother was on his feet. "It's damned incredible!" Eric called to Robert. He smacked his forehead with one palm. "There's no pain at all!" He clapped his left side. "Hell, all the bruises are gone."

Robert nodded. "Thank you," he said to Roderigo Diez. "Sorry if I was rude."

The old man turned slowly and met Robert's gaze. *"De nada, gringo,"* he answered, and perhaps there was a little less hostility in his tone also. He rose from the bedside and took the unicorn horn from Alanna. He ran his hands over its gleaming length, his mouth set in a grim line. When his examination was complete, he gave it back. He looked sternly at both brothers. "Now we must get you out of here at once."

Eric protested before Robert could speak. "Doc, I appreciate what you've done," he said, "but we're not going anywhere until you've answered a few questions."

A look of anger flashed over Diez's face, but the old man kept his voice calm. "Then let me answer them for you as quickly as possible, Americanos. You have stumbled into a world called Palenoc. You are currently in a town called Chalosa in the nation of Guran, which leads an alliance called the Domains of Light. And you are both in greater danger than you know." He pointed to the unicorn's horn in Alanna's possession. "By killing the *chimorg* you have made a fearsome enemy that will stop at nothing to get its hands on you." He paused, drew a deep breath and let it out.

"What you have done is impossible," he continued as if the words were somehow distasteful to him. "The *chimorgs* are immortal. Only the *sekoye* can kill them. Yet Valis tells me you did this, and I believe him. We hope you will give us this secret."

"Us?" Eric asked, raising an eyebrow. "You mean this Guran?"

"I assume a *chimorg* is the unicorn thing we killed," Robert interrupted. "What's a *sekoye*?"

"It's what you call a dragon," Roderigo Diez answered. He turned back to Eric. "The entire Domain will profit from your knowledge. The *chimorgs* are not only monsters, they are the eyes and ears of our foe."

"*Sekoy-yay*," Robert repeated, and Alanna nodded approvingly.

Suddenly someone gave a high-pitched scream, and shouting erupted in the street below. Everyone in the small room ran for the window at the same time to see the commotion. At least a score of black-armored men, their faces concealed behind gleaming masks, swarmed through the streets, casting nets and wielding clubs.

Valis pushed his way out of the room and disappeared down the corridor. Danyel followed.

"Get him some clothes!" Roderigo Diez shouted at Pietka. The innkeeper, paralyzed for an instant with an expression of fear on his face, recovered himself and raced away.

Robert whirled away from the window. "What's happening?" he demanded of the old physician. "Who are those guys?"

Alanna ran to the door, but a shout from Diez stopped her. For a moment they exchanged a few harsh words in Alanna's language. Then she nodded and dashed off. Diez turned to Robert again. "I told you, *gringo*, we are at war."

A bolt of sizzling blue fire lit the sky for an instant, turning the world starkly white. The thunder blast shook the entire inn. Diez thrust his head back out the window and gave a small cry. Robert and Eric bent over him and peered out.

A *chimorg* galloped up the street, tossing its horned head and bellowing. From the other direction, another score of black-clad soldiers charged up from the river. Nets hissed through the air. Clubs and wooden staves rose and fell with ruthless efficiency. Townspeople screamed as they ran to get away.

High in the air, hovering over the scene, limned in a cold, icy light, the black silhouette of a woman laughed and laughed. Her hair streamed and lashed about her head as if the tresses bore life of their own, and as she stretched out her arms, lightning flashed in her palms.

Robert stumbled back from the window and cowered into a corner, trembling uncontrollably. *Shandal Karg,* his mind screamed. *Shandal Karg!* Yet those words meant nothing to him! He knew only that they filled him with fear. More than fear: terror!

Another blast of lightning ripped through the sky. The air crackled. "That hit a soldier!" Eric cried excitedly. A bundle of clothes flew from the doorway and landed on the bed. Pietka didn't linger to be thanked. Eric grabbed the garments of thin leather and began pulling them on as he watched the scene in the streets.

Unnoticed, Robert swallowed his fear and crept toward the window again. He bent down beside Roderigo Diez. He could barely bring himself to look up at the evil shape that floated above them. He didn't understand the unnatural fear that gripped his heart, but he knew its source. "What is that?" he whispered in a choked voice. He couldn't bring himself to say *she*. Whatever it was, it was not a woman.

Diez's gaze bore into Robert with a fierce intensity, as if he saw deeper with those eyes than a man should. His lips curled back as he spat the answer: "That is the Heart of Darkness."

Chapter Five

ERIC followed his brother and Roderigo Diez outside. A pair of sheep, loosed from their pens, scrambled out of their way. The streets were chaos. No sooner were they out the door than a net sailed through the air toward them. Robert shoved the old physician out of the way and knocked it aside with a wide sweep of his arms.

A huge warrior rushed forward. Black armor glimmered in the firelight from a burning building. Large white eyes gleamed behind the carved mask that covered his face. In one hand he held a strange weapon, a kind of heavily weighted baton. The knobs at either end looked like polished wood. He whirled it with a threatening flourish and swung.

Eric leaped in close and threw a forceful block. The baton spun out of the warrior's grip, nearly striking Diez, who quickly ducked as it clattered against the inn's door. Eric struck with his best punch. The mask shattered. The warrior screamed as he clutched his face and fell, blood pouring from his eyes.

"It's lacquer!" Eric cried in surprise. "The damned armor is lacquer!"

Roderigo Diez seized his arm and dragged him back against the wall as a squad of soldiers dashed up the street. A dog ran barking after them. "Its main purpose is to stop a blowpipe's darts," he whispered tersely, leading the way again, "and to frighten poor villagers."

The sky flashed with lightning again, and the thunderblast shook the inn, in whose shadow they hid. Eric smelled the acrid odor of smoke, heard the crackling of flames. Chalosa was on fire.

A woman ran screaming around the corner of the next building. Her ripped bodice fluttered from her shoulders as she clutched her breasts, and blood streaked her left cheek. A pair of black-armored soldiers chased right behind her. One carried a baton. The other whirled a net over his head and prepared to throw.

Robert moved like a silent ghost, brushing past Eric to intercept the pair. A kick sent the netman smashing into his partner, and both soldiers went down while the woman raced away. As the man with the baton tried to rise, another figure darted out of the shadows across the street. A long length of slender wood whistled down, cracking his helmet. Neither soldier moved after that.

Roderigo Diez dashed forward, shouting in the local language as Alanna leaned momentarily on her staff and pointed at the pair on the ground. The unicorn horn, wrapped in cloth again, hung from a leather thong across her back. She bent down and ripped away one of the masks, then looked up at Diez. A brief, heated exchange followed, apparently an argument about the soldiers, until the old physician shook his head.

"What's she saying?" Eric demanded.

"Something's very wrong, Americano," Diez snapped. "These soldiers aren't who we thought they were." He looked desperately around, licking his lips, fire reflecting in his eyes. "Come on," he called, "we've got to get you out."

Eric and Robert traded worried looks as a cloud of thick smoke rolled over them. The night was full of screaming and shouting. They started off down the street with Alanna and Diez. Another net whispered through the air. Alanna gave a shout of warning and swept it aside with her staff. One weighted corner struck Diez a glancing blow, and he clutched at his forehead.

"It's all right," he cried. "Keep going!"

But before they got far, Robert pressed them all into a shadow, flat against a wall. A *chimorg* charged right past them, its hooves throwing up showers of dirt from the unpaved street. A black-armored soldier ran around a corner straight into its path. For an instant he froze. A short scream issued from behind his mask. The unicorn slammed its horn through his armored chest, gave a triumphant bellow, and hurled the body through the air to crash against the side of a barn. The beast ran on down the street as lightning sizzled across the sky.

When the monster was gone, they advanced again, moving as swiftly as they could, crouching in shadows and doorways. Much of the fighting had shifted to another street, at least for the moment. The loudest cries came from the riverfront.

"Where are we going?" Eric demanded as he watched an old man being dragged between two baton-wielding soldiers.

"The *sekoye* are waiting in the field," Diez explained in a hissing whisper. He stared at the old man too. "Sumeek," he whispered, half to himself. He bit his lip.

Overhead, the sky brightened with white fire. Thunder crackled. When it faded, though, another sound took its place. A shrill trilling shivered suddenly over the town, growing in volume, clearly audible over all the tumult.

But Eric still watched the old man and the soldiers. "We're running out?" he shouted. His hand clutched at Diez's long black sleeve, then he let it go. "Like hell."

Robert looked at him, and Eric could tell that his brother was thinking the same thing. Without another word they moved together. In the street, one of the soldiers saw them. He let go of his captive's arm, drew back with his baton, and dealt a savage blow to that white-haired skull. The old man sagged to the dirt with a soft groan, and his killer and his partner turned to meet the challenge.

"Don't kill them!" Roderigo Diez called desperately from the shadows.

Eric easily sidestepped the first blow that whistled down toward his head, but the soldier's instant backswing caught him by surprise. The baton's weighted end brushed his temple, and he barely turned away in time. The pain, however, served only to anger him. Catching his attacker's wrist, he bent it sharply, feeling tendon and then bone snap. The baton tumbled to the ground as the soldier screamed behind his mask. Still, he tried to strike Eric with his other hand. Eric dropped and swept the soldier's feet. A pile of black armor arched high in the air, crashed down on its back, and lay still.

"Not bad, big brother," Robert said quietly, bending over the still form of the old man, "for a teacher of small-town kids and housewives." His foe lay a few yards away, face down in the splintered wreckage of a helmet. He touched two fingers to the old man's neck and frowned. "But we didn't help this guy much."

"He's dead?" Eric asked bitterly. His brother nodded.

"Don't you understand?" Diez shrieked, running up to them. "It's you they want! They've come for you! We've got to get out of here!" He grabbed Robert's collar and tried to pull him to his feet.

Robert's eyes flashed; rising, he whirled around. For an instant his bandaged hand hovered in front of the physician's face, but he didn't strike. Instead, he pushed Diez roughly away.

"He's right about getting out, Bobby," Eric admitted. He glanced down at Sumeek. Maybe if he and Robert had stayed in the shadows, the old man would still be alive. That thought ate at him. "The villagers aren't even trying to fight back. We can't take on a whole army!"

Robert gritted his teeth and shook his head stubbornly. At the same time Alanna gave a shout. She threw herself against Eric, knocking him aside, and they both fell in a heap as something made a sharp, sickening crunch. Someone screamed, but the sound was cut off suddenly. Only a choking, muffled gurgle followed. Eric scrambled up onto one elbow and stared.

A hayrake jutted up from the chest of the soldier he had tackled. The man twitched and shook, but three long wooden points pinned him to the earth like a bug. Gasping, he clawed at his mask and ripped it away. Blood bubbled from his lips as life left his open, fear-filled eyes.

Eric got up and touched the rake's handle in horror, wondering at the tremendous force that could have driven a farm tool clear through an armored man and so deeply into hard-packed earth. "Where the hell did it come from?" he muttered.

Robert gripped his arm. "I swear, the damn thing was leaning against that barn across the street moments ago!" He shook his head again in disbelief. "It just flew!"

"Old Sumeek has his revenge," Diez growled, staring with grim-faced satisfaction at the body of the old man at his feet. "Now let's go!"

Lightning sliced across the sky again. As if in response, that strange trilling that Eric had noticed before swelled even louder. "What is that?" he cried as they ran down the street. No one answered him. He pressed a hand to one ear. It sounded almost like a child's playground whistle, but in three subtly different pitches. Nor was there any pause to it, as if to draw breath. The sound built and grew, sawing through his brain like a sharp-edged knife.

It was another sound, though, that made Eric stop as they rushed past a narrow alleyway. A series of sharp cracks and a cry of pain accompanied loud, rough-voiced curses. At first Eric thought it was the retort of a rifle he'd heard. But in Palenoc? The glow from a burning building lit up the alley enough for Eric to see.

Danyel, wielding a whip with impressive skill, held off two soldiers. A third knelt in the dirt clutching his face. The boy swept his arm tirelessly back and forth, lashing at the eyes behind those masks. The soldiers swung their batons wildly, unable to get close enough despite their armor.

Robert grabbed Alanna's staff and ran at the pair. He struck without warning, splintering the helmet of the first soldier, using the reverse end to sweep the feet of the second. Even before the man hit the ground, Robert brought the butt of the staff down against his mask, breaking it. He raised the weapon again to deliver a final blow.

Danyel leaped in front of him and grabbed hold of the staff with both hands, his eyes narrowing to desperate slits as he shouted a single command. His face gleamed with sweat in the reddish glow of the fire, and his youthful muscles bulged with determination. For an instant, Robert and the boy struggled over the slender length of wood. Then Robert relented and seemed to get control of himself.

Danyel let go of the staff and called to Diez.

"No!" Diez uttered in an anguished whisper. He ran back into the narrow passage.

Robert cast a scornful glance at the soldier that Danyel had downed, and threw a low roundhouse kick, sending him toppling sideways, silencing his cries. Diez ignored him and ran right past.

Eric moved forward with Alanna. For the first time, he noticed the still figure that lay on the ground in the gloom at the rear of the alley. Pietka. There was little anyone could do for the old innkeeper. A bloody hole, perhaps a quarter of an inch in diameter, oozed a thick stream of blood just above his right eye.

"What happened?" Roderigo Diez moaned, dropping down beside his friend. Tears welled up in his eyes. He brushed them away, but new ones took their place as he lifted Pietka's head in his hands and rocked him. He spoke again, looking at Danyel, using the boy's own language.

Danyel's voice took on a strange calm. He answered as if he were issuing a report, and he stared at the body with a cool detachment as he coiled his whip.

Eric found it an odd, disconcerting transformation. "What did he say?" Eric asked, kneeling beside Diez.

Diez tried not to weep as he explained. "Pietka and Frona apparently tried to hide back here, but these soldiers saw them. When Pietka tried to defend his mother, somebody shoved him." He rose slowly to his feet and went toward the wall at the back of the alley. He peered at it closely for a moment until he found what he was looking for. "His head hit this." He pointed to a large, jutting nail and drew his finger along it to show them the dark wetness.

Alanna called back from the mouth of the alley. She had claimed her staff from Robert and had taken a position to watch the street.

"The fighting's coming this way again," Diez informed him wearily. "We can't stay here."

"I'll carry him," Eric offered. He took Pietka's hand and prepared to lift the innkeeper onto his shoulder.

Diez caught his arm. "Leave him," he instructed with a firmer voice. "He'd understand."

Another pair of soldiers strode past the alley, dragging a screaming woman in a net between them. Alanna and Robert moved as a swift, efficient team, catching the soldiers by surprise, taking them out before they knew what had hit them. Robert flung the net off the woman. She stared openmouthed for an instant and raised one hand to touch Robert's hair. Then she scrambled up and ran.

Eric raced to his brother's side. But when he passed one of the fallen soldiers, he noticed the smear of blood and the empty black socket behind a broken mask. Danyel's whip had claimed an eye from that one.

As they ran out into the street again, a fiery wall crashed behind them, causing them all to turn and look over their shoulders. Visible through the flame, smoke, and embers, farther back up the street, the *chimorg* bellowed as it trampled a black-armored shape.

Eric had never been in a war. For a moment, the cacophony threatened to overwhelm him. The screams, the crackling of the dozens of fires, the crash of timbers, the thunder and lightning, and that terrible trilling assaulted his ears. Everywhere he looked, soldiers and terrified villagers ran or fought. Sheep and cattle, pigs and dogs bleated and squealed and barked, loosed from their pens or barns or leashes. The sky itself turned red with heat and fireglow and lightning flash.

Finally they reached the very edge of Chalosa. Far out across the field, three dragons clawed at the earth and beat their shining wings as they stretched their necks high into the air. They were the source of the trilling. Eric recognized it now. Singing! The dragons sang! He followed the fixed gaze of their diamond-faceted eyes and stared once again at the woman Diez had called the Heart of Darkness.

She appeared smaller now, though no less dangerous. Lightning still flashed in her hands, and her chill laughter still pierced the night. The sky around her seemed almost like a hole, and the dragons' song was pushing her farther and farther into it. The louder and higher they sang, the more distant she became.

But another a bolt sizzled earthward out of that hole and fried an armored soldier.

"I understand now!" Roderigo Diez cried suddenly, glaring at the soldier's charred and smouldering remains.

He didn't get a chance to explain, though. On either side of the field, armored warriors rose up from the deep grass and charged at them with nets and batons. Another squad of attackers gave a shout and came at them from behind.

Eric barely had time to glance at Robert. A net flew past his head, and he ducked. A huge figure rushed him. A baton whistled down toward his skull. *Perhaps this is the greatest terror of war,* he reflected as he threw himself at his attacker, *the discovery of one's own capacity for rage.*

Until now all his fighting had been a game, an exercise, a competition. Go to class, take a lesson, teach a student, win a trophy, have a laugh and a beer afterward. He knew that life. He knew that Eric Podlowsky.

But did he know this one? He thought of Pietka, and, God help him, he *wanted* to hurt this soldier that came at him. He caught the descending arm in a double block. With a shout, he smashed his elbow into the man's solar plexus, finding an almost erotic joy in the way the thin, lacquered chestplate shattered. Without hesitating, he slammed the heel of his right hand upward, snapping a helmeted head back with tremendous force.

"Don't kill him!" Roderigo Diez screamed.

Two more attackers rushed Eric. The first swung at him with a baton. Eric dodged the blow easily. He felt detached, almost as if he were watching himself from outside his body. With a quick side-step and a kick he broke the man's knee. The second soldier carried a different weapon, some kind of short rope with a heavy knot in one end. Before Eric could get his balance the knot caught him a glancing blow on the cheek. He shrugged off the pain and threw a powerful reverse punch straight to his foe's face. Pieces of the black sculptured mask flew in all directions.

Eric eased off and looked around, searching for his brother. To his surprise, a handful of villagers had joined them. The Chalosans fought poorly, but now their screams were filled not with fear but with fury. He spied Valis too, fighting with them, wielding a staff like Alanna's. He and Danyel waged furious combat shoulder to shoulder, while Diez crouched half-hidden in the shadow of a nearby building, his old eyes wide with fear and anger. Alanna had lost her own staff. She swung a net around and around, using its weighted corners against any black-clad figure within reach. Another dark-haired woman fought close beside her, using another net the same way.

A sharp *kiai* caused Eric to whirl about in time to see Robert execute a block with such force that a baton went spinning from a warrior's numbed grip. With fluid grace, his brother grasped his attacker's arms, turned, and dropped the man with a flawless throw. The soldier struck the ground with bone-breaking force as Robert met his next foe. A sweeping crescent kick flung that one off his feet.

The look on Robert's face was serene and cold. He did not wait for his attackers. He went to them, cut them down with perfect technique and an icy joy. An armored fighter ran past him, intent on a Chalosan man. Robert caught the soldier with a bent elbow around the throat, swept him to the ground, and heel-kicked his chest. Another baton whistled toward Robert's head. Even across the distance, Eric heard armor and bone snap and a soldier's surprised scream as his brother blocked the blow.

A flicker of memory rushed through Eric's mind, and he remembered Robert on the rim of the clove back in the Catskills, doing kata, framed against a full moon. There had been a coldness, an otherworldliness to it that at the time had eluded him in his beer fog. In retrospect, it seemed like a portent of things to come.

Something brushed Eric's shoulder, and instinctively he ducked. A net sailed through the air, ensnaring Alanna. She gave a sharp, angry scream as a pair of armored fighters bore her down. Before Eric could run to her aid, another attacker charged at him, wielding a staff as if it were a spear or lance.

"Thanks," Eric muttered, grasping the offered end. A side-kick to the warrior's chest, and the weapon was all his. Eric tucked the staff under one arm and faced Alanna's attackers. She struggled, pinned to the ground under the net, while one of them tried to secure her feet with a cord.

Giving no warning, Eric dealt a blow to the helmeted skull of the soldier at Alanna's feet. The laquered cap split in two and the soldier sagged on top of her. Her second captor turned to meet Eric, pulling two batons from his belt. He spun them twice with an audacious flourish.

Eric spat in the soldier's eyes. Most of his saliva splashed on the mask, but it was enough to momentarily disconcert his foe. He brought the low end of the staff straight up into the man's crotch with all the force he could summon. The batons fell to the ground. The soldier sank to his knees, folded forward, curled into a fetal ball and emitted a shrill cry.

Alanna threw the net off and got her to her feet. Immediately she ducked again. There were nets everywhere now. They *shhhsssed* through the air. Half the Chalosans lay helpless. The other half ran like frightened rabbits toward the foothills and the mountains. The black-clads were everywhere, waiting to intercept them.

Roderigo Diez gave a shout. Across the street, a pair of soldiers dragged the old physician from his hidey-hole. He kicked at their shins, spat on them, cursed, and tried to bite. One of the warriors slapped him hard.

Before Eric could move, Robert took the first one down with a flying kick. The force of his attack sent all three, even Diez, sprawling in the dust. Robert bent and ripped the helmet off the second man, raised the knife-edge of his left hand, and fixed his gaze on the soldier's soft, exposed throat.

"Don't kill him!" Diez screamed, staring in wide-eyed dread. Robert barely seemed to hear. But the anticipated blow didn't come. Mercifully, Robert straightened and turned his back. As he offered his hand to help the old doctor up, the warrior scrambled to his knees and reached for a baton. Robert's back-kick took him full in the face.

"You mustn't kill!" the physician shouted, waving a finger wildly under Robert's nose. Then he gazed around the streets in wide-eyed desperation, biting his lip. "We can't win here," he cried hopelessly. "Run to the *sekoye*! Run!"

"And let these people be slaughtered?" Eric raged as he rushed to his brother's side. "We can't run away!" He could hardly believe the words coming out of his mouth. Only moments before, it seemed, he'd told Robert they couldn't fight a whole army. Still, he didn't want to run!

Alanna spoke rapidly to Diez and waved a hand toward the dragons.

"They won't be killed!" Diez shouted back at Eric. He shot a look past the brothers. In the sky, the Heart of Darkness stared down at them. From far, far away, from some deep well of blackness, an electric serpent shrieked across the night. Diez screamed and knocked them all aside. The world flashed blue-white, and the air hissed.

For a split second, an armored soldier glowed like a sun as the bolt consumed him.

Diez struggled visibly to control his emotions. Then he seized both brothers by the arms. "*Apurese!*" he urged, lapsing into his native Spanish tongue. "We must go before Darkness claims us all!"

"No!" Robert shouted furiously, staring at the woman in the sky. His whole body tensed. The muscles and veins in his neck and face showed lividly under the flesh as he clenched his fists. "No!" he cried again.

Eric caught his brother by the arm. The intensity of Robert's defiance hit him like cold water. "Stop,

Bobby!" he urged, regaining his own reason. "We can't fight these odds! It's time to go!"

"They won't be killed!" Diez cried again, dragging at Robert's other arm. "They won't be killed!"

"What do you mean, they won't be killed!" Robert shouted back, jerking his arms free. "What about that soldier? She fried him!"

"She is not the danger here!" Diez shouted back. "She kills, yes! But the soldiers won't!"

"What about Pietka?" Robert reminded him cruelly.

"They won't be killed!" Diez shrieked, on the verge of a hysteria to match Robert's. Tears streamed suddenly down his old face. Still, he reached out and caught Robert's arm again.

"All right!" Robert answered, relenting. But a violent trembling seized him. He shot a look back up at the sky, then reached out and gripped Eric's shoulder for support. His eyes still burned with some hidden emotion, and the momentary weakness swiftly passed. "We run for the dragons," he agreed, "but we take as many down as we can on the way."

Farther out in the field, Valis was still on his feet. The big dragonrider fought with a ferocious strength, lashing out with the broken halves of a staff at a circle of black-clads trying to get a net over him. Together, Robert and Eric made short work of his attackers.

They ran as fast as they could. The grass, rising halfway to their knees, hampered them, and old Diez slowed them down, but those few warriors who saw and dared to follow found Robert waiting, crouched in the weeds like a silent, vengeful tiger.

Danyel was waiting nervously with the dragons.

He jabbered something in an apologetic tone to Alanna and Valis and hung his head. There was no sign of his whip, and Eric guessed that he had lost it in the fighting. "Tell him there's no reason to be ashamed," he said to Diez. "I saw him fight. He was just the first to see how hopeless it was."

Diez looked at him with a new, appreciative expression, then said something to the boy. Danyel's face brightened a little.

Abruptly, the dragons stopped their singing. Eric gazed up toward the sky again. There was no sign of the woman from his dream. If she was a woman at all. In fact, he wondered now if it had been a dream. "What did you mean—she wasn't the danger?" he said to Diez.

The old physician looked over his shoulder toward the smoke-filled sky. "These soldiers are not from the Dark Lands where she holds sway," he answered with a shiver, "but from the Kingdoms of Night. She came to save you from them." He fixed Eric and Robert with a fearful gaze. "To save you for herself." He fell silent for a moment as he looked from brother to brother, and a puzzled frown warped the corners of his mouth. "I'd have thought she would've killed you rather than risk the secret you carry falling into our hands." He scratched his chin, his frown deepening. "I wonder why she didn't?"

Robert gave a sharp intake of breath. "The Dark Lands," he murmured. There was a mysterious edge to his voice. "The Kingdoms of Night." He opened his hands and stared at his palms with a strange expression. The bandage on his right hand was bloodied. He had opened his cut.

Eric bit his lip. "I had a dream of her," he confessed. "I think she has something a lot more unpleasant in mind."

Robert looked up sharply. An unmistakable fear filled his brother's eyes.

Valis interrupted with a shout and pointed back across the field. A squad of black-clads rushed toward them, waving nets and weapons. Alanna saw them too and sang out a sharp note that set Eric's ears to ringing. The amber-winged dragon stretched down its neck. Wasting no time, she put one foot into the stirrup and swung into the saddle. Robert sprang up behind her.

Valis and Danyel sang out, each in his own distinct voice, and their dragons bowed their heads. Valis and Roderigo Diez mounted the fire-winged beast. Danyel climbed onto his opal-colored dragon, the largest and most beautiful of the three. He held a hand toward Eric.

"It's now or never, big brother," Robert called when he saw Eric hesitate. Eric licked his lips, then grasped Danyel's hand and rose up into the saddle behind the boy.

One after the other, the *sekoye* lifted into the night sky. Eric felt a surge and the rush of wind against his face as his stomach flip-flopped. His arms tightened around Danyel. In a dim corner of his mind, he realized that the boy hadn't lost his whip at all but wore it coiled about his waist like a belt. Half-standing in his stirrups, Danyel sang his beast higher and higher into the darkness.

Far below, Chalosa burned like a sad, lost star.

Chapter Six

Sing woe! Remember,
And pity us our plight;
The dead dwell in the Dark Lands,
And the Kingdoms of Night.

WITH that quatrain he had ended *A Pale Knock*. Robert repeated it again and again, unable to get the words out of his head. *The Dark Lands*. A chill ran through him, and he shivered violently. *The Kingdoms of Night*.

He'd never been afraid of anything in his life. At least, he'd always told himself that. But now he couldn't help it. His guts crawled as if something inside were gnawing to get out. There were too many resonances between his novel and this strange world. Too much in Palenoc that seemed familiar to him. Too much that terrified him.

That *thing*—that woman—in the sky. Why did it paralyze him with fear to look at her? To even think of her? *Shandal Karg*. Those words echoed in his head. What did they mean? Was it a name?

Yes.

Her name.

Robert squeezed his eyes shut and bit back a scream. He didn't understand. How could he know that?

He wrapped his arms around Alanna's slender

waist and clung to her, using the touch of her, her nearness, her smell to drive away his fear. He felt the strength of her body, her sheer physical power, greater than any woman he had ever held. Her pale face and black hair shone in the bioluminescent glow of the beast's wings as she sang to it. He wanted to catch that face between his hands, pull her back and press his cheek to hers. Maybe that would stop his shivering.

But between them, wrapped in a cloth and hung on a thin cord over her shoulder, was the unicorn horn. It only reminded him of the evil that was out there, waiting. He swallowed hard and curled his fingers around the concealed shaft. He would not let his fear master him.

The wind whipped sharply at his face. The night chilled and stung him. His leather garments offered some protection, but his cheeks burned with a cold fire and his fingers tingled. He wiggled them into the folds of Alanna's tunic and, despite the horn between them, drew her even closer.

The dragons swept northward away from Chalosa, then arced toward the west. The black peaks of the mountains sped past below. Danyel and Eric flew on Robert's right side, Valis and Diez on his left. Wingtip to wingtip, the three *sekoye* raced through the dazzling night.

Robert could not distract himself by admiring the beasts for long, though. Dark thoughts closed in again, filling him with foreboding. He remembered Pietka, dead now. And crazy old Frona, casting leaves over his brother. What had become of her? And what had become of Brin? He felt like a coward for running and leaving them behind.

Alanna's braids snapped at his face. He leaned

his head down against her shoulder, trapping one of them under his cheek, and rolled his eyes up toward the azure ring that stretched from west to east across the starlit sky. Just above it floated a fat moon no longer quite full.

Thanador, it was called. But how did he know that?

Alanna's song changed subtly. They left the mountains behind. The *sekoye's* left wing dipped. Robert's grip tightened around the dragonrider as, for a dizzying instant, he saw the ground far below and thought he was falling. The stars spun, and the blue ring shifted. He started to cry out.

Alanna's hands closed firmly over his, and she pulled him securely against her body. Again he felt her strength, the same strength that had dragged him from a hidden, ghost-haunted pit, and he knew he had never been in danger. He felt like a fool as well as a coward.

Now they flew southward. A darkly silver ribbon cut a swath through the land below. Robert started as he spied a trio of lights racing along underneath them. Then he realized what it was that he saw—reflections of the dragons' wings on the river's rippling surface.

Alanna let go of his hands, reached back, and tucked her braids down inside her shirt to keep them from lashing him. That done, she pointed to the land on the west side of the river. "Chylas," she called over her shoulder, following it with something more he didn't understand. Next, she pointed downward to the east. "Guran."

He knew her meaning, though, or thought he did. The land west of the river was Chylas. To the east lay Guran. Roderigo Diez had told them they were in a nation called Guran.

"Rasoul?" he shouted into the wind, the word drying in his mouth before he could get it out. How could anybody sing against such wind, he wondered. He swallowed and called the name again. Then, abruptly, his jaw snapped shut.

What was Rasoul? *A city,* came the answer from somewhere deep in his mind. *An important place.* But how did he know that?

Alanna pointed down at the river, then drew her finger straight ahead. "Rasoul," she repeated, nodding. The river led to Rasoul. She didn't seem surprised that he knew the name. But why should she? He might have picked it up from Diez or Pietka or any of the other villagers.

Only he hadn't.

Alanna's hands closed over his again, and she began once more to sing in a rich alto range. Robert listened. If there were words, he could not understand them, but her voice was razor-edged velvet. It cut through the wind, through the night itself. In response, her dragon surged forward. Even Robert flung back his head to feel the rush on his face. He discovered he wasn't quite so cold anymore.

Far ahead, another dragon shimmered faintly in the black heavens. Off to the east, still another. On wings of cool emerald the two beasts floated, scarcely seeming to move against the speckled backdrop of stars. Robert tapped Alanna's arm and pointed the pair out to her. She nodded and pointed to a third that he had not seen. Flying below and a little to the left, at a height that must have ripped leaves from the trees, another dragon followed, pacing them. From above, it appeared to be no more than a racing shadow. Only the firelight that burnished those treetops revealed the color of the *sekoye's* ruby underside.

Alanna spoke to him again, and Robert fervently wished he could understand her language. She pointed. In the distance the river flowed into a vast, glimmering body of water, a sea or a huge lake. A moment more, and they left the land behind and swept out over the waves. Alanna half rose in her stirrups and sang. Her dragon swooped low, skimming the surface.

Robert twisted around to see what had become of the dragon below them. It followed just behind, its wings blazing brilliantly. The rider waved to him.

He glanced up, searching for his brother, and nearly gave a shout. Danyel's dragon came screaming out of the night in a steep dive. The boy stood erect in his stirrups, leaning back to resist gravity. Eric clung for dear life, his face screwed up, eyes squeezed shut, mouth open in a long wail.

Just when Robert was sure the dragon would smash into the lake, it leveled out. The tips of its fire-opal wings touched the water, hurling up streams of spray and mist, before it began to climb again. Its mighty tail cut a trough through the waves before it lashed the air.

"If Eric survives the ride," Robert called into Alanna's ear, "he's going to kill that kid."

Overhead, Valis's dragon kept pace effortlessly. Valis was the odd one, Robert reflected. Quieter than Alanna or Danyel, strangely reserved, Valis had a talent for merging into the background. A cultivated talent, Robert suspected.

In the distance up ahead, the pair of emerald-

winged *sekoye* made gradual turns. Alanna overtook
them, and the two new riders fell in with the rest
of the party. Six dragons soared together in a loose
formation, the mingled light of their wings making
liquid fire of the lake beneath them.

Abruptly, they were over land again, but the lake
remained visible, rippling in the moonlight, just to
the west. Alanna tapped him on the knee to draw
his attention. "Rasoul," she called back.

At first he saw nothing. Then, straight ahead, he
picked out a collection of tiny glimmering dots in
the darkness. Like the lights of a modern city seen
from the air, he thought, though he knew that was
impossible. Or was it? This was Palenoc, where
nothing seemed impossible.

The lights grew rapidly, spreading over the countryside as they approached. Yet another pair of *sekoye* gyred with slow grace above the city. Alanna
began to sing again, and her dragon slowed its
flight. Valis and the emerald dragons surged past,
then they also slowed and fell back into formation.

Rasoul was far larger than Chalosa. Robert gazed
down into the maze of streets and alleys. Most of
the buildings were low and dark, seldom more than
two stories. Here and there, however, a minaret or
a tower thrust up against the night. Globes of
weird colored fire dotted the streets. Some rooftops
displayed similar, but larger, globes. Others shimmered with the light of flickering watch fires,
which burned in huge metal cauldrons.

At the heart of the city, one tower soared above
all the others. Alanna aimed her dragon straight
for it as she patted Robert's hands where they
rested on her stomach. Words he couldn't understand drifted back to him. From her tone and the

warm relief in her voice, however, he knew her meaning. She was coming home.

The dragon opened its wings and glided downward in ever-narrowing circles. Just above the tower, it beat its wings again. Robert stared downward. In the center of the tiled roof a huge ball of softly glowing light burned upon a giant metal tripod, the only feature that he could see, except for the low, thick wall that ringed the top of the tower. Alanna guided her dragon down while the others circled above.

Massive claws caught hold of the wall. Wings fluttered, then stilled and folded. Perched like any bird on a fence, the dragon stretched its neck down to the roof.

Alanna tapped Robert on the knee again and spoke. He didn't need to understand her language. Almost reluctantly, he unwrapped his arms from her waist, swung one leg over, and dropped. Though it was only a few feet, the impact shivered up through his ankles and knees, and he wobbled for a moment on rubbery legs.

Alanna unlashed a pair of leather packs from her saddle, then dropped lithely beside him. Turning, she sang a trio of notes and waved to her beast as it sprang away from the wall, spread its wings, and climbed alone into the night.

"Where's it going?" Robert asked, watching it fly southward.

Alanna shouldered her packs, grabbed his arm, and led him to the waist-high wall. Rasoul spread out in all directions. Some sections of the city, he noted, were darker than others. To the south stretched yet another great body of water.

Danyel's opal-winged dragon swept low above

the tower. Robert heard the young boy's strong tenor singing to the beast as claws scrabbled sharply on stone. Robert caught his breath as the wind from its wings blew on his face and snapped at his clothing. It was an awesome spectacle. The dragon folded its wings and stretched out its neck. Eric slipped to the rooftop. He looked pale and clutched his midsection with one hand as he stumbled toward Robert. The boy did not dismount, but flew off with his beast.

"I'm gonna kill him," Eric muttered as he reached Robert's side. "I swear I'm gonna kill him."

The furious beat of wings alerted them that Valis was descending from another direction. His bass voice boomed as he guided his mount lower. It came in faster than the others, its legs, held tight against its streamlined form, unfolding only at the last possible moment. Immense claws found purchase on the wall. Wings fluttered, then folded. Perhaps because Roderigo Diez was so old, the dragon stretched its neck and laid its massive head flat upon the tiles. With one strong hand Valis steadied Diez as the Spaniard climbed down, and Alanna ran to his side. Like Danyel, Valis departed with his dragon.

Overhead, the remaining dragons—their escort— wheeled away.

"Exhilarating," Diez said breathlessly when he joined them. "Is it not, *hermanos*?"

But Eric was not listening. He moved toward the huge iron tripod that stood at the roof's center. It reached nearly twice Eric's own six-foot-plus height. Atop the tripod perched a massive globe, seemingly made of glass. The liquid within radiated a gentle glow that softly illuminated the rooftop.

"What is that stuff?" Robert asked Diez as Alanna steered him toward the tripod.

"Call it dragon piss," Diez answered, with an amused shrug. "There's no time for a better explanation. I must take you to Phlogis."

Alanna caught Eric's arm and pulled him back a step while Diez ran a hand along the underside of one of the tripod's legs and located a concealed lever. Robert heard the faint hum of gears. A mild tremor shivered through the tiles under his feet. Directly beneath the tripod, a section of the floor rose slowly upward, revealing stairs that descended into a well-lit chamber.

"Welcome to Sheren-Chad," Diez said, hustling them down the stairs.

"Sheren-Chad?" Robert asked suspiciously. "I thought this was Rasoul."

Alanna said something to Diez, and he replied. "Every Domain city has its Sheren," Diez explained, coming down the stairs after Robert. "Relax, Americano. You are not prisoners, and we are not your enemies." He put on a sardonic grin that Robert found vaguely irritating. "You've already made enough of those."

Robert reached the bottom of the steps. The chamber was illuminated with a dozen smaller globes mounted at equal intervals on plain stucco walls. A long table occupied the center of the chamber. Upon it rested large, heavy basins of water and stacks of soft towels. Around the room, against the walls, stood several wardrobes and chests.

"Please wash yourselves," Diez instructed. "Especially you, Eric Podlowsky. You have the stink of cremat leaves about you."

"Cremat leaves?" Robert asked.

Diez said something to Alanna. She dropped her packs in the floor, reached into the small pouch at her belt, and withdrew a handful of the tiny brownish leaves she had thrown at the *leikkio*—the same leaves old Frona had scattered about Eric's room.

"Cremat leaves," Roderigo Diez repeated. "The *fantasmas* will not tolerate their odor."

"*Fantasmas?*" Eric said.

"Ghosts," Robert translated. He knew a little Spanish, along with several other languages. He took a leaf from Alanna's palm and sniffed it. The odor was very faint, vaguely minty. She took it back and returned it with the rest to her pouch.

"Ghosts," Diez affirmed. "In Palenoc, they are very real."

The four of them said no more as they prepared to wash. Eric dipped his hands and face into the water, then started to dry himself, but Alanna reached out a hand and shook her head. She gestured at his shirt. When he obviously didn't understand, she made a grab at the buttons of his trousers. Wide-eyed, Eric caught her hands.

"Wash everything, *amigo*," Diez explained, removing his own shirt. "There are clean garments too. Please hurry. Dawn is not far off." He said something to Alanna then. The dragonrider grinned, unslung the unicorn horn from her back, and thrust it into one of her packs. Then she glanced at Eric and grabbed the hem of her own shirt, pulling it over her head in a single easy motion.

"Oh, shit," Eric muttered.

Alanna was out of her clothes in no time. Robert wondered what Diez had said to her, for she kept glancing up at Eric as she bent over her basin and scrubbed her face. Her braids fell into the water. She slung them around, scattering droplets as she dipped and wet a cloth. There was a soundless trace of laughter on her lips through the whole process.

"Please, Eric," Diez urged as he shed the rest of his garments. "Hurry." Naked, the old Spaniard began to scrub himself.

Robert raised one eyebrow and looked at his brother, then tugged off his shirt. The light from the globes shone on his smoothly muscled chest and arms. He bent and pulled off his boots, then stepped out of his trousers.

"You couldn't at least provide a loincloth or something?" Eric snarled as he gave in and reached for his boots. His face was beet-red. "Privacy curtains?"

While he cleansed himself, Robert watched Alanna. She had a magnificent body, lean and superbly muscled. Beads of water rolled down the deep cleft of her spine and between her buttocks as she bent and worked the wet cloth over her calves. She seemed absolutely without modesty. Robert turned away quickly, surprised at the intensity of his own reaction. He bathed swiftly and wrapped himself in a towel.

"Over here!" Diez called from a row of wardrobes on the far side of the room. "Come! Hurry!" The old Spaniard was still naked and dripping. A puddle of water grew around his feet as he opened a couple of the doors. "Choose something quickly."

The wardrobes contained shelves piled high with folded garments, all of the same supple leather as their dirty clothes, only bleached to an off-white shade. Diez pulled down a couple of shirts and tossed one each to Robert and Eric. "Do not worry about the fit. We must hurry!"

"What is this hide?" Robert asked, running his hand over a pile. But Diez was too busy drying himself to answer. Robert shrugged and drew down a shirt.

Eric slithered into his shirt as fast as he could. It was his luck that it fit perfectly. Robert found his too loose and the sleeves too long. Rather than search for another, he rolled the sleeves up to his elbows. Alanna was beside him now. She rifled through another wardrobe, found trousers, and tossed them to him. They were a much better fit than the shirt, and he tucked it deep into the waistband. The first pair his brother drew down were too small and tight. Diez shoved another pair into his arms.

Next, the Spaniard and the dragonrider chose outfits for themselves. Alanna snatched up her packs again and headed for a door in the north wall.

"Shoes?" Eric called. "Or boots?"

"Later!" Diez snapped. He ushered them to the door, pausing long enough to take the nearest lightglobe from its sconce on the wall. Holding the shining glass ball high, Diez led them into a narrow corridor.

They did not go far before they came to another flight of stone stairs. Diez led the way, with Alanna in the rear. The steps were steep and narrow. At the bottom Diez flung back a thick wooden door. A dim yellowish light pervaded the new corridor. A single globe rested on a narrow tripod, but its glow was weak. *Old*, Robert thought to himself. Diez's light seemed almost an invasion. Heavy tapestries adorned the walls. The floor was plain stone tile, cold against Robert's bare feet.

At the other end of the corridor loomed a pair of huge doors, iron-bound and reinforced, painted with arcane-looking symbols. Robert felt a sudden apprehension. For his novels, he had done research into magic. He didn't recognize these particular markings, but he knew about wards.

Eric crept up beside him. "Looks like those Dutch things I've seen painted on Pennsylvania barns," he said uneasily.

"Hex signs," Robert supplied in a whisper.

Diez seized the ring of an iron knocker with one hand and slammed it down against the plate twice. The sound reverberated ominously through the corridor. For an instant, nothing happened. Robert felt his heart quicken as Diez started to lift the ring again. His mouth felt dry.

The door opened a crack, paused, then creaked slowly open.

Robert felt the pressure of Alanna's hand in the small of his back. Reluctantly, he let himself be ushered inside. The doorman, a huge, ugly brute whose hair was shaved close to his head and who had but maybe three good teeth, regarded him with cool eyes that suddenly widened in surprise. The man's jaw dropped. He started to stammer something, then stopped himself.

Robert felt his gut begin to crawl again. The doorman's reaction unsettled him. Worse, some dark sense of dread stole upon him as he crossed that threshold, the same fear he had felt in Eric's room when he first gazed out the window and saw . . . He had trouble saying her name. *Her*. He realized he was clenching his teeth, a habit he thought he'd broken years ago. He forced himself to stop. Still, he gave an involuntary flinch when the door boomed shut behind them.

The chamber was gloomy and stiflingly hot. Thin smoke filled the air; tendrils of it wafted about on unseen drafts. Robert couldn't guess where those drafts came from. There was no window in the room.

A huge circle had been painted on the floor in the room's center, another hex sign like the ones on the door but far more elaborate. The lines were formed of gold that had been melted to a liquid and poured. Within the hex sign were painted other sigils and glyphs, all with meanings unknown to him.

"Holy . . . !" Eric said as he approached the edge of the circle. Something held him back from quite stepping over it. Nevertheless, he pointed, the breath whistling between his lips. Set among the painted symbols were gemstones—diamonds, emeralds, rubies, sapphires, and more—larger than any ever seen on earth. They shimmered in the light of Diez's globe as he came to stand beside Eric.

Robert turned slowly, feeling a sudden draft upon his hands. To his left and right, where the light from Diez's globe barely reached, narrow sections of the stone wall swung silently back. Twelve white-robed figures, faces concealed under voluminous hoods, slid out with soundless tread and formed a circle in the room. They did not speak or give acknowledgment to anyone.

A red light erupted from the left side. Two black cauldrons sat side by side on squat clawed feet, pouring the ruby glow from their bellies. Each was ringed with its own gilt circle. Robert would have sworn they hadn't been there before, yet the smoke and heat that permeated the room seemed to exude from them. There was no flame that Robert could see. He started toward them for a better look, but Alanna brushed his arm and shook her head. For some reason, Robert obeyed.

"What the hell is this place?" Eric muttered nervously.

Alanna spoke in soft tones, as if trying to reassure them. Robert didn't feel reassured, though. He swallowed hard. A cold sweat beaded his face and throat. A single drop crawled like an insect from his hairline, past his temple, toward his jaw. His hands automatically stiffened and his fingers went rigid, ready to strike.

Impossibly, a wind swept through the room. Streamers of smoke swirled like living wisps. The light seemed to recede, and darkness closed about like a monstrous hand. A chill shivered up Robert's spine. His heart raced, and inside he screamed as the razor edge of some terrible memory suddenly scraped against his mind. He retreated a step, but Alanna was there, her hand on his back. Somehow, he knew her touch and drew strength from it.

"Do not fear, Roberto!" Diez called, his eyes narrowed against the unnatural gale.

In the center of the hex sign, something began to form from the whirling smoke. A human shape. Its features remained indistinct in the vapor and the gloom, but a pair of darkly burning eyes glared at them. Robert felt his knees weaken. The creature radiated a rage that struck him with an almost physical force.

How did you kill the unicorn?

The voice serrated through Robert's head. He clutched at his left temple, barely able to draw a breath. Alanna moved suddenly beside him. She dropped her packs on the floor, opened one, and drew out the black, twisted, blood-caked spike. She set it at the golden edge of the circle.

"I understand you!" Robert shouted, fighting to master his fear. He shot a desperate glance at Eric, who nodded. He understood too.

A whorl of smoke curled around the horn, as if it were an extension of Phlogis's will, and lifted it to eye level. The creature at the center of the hex sign made no effort to approach it, but he examined it just the same. The horn tumbled slowly end over end with nothing but the smoke to support it. *I can touch your mind, Son of Paradane, which you call Earth.*

"Why not?" Eric muttered with nervous sarcasm. "This is all in my mind."

Alanna said something to Diez, and the old physician called out over the wind that rattled about the chamber. "Phlogis!" he cried. "Be easy with them. They haven't had time to grasp all of this!"

But the monster called Phlogis paid the old man no heed. *How did you kill that which cannot be killed?* it demanded.

"What are you fucking talking about?" Eric shouted back. There was an edge of anger in his voice. He held his fists clenched at his sides.

The chimorg *cannot be killed, except by the* sekoye. *Yet you killed one. Explain this.*

Robert struggled with his fear and fought it down. He glanced at Alanna beside him and found in her eyes no menace or deceit, only courage. Something dark and horrible had surged up from his memories for an instant, but it was gone now. He couldn't even be sure what it was. Instead, he felt angry for letting such fear grip him and angrier with this creature, Phlogis.

"I broke the damn thing off!" Eric shouted defensively.

"And I ran it through the monster's heart!" Robert reached out and snatched the horn from the air. It was his, after all. Or his brother's. A trophy of battle.

And it died?

The wind whipped about the chamber with renewed intensity. Smoke swirled, stinging Robert's eyes. He felt his gut tightening again as the gale physically forced him back a step.

"Stop it!" he screamed, raising the horn like a club. He didn't *like* feeling afraid. He didn't like *people* who made him feel afraid.

The wind ceased. The smoke stilled. The creature called Phlogis stared at him with those hellish eyes. Robert felt the weight of Phlogis's interest bearing down on his mind.

You intrigue me, Sons of Paradane. The creature shifted its attention to Eric and appeared to study him. *You broke the* chimorg's *horn? How?*

Eric shrugged, trying to appear calm despite his trembling. "Lucky, I guess," he answered.

A quiver of amusement brushed with tickle-softness through Robert's head. *I mean, what weapon did you employ, Eric Podlowsky?*

Eric stuck a tongue in his cheek and rolled his eyes toward Robert. "My hand," he answered finally. He cocked an eyebrow. "A bit flashy, in retrospect," he said to his brother with a small grin. "More your kind of trick."

Phlogis did not resort to words. His doubt and disbelief hovered like a hammer waiting to fall.

Diez stepped to the gilt edge of the circle. "These *hermanos* are warriors of great skill, Phlogis," he said, intervening. "They fight like nothing you have seen. If he says he broke the horn with his hand, believe him!"

A silence fell over the chamber. Finally, Phlogis spoke again. *I believe,* he said, his harsh gaze focused on Eric. *I see the truth deep in this one's mind.* The creature turned. For the first time, Robert realized it did not touch the floor but floated a few feet above the tiles. Its movements were as subtle as the smoke of which it was composed. It reached out a hand and gestured toward the cauldrons.

The smoke began to eddy and shift, and the ruby light wavered. Above each cauldron, shapes began to form.

"Pietka!" Roderigo Diez cried.

One of the smoke-shapes lifted its head. Indeed, it did resemble the little Chalosan innkeeper.

Your friend, Pietka, has won his vengeance, Phlogis stated. *As has Sumeek.* The second shape raised its head and regarded them. It was with the white-haired old man.

Diez took a step toward Pietka. "Old friend . . ." he started.

Do not speak to him, Phlogis interrupted sharply. *He prepares himself for Or-dhamu.*

Diez halted. He continued to stare at Pietka, but he stepped back and took his place next to Robert again.

"I saw him die," Robert whispered uneasily as he watched the ghostly form of Sumeek floating in the ruby glow.

Roderigo Diez shrugged weakly. "This is not the world you know," he answered quietly. It was enough to send another chill up Robert's spine, for he remembered something else Diez had said earlier. *In Palenoc, ghosts are real.* He turned and stared with sudden, dreadful understanding at the monster called Phlogis.

Do not fear, the monster said to Robert's mind, which put him immediately on his guard. *Pietka and Sumeek, though they are dead, are come to help you, Sons of Paradane. From this moment on, all who hate the Darkness will call you friend.*

Pietka and Sumeek drifted, smokelike, out of the red glow of their cauldrons, across the room and toward the brothers. Again Robert felt fear, but Alanna's hand found his, and their fingers intertwined. Eric glanced at him, stiff and tense, with the gleam of fear in his eyes.

Phlogis's voice rumbled in their heads. *The sekoye is the chimorg's natural enemy. So you, Eric and Robert Podlowsky, shall be Brothers of the Sekoye. Brothers of the Dragon.*

It was too late to run. The smoke-shapes folded around them. Robert tried to hold his breath, but the fumes crept up his nostrils, down into his lungs. For an instant, Pietka's face hovered right before his, and he peered deep into the dark pools of the little innkeeper's eyes.

"Stop!" he screamed. He tried to pull free from Alanna, but she held his hand tightly.

A cold wind whispered through his brain. Images flashed through his head, memories that were not his own but Pietka's, fragmented visions that made him cry and laugh and rejoice and grieve, all in the space of a single heartbeat. He shivered in the grip of something he couldn't resist as invisible fingers examined him, opened a private part of him and deposited something, then folded him together again with an almost gentle pat, leaving him no longer afraid.

Like a soft breath, the essence of Pietka planted a feathery farewell kiss on the place where Robert's fear had resided. The innkeeper smiled and faded away, taking his memories with him, leaving Robert full of a calm that he had not known for days. A bit of smoke hovered in the air before him, slowly diffusing.

Diez took a step and put his hand up to touch the last of that smoke, a final farewell gesture to his friend.

Robert smiled at Alanna beside him and looked to his brother. Eric stood in a seemingly precarious pose, limp as a rag doll that someone had propped up. His eyes were closed. As Robert watched, his brother opened his mouth and exhaled a thick white smoke that took Sumeek's form for just an instant before it wafted into nothingness.

"Robert!" Alanna squeezed his hand. Her large brown eyes, full of concern, peered into his. "How do you feel?"

He understood her language now. That was the gift Pietka had left him.

"He's gone," Eric said quietly in the language of Palenoc.

Robert knew who he meant. Not Sumeek, but Phlogis. The chamber felt calmer, no longer permeated with an aura of anger. He looked toward the empty circle. Without a word or a sound, the twelve white-robed figures that ringed the room lowered their heads and exited through the narrow doors.

"No," said Roderigo Diez to Eric. "Phlogis is still here. But it is dawn. When the sun rules the sky, all ghosts seek their rest."

Robert felt a feathery breath upon his brain again. Phlogis, he knew, and he waited for the monster to speak. It said nothing though, sparing him its saw-edged voice. Instead it stroked and probed, then withdrew.

"You said *ghost*," Eric muttered.

Diez nodded as he led them from the chamber. "Dead these past five hundred years," he affirmed.

Robert stared over his shoulder at the circle on the floor as Alanna pulled him along. *What,* he wondered, somehow certain that Phlogis's eyes were still upon him, *was that all about?*

Chapter Seven

ERIC woke slowly from a long and troubling dream. The details eluded him, slipped like vapor from his mind's grasp, but a face lingered in his memory. Blond hair. Blue eyes that shone like stars. He had seen that face once before in his delirium, so like his brother's but not. Pain. He had dreamed of pain. The blond boy's? Or his own? He couldn't remember.

He rose up slowly on one elbow and felt the thin ridge of the scar above his left eyebrow. It was real. It was all real. One didn't dream of dreaming. He peered around, his eyes still matted with sleep. A few beams of sunlight leaked around the edges of the sealed shutters on the room's only window. His candle had long ago burned itself out while he slept. Only a melted stub remained on the small table by his bed.

It was a gloomy room with stone walls and a cold hearth. In winter, a good fire no doubt cheered the chamber considerably. A couple of padded chairs were set by one wall. A wardrobe and a writing desk stood against another. A polished mirror hung upon the wall near the wardrobe. Beneath the mirror on another small table, a basin and pitcher of water rested. The only things that lent any gaiety to the room were the heavy, hand-braided carpets that covered the floor. Their colors were natural, but elaborate whorls and curls, reminiscent of sea waves, ran through the weave.

He threw off the light blanket that covered him and rose out of bed. Naked, he trudged to the mirror. The scar would be the first thing he noticed for some time. He needed a shave badly. He'd never had much of a beard. His stubble grew in patches and clumps, and several days' growth only made his chin look dirty. He poured cool water from the pitcher into the basin and laved it over his face.

The gloom was too oppressive. He went to the shutters, unfastened the small latch, and pushed them open. The bright sunlight caused him to blink. It must be past noon, he figured, glancing at the blue, cloudless sky. A warm breeze blew over him.

Far out above the rooftops a dragon glided. How different they appeared in the sunshine. Eric watched the creature float higher and higher in a slow arc toward the sun. Its slender gray body undulated as it climbed, its wings were opaque in the sunlight. Gone was the bioluminescence that had burned in those pinions at night. Still, even without that fire, the beast was a marvelous and powerful sight.

In the streets below, some celebration was in progress. People danced, packed against each other, their heads tossed back with laughter. The sounds of music rode the breeze to his window. A sharp cackle rose briefly above the rest of the noise, reminding him poignantly of old Frona.

He had dreamed of her too, he remembered, of

her incense and cremat leaves and faded blue apron.

Eric turned away from the window and went to the wardrobe. Slowly he pulled open the doors. Several pairs of trousers were folded on one shelf. He rifled through them, half grinning. Black leather and gray leather and pale, bleached leather. At least there was greater variety in the shirts. The leather was there, but so were some cloth fabrics with long, loose sleeves and lace-up fronts. He chose gray trousers and a white cloth top.

He found his boots in the bottom of the wardrobe. Someone had brought them while he slept. But as he bent to pick them up he noticed something else there—his khaki shorts from L. L. Bean and his hiking boots. He recalled Alanna's packs. She or Danyel must have brought them from Chalosa. He decided against wearing them though. They somehow seemed out of place in Palenoc.

He picked up the shorts. There were a couple of things in the pockets that might prove useful. Then he realized that they were not his shorts but Robert's. Eric carried a small Swiss army knife. What he found in the right front pocket was his brother's Boy Scout penknife. Robert had owned it for years. His brother's wallet was in the left hip pocket.

In the left front pocket, he found a few crumpled dollars and some change. Then something else caught his attention—a carefully folded newspaper clipping. Why would Robert carry that? Curious, he walked over to his bed and sat down. Dropping the shorts, knife, and money on the blanket, he leaned toward the sunlight to read.

MAN SHOT TO DEATH OUTSIDE BAR

A twenty-five-year-old man was attacked and shot to death as he exited a popular West Village bar at Seventh Avenue and Grove Street about 10:20 p.m. last night.

The man, who was not identified pending notification of family, had just left the bar when witnesses say a gang of five youths, approaching from the opposite direction, attacked him without apparent provocation. Two witnesses reported that when the victim attempted to fight back, one of the youths drew a pistol and fired three shots. The youths then fled.

The victim was taken by ambulance to St. Vincent's Hospital, where he was pronounced dead on arrival of gunshot wounds to the chest.

Eric read the clipping twice, puzzling over its significance. It had been cut, not torn, from the center of a page and had no date affixed. Nor was he sure which paper it had come from, though it felt like the cheap, brittle pulp used by the *New York Times*. Frowning, he folded it carefully again and pushed it back into the pocket where he'd found it.

He picked up his brother's wallet, stared at it, tapped it on his palm. The urge to search it was almost irresistible, but at last he returned it to the hip pocket of the shorts, its secrets intact. He put everything back in the appropriate pocket.

Just as he replaced the penknife, a knock sounded at his door. He gave a guilty little jump and rose to his feet. "Come in," he called.

Roderigo Diez stepped into the room. "I see you are awake," the old Spaniard said.

Eric folded Robert's shorts neatly, placed them on the bed, and went back to the wardrobe for the boots his new friends had provided for him. "I don't usually sleep so late," he said as he carried them to one of the two chairs, sat down, and pulled them on.

"I gave orders to let you rest," Diez answered. "You've had much to adjust to and more to think about. If you're up to it, there is someone I wish you to meet."

Eric finished the lacings on his right boot and sat erect. "What's going on outside?" he asked, marveling again at the strange words that rolled off his tongue, at the ease with which he spoke the Palenoc language.

Diez strode toward the window and peered down. "They have heard that a *chimorg* has been killed, that a blow has been struck against Darkness by two young men called the Brothers of the Dragon." He turned back to Eric and folded his arms across his chest. He wore a half-amused grin. "All Rasoul is celebrating. You and *su hermano* are heroes."

"Don't use that Spanish stuff on me," Eric warned in mild irritation. "I don't speak it the way Robert does. He's good with languages. He'd have figured this one out on his own, given time. But it's a talent I don't have."

"My apologies, Eric," Diez said with a slight nod. It was only the second time he had used Eric's name, and he pronounced the second syllable as if he'd just seen a mouse.

"No problem," Eric answered with a shrug. "But

I'm curious. When we first met I had the feeling you didn't much care for us."

Diez paced to the center of the room. He rubbed his chin with one hand, and his expression darkened. "I had a daughter," he said with quiet unease. "Younger than Roberto. In Rota, Spain, we lived, and she worked as a waitress at a little cabaret where many sailors and soldiers from the American naval base would come. One night, as she left work . . ."

Diez stopped and squeezed the bridge of his nose with a thumb and forefinger. When he continued, his train of thought had shifted subtly. "She always walked home . . ." He stopped again in obvious distress and shook his head. "Some of your sailors, Americanos . . ."

"That's okay," Eric said with rough sympathy as he got to his feet. "You don't have to paint a picture."

Diez clenched his fists at his side. His eyes were open again, but he was plainly seeing a different scene in a different place and time. "My Paloma, she tried to fight back. She managed to take a fingernail file from her purse."

Eric was startled by the hardness of Diez's expression and the hatred that suddenly emerged in his voice. Yet he felt himself sharing the old man's anger. At the same time, he felt shame for his countrymen.

"That file, it wound up here," Diez said bitterly, jabbing himself in the throat with the index finger of his right hand. "Paloma bled to death in a dirty, stinking alley before anyone could get help."

"What about the sailors?" Eric asked thickly.

Roderigo Diez shrugged. "They sit in a prison

somewhere," he answered wearily. "I don't know. I came to Palenoc shortly after the trial." He looked at Eric, and the anger ebbed out of his face, leaving him looking tired. "When I saw you and Roberto, two Americanos, all this came back to me. I was rude and now I ask forgiveness."

"Not necessary," Eric answered. "But I'm glad we got it out of the way."

"I saw how you fought for the people of Chalosa," Diez went on. "You and your brother are good men."

Eric gazed at Robert's shorts on the bed on the far side of the room and chewed his lower lip. Diez's story bore startling similarities to the mysterious clipping in his brother's pocket. An apparently random attack, outside a cabaret or bar, resulting in death. He grew even more curious as to what it was about. Robert was such a private person though. Eric wondered if he should ask.

"How did you get to Palenoc?" Eric asked abruptly.

Roderigo Diez slapped his forehead with one palm. "That is a longer story for another time," he answered. "Someone is waiting for us. Her name is Blor, and she is hugely fat, but she has much to teach you."

"It figures," Eric said, forcing a grin. "Robert winds up giving lessons to the most stunning beauty that ever straddled a dragon, and I wind up getting lessons from the local fat lady."

"You will like her very much," Diez responded as he clapped Eric reassuringly on the arm. "She is Phlogis's assistant, and after you have spoken with her, we will find you something to eat."

Eric bristled. "Not another ghost?" he said dubiously.

"Quite mortal," the Spaniard assured him. He paused for a moment, then put on a grin of his own. "At least, as you understand that word."

Eric puzzled over the meaning of that as Diez led the way out of the room. A cool breeze swept through the corridors as they wound their way several levels lower. The tower called Sheren-Chad was essentially a series of large rooms stacked one on top of the other with a number of smaller quarters and stairways winding up the sides. It was simple in its construction, functional in design, and quite plain in decoration. Large blocks of unmortared stone made the walls, each fitting with utter perfection into its space. Here and there, huge wooden beams stood bare and undisguised.

"Not much on interiors around here, are they?" Eric commented, giving one of the beams a slap as they passed it.

Roderigo Diez did not bother to slow his pace or look around. "Palenoc is a world at war, Eric," he answered. "And Sheren-Chad is, as you would say, Central Command."

"War?" Eric responded.

"For one thousand years," Diez affirmed. They passed under a stone arch and down another flight of stairs.

"Who's the enemy?" Eric asked, recalling the black-armored warriors that had attacked Chalosa.

"Darkness," came the Spaniard's enigmatic reply. They stopped abruptly before an ordinary door. Diez put out a hand and pushed it open. He led the way inside.

Shelves of books lined the walls. Half a dozen large tables stood in the circular room, all piled with maps and charts and opened volumes. More maps and charts hung stretched in wooden frames on nails driven into the walls or into the shelves themselves. The melted stumps of half-burned candles thrust up among the clutter. A number of cresset lamps hung on chains from the ceiling. Three unshuttered windows filled the room with sunlight and fresh air. Even so, it smelled of ink and old paper.

An immensely fat woman bent awkwardly over the largest table in the center of the room. Her colorful cloth skirts swirled with every small movement, and her breasts dangled like huge pink watermelons inside her loose blue blouse. A score of thin bracelets adorned one wrist, and a gold hoop hung from one ear. Her salt-and-pepper hair was pulled back in a tight bun.

She seemed oblivious to their entry.

"Blor?" Diez said softly.

She looked up from her work, an ink stylus in one hand. She stared blankly at Diez, then her eyes seemed to focus, and a pleasant smile parted her full lips. She set the stylus carefully aside and came toward them.

"Roderigo-*kaesha*," she said by way of greeting. She turned immediately to Eric and held up her palms. "Welcome, Eric Podlowsky," she intoned formally, but she peered closely at him. "By Taedra, the Mother-dragon," she said with breathy excitement. "His eyes *are* green!"

Eric touched his palms to hers. He had seen the greeting before in Chalosa. He smiled at her, somewhat embarrassed by her scrutiny. "I'm pleased to meet you, Blor."

"Wait until you see his brother," Roderigo answered with something like a smirk.

Blor couldn't seem to tear her gaze away from Eric's face. "You say he is blond? *Kaesha,* is it possible? Could he be the one?"

Eric felt the heat of a blush in his cheeks as he broke both palm and eye contact. He looked toward Roderigo Diez in confusion. What was she talking about? Could Robert be the one *what*?

"No, *Kaesha,*" the old physician answered patiently. "They come from Paradane. It is enough that they are heroes."

Blor put a hand to her lips and shook her head thoughtfully as she continued to stare at Eric. Then she gave a little sigh and beckoned them toward the table. "I was recording the loss of Terreborne," she told them. "It is a sad thing, to lose so great a kingdom."

"A worse thing to have an enemy on our northern border," Diez added, grim-voiced.

Blor used her arm to push aside a pile of books and papers so Eric and Diez could see the map she'd been working on. An ink bottle teetered treacherously. With surprising speed, she shot out a hand and righted it. With another sigh, she shoved a cork stopper into the bottle and put it in a safe spot. Her bracelets jingled as she gestured toward her labors.

Eric leaned over the table. The smell of fresh ink hovered like a cloud. Sunlight from the middle window fell directly upon her workspace. A chart made of something akin to linen lay amid all the clutter, stretched in a frame. A black patch of ink gleamed wetly.

The outline of the map was familiar to Eric. Too familiar. His jaw dropped. Straightening, he turned and stared at Roderigo Diez and Blor. "What the hell is this?" he demanded.

Blor pressed closer to the table and swept her hand over the chart. "It is the continent of Sinnagar," she answered simply.

Eric became acutely aware of Roderigo Diez's gaze upon him, and he returned the Spaniard's look angrily. "The hell it is," he shot back. "It's fucking North America!"

"The similarity is most interesting, is it not?" Diez replied, bending nearer to the map. He drew one finger along the northeastern seaboard, across the Great Lakes and the upper portions of what might have been the United States. "All these nations in yellow," he said calmly, "are the Domains of Light. These in black"—he indicated most of the Far West and the Southwest, then portions of the Deep South—"are the Dark Lands and the Kingdoms of Night."

"The Domains and the Dark Lands are bitter enemies," Blor informed him.

"And the Kingdoms of Night?" Eric said sharply. He glared at Diez without quite knowing why. The old man might have prepared him for this surprise.

"States in rebellion against Darkness, but just as evil," Blor answered. "They are ruled by Keris Chaterit, who has designs on the Onyx Throne of Srimourna."

Eric bent over the map again, his jaw clenched. "This one," he said, jabbing a finger at the area of Texas. It was marked in yellow ink. "It's part of the Domains? It seems so isolated."

"The kingdom of Vanyel is a large and strategic part of the Domains," Blor explained patiently. "But it's a nation under siege with the Dark Lands on one side and the Kingdoms of Night on the other.''

''What about these?'' Eric said, sweeping a finger along the middle states and the Midwest and in an arc that trailed down to the Florida peninsula. More than a score of outlined nations there bore no color at all.

Brushing against him, Blor pushed back another stack of books and moved closer to the map. ''Those are the Gray Kingdoms. Their alliances are ever shifting, ever unpredictable.''

Roderigo pressed against Eric's other side. ''This is Guran,'' he said, waving a hand over a yellow nation that occupied most of the upper Northeast, ''and this is Terreborne.'' He thrust a finger at a huge area that in Eric's own world would have been Quebec. It was there that Blor had just applied her fresh ink. ''It was from Terreborne the warriors came who attacked Chalosa. We know now they sailed in boats down this river.'' He pointed to a thin blue line.

Blor shook her head. Wisps of gray-black hair stirred about her neck. ''Terreborne has long been part of the Domains. We do not yet know how or when it surrendered to Darkness.''

''Not to Darkness,'' Roderigo Diez informed her, ''To the Kingdoms of Night. Shandal Karg herself struck down some of those soldiers, and a *chimorg* harried them as well.''

Blor reached up and clapped a hand over his mouth. A genuine look of fear flashed over her face. ''Do not say that name!'' she snapped in a sharp whisper.

Diez pushed her hand gently down and kissed it. ''Nevertheless, what I tell you is true,'' he assured her. "The soldiers were masked, too, in the manner of the Kingdoms." He glanced toward Eric. "They think that if they are careless and kill someone, no ghost will recognize them." He shrugged. "A foolish idea, but then, Keris Chaterit is a fool to challenge the Heart of Darkness."

"Why?" Blor persisted. "Why would she interfere?"

"She didn't want Robert and me to fall into their hands," Eric answered before Diez could say anything. "She has her own special plans for us. We killed one of her pets." He frowned and turned uneasily back toward the map. "How do you know they came down the river?"

Diez looked at Blor and exhaled a slow breath as he spread his hands. "We consulted what you would call 'the spirit world.' "

"What?" Eric pushed back from the table and rubbed a finger over the scar on his forehead. "You expect me to believe all this shit about ghosts? And now you're trying to tell me they're all on your side?" He slammed a hand down on the edge of the table. "This is all crazy!"

"You have seen Phlogis for yourself," Diez argued reasonably. "And you yourself have been briefly possessed by a spirit. That is why you now can speak our language. Roberto knows the truth I speak. He saw the *leikkio*. And you know it too. This is not the world of our birth, Eric Podlowsky. It is Palenoc, and here ghosts are quite real."

Eric felt the muscles in his jaw tighten. Suddenly, he remembered leaning out the window of his room in Chalosa, seeing a man in the street below. The man had looked up at him, as if knowing he was there, then *disappeared*.

"So, you've got the ghosts on your side?" he

asked. "They were watching us in Chalosa, weren't they?"

"Not all ghosts," Blor answered. She paced across to another table, rummaged along a pile of books, and extracted a thin volume. "It is very complex. Roderigo-*kaesha* ..."

"*Kaesha?*" Eric interrupted. He understood most of the Palenoc tongue, but there were still a few words that were beyond him.

Diez blushed a little. "Less than a mate," he explained, "but much more than a friend. Soul mate, as you Americanos might say."

Blor smiled and handed Eric the book. It smelled of dust. "Roderigo-*kaesha* will explain it to you, and this book will help. But remember this, Eric Podlowsky," she said, her face turning stern with warning: "In Palenoc, you must be very careful never to take a human life."

Eric recalled how Diez had screamed at Robert during the Chalosa battle, and he thought suddenly of the weapons the attackers had used: clubs, staves, whips, nets. Not a blade or edged weapon of any kind. "Why?" he asked, feeling strange even as the words left his lips. He had never killed anyone in his life, never even thought of it before coming to Palenoc.

Blor touched Roderigo Diez's hand. Their fingers intertwined. "When most of us die," she told him quietly, "our spirits seek the peace of Paradise. In Paradise, the spirit rests until it is ready to merge with Or-dhamu."

"Is that your god?" Eric interrupted again.

"Not in the way you mean God," Diez answered. "Or-dhamu is Responsibility. It is the great balancing force that keeps order in the universe. For a time we rest in Paradise, but eventually we all become part of Or-dhamu."

Blor took up the conversation again. "Except for those who suffer violent death or sudden accident," she explained. "For them, there is another course."

Eric blinked. "Another course?"

Roderigo Diez nodded. "The spirit of someone who is murdered or slain becomes a *dando*, a terrible ghost that will not rest until it wreaks vengeance on its murderer. That is why you must not kill, Eric. You and your brother are great fighters, but you must always be very careful."

Eric frowned again and moved back to the map with its many countries in black and yellow. "How can you be at war if your soldiers can't kill each other?" he demanded.

Blor gave a long sigh and brushed a hand over her hair. Her bracelets jingled, and the fat folds of skin on her arm quivered. "Much can be done to strangle a nation economically," she said. "And much can be done by covert forces to subvert a government."

"Yet you do fight," Eric insisted. "I was there! I was in Chalosa!"

"You did not see bloodshed," Diez reminded him.

"Pietka was killed!" Eric found himself shouting. Abruptly he stopped, remembering Pietka's ghost. Phlogis had said Pietka had won his vengeance. Sumeek, too, with a hayrake that had flown, seemingly of its own accord, from its resting place against a barn wall to skewer a murderer.

He tried to shake the image from his mind, and his thoughts shifted to Frona and to Brin the blacksmith. "What became of the other Chalosans?" he asked quietly.

"Phlogis is working to learn their fate now," Blor reported.

"He's awake?" Eric said with some surprise. "It's daylight."

Blor smiled faintly. "Phlogis never truly sleeps, Son of Paradane. He has powers and contacts you do not yet understand. He has but one goal, and that is the overthrow of Darkness. In the daytime, though, it is harder for him, and he does not waste his energies to maintain a corporeal form." She hesitated for a moment and bit her lip in worry as she glanced at Diez. "I fear he is so close."

"Close to what?" Eric pushed.

Diez gave a little frown and put an arm around Blor's shoulders. "You must realize," he said slowly, "that Phlogis is a *dando*. What he does for the Domains of Light, he does because it is the only way to gain vengeance on his murderer. You surely sensed the powerful aura of his anger when you stood in his presence, did you not?"

Eric nodded. *Not just anger,* he thought without saying anything, *but insanity*.

"A *dando* that cannot achieve its vengeance may lose its focus," Diez continued. "After a while, it goes crazy and becomes an *ankou*, a thwarted spirit filled with blind malevolence." He glanced sideways at Blor and hugged her tighter. "There are some of us who fear Phlogis is approaching this transition. The golden circle and the symbols and all the great stones of power you saw in his chamber are designed to help him maintain control. Yet each day his fight grows more desperate."

"But Sumeek and Pietka avenged themselves so

quickly!" Eric argued. "What's wrong with Phlogis? Doesn't he know his killer?"

Blor and Diez exchanged looks. "A spirit always knows its killer," Diez answered. "But the one who murdered Phlogis commands the blackest and most potent of sorceries. His murderer is none other than the Heart of Darkness, the Queen of all the Dark Lands, and though Keris Chaterit would deny it, the Kingdoms of Night."

Blor moved away from Diez and stepped into a beam of sunlight, hugging herself as if she were cold. "Shandal Karg," she said in the barest whisper.

Eric repeated the name to himself as he began to pace about the room. Everywhere he turned now he saw the maps and charts upon the wall. He recognized Africa. It too was dotted with patches of yellow and black and empty outlines that represented unaligned states.

Asia, upon another wall, was all black. Most of Europe, too, except for the region that might have been Scandinavia and the area around Greece and the Aegean Sea.

How? he wondered. *How could it all be so like his own world?*

South America was much the same as Asia. Only a thin band of states along the west coast glimmered with yellow ink.

"You are quite correct in what you are thinking," Roderigo Diez said, coming to his side as he regarded the maps. "We are losing the war."

Eric turned slowly about the chamber. To him, the charts were mere lines and splotches of ink. He moved back to the table where the North American map lay, leaned forward, and peered at it without saying a word.

He studied the yellow nations and read the names to himself: *Guran, Chylas, Aegren, Vormysta, Virashai, Wystoweem, Pylanthim, Imansirit.* A few more. Lonely Vanyel. These were the Domains of Light.

The Dark Lands and the Kingdoms of Night claimed far more territory. Dargra, Markmor, Durazador, Shadark, Srimourna, Patmos, Chule, Chol-Herod, the Grieve. The list of names went on.

Something about the land called Srimourna caused him to look closer. Blor had mentioned an Onyx Throne. In his own world, it might have been Arizona. Near to where the Grand Canyon would have been was a circle of red ink.

"What's this?" he asked, stabbing a finger at the spot.

"Boraga," Blor answered.

"The Throne of Darkness," Diez translated needlessly.

Eric closed his eyes again. A world at war, and a very strange war it was. Yet all he could feel, all he could think about, was Pietka and the farmer Sumeek, and Frona, and Brin. Traces of Sumeek's spirit seemed to linger in his mind, like a taste or a smell he couldn't forget. He could almost feel the blow on the back of Sumeek's head that landed too hard, feel himself falling sideways, see the nail jutting from the wall an instant before it penetrated his skull.

Sumeek, with a hayrake, had won his vengeance. Well, Eric had not won his.

"I can't pretend to understand all of this," Eric said uncertainly. "This isn't my world or my war." He gave Diez a troubled look as he moved away from the map. "But the Chalosans were kind to me.

If they were attacked because somebody wanted the Podlowsky brothers, then I've got a big debt to pay." He turned his gaze on Blor. "When Phlogis finds out where the Chalosans have been taken—whatever his means—I want to know about it."

He went to one of the windows, feeling the weight of Blor's and Diez's gazes on his back, listening to them mutter between themselves. In the sun-washed streets of Rasoul the people were still celebrating, dancing their dances and singing their songs.

All he saw was darkness. All he heard were cries and the soft, slithering hiss of rope nets in the air. And he thought of how he had fled. At the time, he had told Robert it was the wise thing to do. Now, though, it was a different time.

He muttered a name under his breath.

Shandal Karg.

Chapter Eight

ROBERT, Alanna, and Danyel pushed through the throngs of people that crowded Rasoul's streets, trying not to lose each other in the press. The beating of drums and tambourines was almost deafening. The high-pitched screeching of flutes, the wail of several kinds of stringed instruments, the multitude of voices all swirled in one tumultuous symphony.

Several times, jubilant women grabbed Robert and tried to dance with him. Each time, they turned enthusiastic gazes up to meet his face—and froze. Each time, Robert moved swiftly away without looking back, filled with a queer sense of unease.

"It's your hair," Alanna told him, pausing long enough to push a few of his blond wisps back up under the soft brown cap she had given him. "And your eyes."

A throng of colorfully-skirted, whirling celebrants danced past, separating him from Alanna and Danyel. He turned slowly, taking in the scene. Sheren-Chad loomed behind him. A sea of unfamiliar faces surged in every direction. In all his Orient travels he'd seen nothing quite like this. He felt strangely lost.

Someone made a grab for his hand. Danyel flashed him a quick smile and dragged him through the crowd to where Alanna waited. She was leaning against the door of some shop that had closed for the festivities. Her lips curled upward in wry amusement.

"We'll be free of this soon," she promised. "There is so much I want to show you, Robert Podlowsky."

Polo, he almost corrected. But then he thought better of it.

Robert had risen early while the sun was still climbing into the rich, blue morning. He was eager to see Rasoul in the daylight, so he'd pulled on his same clothes from the night before, gone straight to the roof of the Sheren-Chad and stared out over the parapet.

Guran's capital sparkled in the sunshine. Most of its structures were made of white sandstone. Everywhere he looked, the stores and houses, the walls and the street pavings glimmered. The effect was dazzling. In places, where the sun touched directly, it almost hurt his eyes.

From the top of the high tower he could see most of the city. To the east it sprawled outward and upward into the hills. To the south and southwest, past the distant rooftops, a vast blue ocean stretched to the horizon, dotted here and there with the white sails of ships and fishing boats.

The streets below Sheren-Chad were already filling with people. He had guessed at first that it must be some holiday in Rasoul. Only later, when Alanna had found him on the roof, did he learn that he and his brother were the cause of their joy.

"Let me show you the city up close," she had said with quiet enthusiasm.

He looked at her now, in the shadowed doorway, her black hair stirring ever so slightly in a random breeze. Her eyes were rich as chocolate drops, gleaming as she gazed out over the crowd. Robert looked away, afraid to be caught staring.

Overhead, a dragon glided in the cloudless heavens. The great beasts were no less majestic in the daytime, even without the fire in their wings. He watched as a particularly large one drifted southward, its shadow rippling over the celebrants, and disappeared below the line of roofs. He could only guess that it had landed somewhere near the ocean's edge.

"Where did it go?" he asked without quite realizing he'd given voice to his query.

Alanna touched his arm, excitement brightening her expression. "Would you like to see a nest?"

"I want to see it all," Robert answered. "Show me everything."

They left the doorway and plunged into the crowd again. Though he was eager to see the sights, the noise wore at him, and he was growing quite thirsty. Atop Sheren-Chad the day had seemed balmy, and soft winds had played on his skin. At street level, it was sweltering, and the breezes were few. He wiped the back of his hand across his face to catch a bead of sweat that threatened his left eye.

Unexpectedly, someone jostled him. Something brushed against the back of his head, and his cap slithered off. It was quickly trampled and ruined.

A white-robed old man with gray hair that spilled past his shoulders stared at him in utter shock, then, oblivious to the crowd and the danger, threw himself down at Robert's feet. "Shae'aluth!" he cried, prostrating himself. "Shae'aluth!"

Unnerved, Robert tried to back away, but the crowd prevented it. He shot a desperate look at Alanna, embarrassed and angry. The old man clutched at Robert's ankles and tried to kiss his feet. Others in the crowd, hearing the madman's cries, turned also and stared. A collective gasp went up.

"Tchai!" Alanna shouted as she kicked at the old man's hands. A murmur ran through the assemblage. Someone screamed. Alanna and Danyel pulled Robert away, leaving the sun-smitten old fool groveling and muttering in the road. Swiftly, they pushed through the crowd, putting distance between themselves and all those staring eyes.

"What did he call me?" Robert demanded. "I couldn't understand him!"

"It's a Doven word," Danyel explained as they hustled him along. "But pilgrims from all over the Domains of Light use it, and they all come to Rasoul seeking the Shae'aluth." He paused long enough to steer a course around a circle of tambourine beaters. "It means 'Son of the Morning.' "

Robert was beginning to think he should have stayed in Sheren-Chad. Other faces turned his way as he passed, and he noted with growing unease the reaction he caused. Maybe it hadn't been a good idea to come down to the streets. His looks had attracted some attention in Chalosa too, but nothing like this. "Why do they stare at me?" he snapped.

"All the city knows that two green-eyed brothers,

Sons of Paradane, have killed that which cannot be killed," Alanna answered.

"That's what this is about?" he explained irritably, waving a hand at the crowd.

Danyel walked ahead of them now, clearing a path. "You don't know what a great thing you've done," he said over his shoulder. "You've brought them hope."

Alanna steered him suddenly down a narrow alley, so narrow they were forced to walk single file, their shoulders brushing the white stone of the buildings on either side. But when they emerged at the other end, there were fewer people in the street. Another block, and there were fewer still.

"Where are we heading?" Robert asked, growing calmer now that he had some space about him. On this street a few shops were open. They passed a basket vendor, an ancient gray-haired woman who watched with narrowed eyes as they went by. She nodded but said nothing. Yet Robert felt her gaze on his back until they finally turned a corner.

"You should be used to being admired," Alanna said, a smile curling her lips. She tilted her head and regarded him out of the corner of her eye. He had the vaguest impression she was laughing at him.

"What is that?" he asked, pointing beyond her to a building that looked like something out of Greek myth. It was set on a low hill. Rows of sparkling columns supported a great roof and an ornately carved cornice. A line of people curled up the slope, patiently awaiting entrance through a pair of huge bronze doors.

"That is the temple of Taedra, the Mother-dragon," Danyel said with reverence. "The Son of the Morning resides there."

Robert ran a finger along his lower lip as he watched the people file up the hill and go inside one by one. "It looks like a church," he commented.

"A church?" Alanna replied, hesitating on the word and giving a thoughtful look as she followed his gaze. "I don't understand, Robert. The temple of Taedra is a place for healing. Would you like to see it?"

Robert nodded with interest. He had visited a lot of temples during his travels in the Far East. They always fascinated him. This time, though, he felt some slight, unexplainable trepidation. He walked a bit behind his two new friends as they moved to take their places at the end of the line. The people there looked at Danyel, then at Alanna, and they parted graciously, as if they recognized the pair.

Then the nearest ones noticed Robert.

A woman with a small child at her breast clapped a hand to her mouth and took a step backward. A strong, broad-shouldered man squeezed his eyes shut and bowed his head, tapping the arm of the man beside him, who instantly did likewise. Yet another gathered the neck of his white robe in his fists and raised it to hide his face.

Robert felt a crawling sensation in his gut as he walked up the hill toward the bronze doors. The looks of awe he drew unsettled him. He lowered his gaze and paid strict attention to every step, refusing to look at anything but his feet. Yet he felt the eyes on him like brands as the crowd parted, wavelike, at his approach. And he heard their murmurings.

"Shae'aluth."

"The Son of the Morning!"

"Holy One!"

There was no line now before the great doors.
The people farther up the hill heard and turned to
stare. The citizens of Rasoul made a path for him,
a path that closed quickly as they gathered behind
him and followed him to the doors. Robert felt the
gentle brush of hands upon him as he passed. He
tried to shy away from the touches without showing fear and without giving offense. Finally, he
caught Alanna and Danyel by their arms and
pulled them close.

"Why are they doing this?" Robert whispered
tensely to Alanna.

"They believe you are the Son of the Morning,"
she answered in a calm voice.

"You are, aren't you?" Danyel asked, turning his
big brown eyes upon Robert as they reached the
bronze doors. There was a gleam in those young
eyes, a look of fervor that frightened Robert.

"I don't know what you're talking about!" he protested in a low, tight voice. He glanced nervously
from side to side at the expectant, worshipful
faces that pressed around him, then turned on
Alanna. "You knew this would happen!" he ac-
cused. "You lured me out of Sheren-Chad to put
me on display!"

Back down the hillside a woman began to sing in
a high, sweet voice. Others took it up, and the song
swelled, spreading from person to person, like some
kind of anthem. Alanna slipped her hand into his
and regarded him with that same intense gleam.

"Make them stop!" he told her, gripped by a fear
he couldn't comprehend.

"Nothing can make it stop," said a new voice

from just inside the doors. It was a patient, calming voice, gentle with understanding and sympathy. Robert felt its power. It soothed him somehow, and eased his fear. The speaker continued. "They will realize soon enough that you are not the Son of the Morning."

Robert turned to face a thin, middle-aged man with short, dark hair that tapered to a long point down the back of his skull and neck. He wore an easy smile and a simple robe of white linen. His only other adornment was a necklace of varied stones and crystals. In his right hand he held a wooden tray upon which were the remains of a loaf of bread. Alanna and Danyel each broke off a small piece and swallowed it.

The speaker touched Robert's elbow and led him across the threshold into the temple of Taedra. Large skylights of stained glass adorned the ceiling. Sunlight flooded the interior with muted colors. There was no altar, no furnishings of any kind. Stretched upon soft pallets, dozens of citizens reclined. Upon the brow of one a small powder-blue stone was balanced. Upon the bare chest of another was a quartz crystal. One man lay in apparent sleep with two flat green stones on his open palms. Robert recognized the stones as malachite.

Other priests like the one beside him moved quietly among the worshippers. Try as Robert might, he could think of them in no other terms. The priests each carried a small bag of stones. Sometimes they would pause to observe a worshipper, bend and exchange one crystal for another, or whisper something in soft, reverent tones. When one worshipper was done, a priest collected the stones, helped him to rise, and conducted another to the vacated pallet.

"You are a Son of Paradane," the priest beside Robert said. He placed his tray with the half-eaten loaf of bread down on a slender pedestal that stood near the entrance. He stared at Robert's face. Unlike so many others, though, there was no fervency in his gaze. "I've heard that you and your brother both have green eyes but only you have the blond hair."

"That seems to make me an oddity around here," Robert commented, trying to sound lighthearted.

The priest allowed himself the smallest hint of a smile. "It is more than rare," he answered. Their gazes met for a moment, and before Robert realized it the priest had reached out and gently taken hold of his arm again. "You must put aside your fear," he said.

"It is true, then, Father?" Alanna spoke in hushed tones, but disappointment filled her voice. "He's not the Son of the Morning?"

The priest regarded Alanna and Danyel with infinite patience. "He has the eyes and the hair," he told them. "But he is not the Shae'aluth."

His voice had a mesmeric quality. Part of Robert began to relax, but another part felt the first needle pricks of panic. Nevertheless, he let himself be guided deeper into the temple. With the priest on one side, still holding his arm, Alanna on his other side, and Danyel behind, he moved among the pallets to stand in a beam of sunlight that spilled through the largest and centermost skylight. He felt its warmth on his neck and face.

Several of the other priests drifted closer. A few of the worshippers sat up on their pallets to watch.

"You have pain," said the priest beside Robert. He reached out and accepted a stone that another priest passed to him, pressing it into Robert's right hand. Robert winced. The gash that he had taken across his palm from the unicorn's razor-sharp scales was still red and tender. But the priest held Robert's fingers tightly around the stone. He closed his eyes and began to hum, and his brothers joined him. The worshippers, too. Then even Alanna and Danyel.

The pain that he had shut away flared briefly. He gave a short gasp. Then it was gone before he could even pull his hand away. The humming stopped. The priest took back the stone and let go of Robert's hand. Mystified, Robert flexed his fingers and stared at the skin where the gash had been. No scar, no sign of a wound.

The priest reached for his left hand. "Let me heal this one, too," he said. "The wound is old, but I can remove that scar as well."

This time Robert snatched his hand away. "No," he snapped, curling the fingers into a fist and hugging it to his chest.

"I see," the priest responded, his eyes lighting with understanding. "It is a mark of blood bonding, is it not?"

Robert's jaw dropped. How could this priest know about his scar or its significance?

He opened his left hand and stared at the fine white line that stretched from one side of his palm to the other. One rainy night in China he had cut himself with his penknife. Scott Silver had done the same, and they had pressed their hands together, sharing blood between them in a solemn ceremony as they knelt on a bare floor while clouds raced across the sky outside the window of their darkened, dirty hotel room.

"Who are you?" he said quietly, numbed by the memory.

The priest smiled more with his eyes than with his lips. "One Who Waits And Serves," he answered enigmatically.

"They do not take names," Alanna explained, "who serve in the House of Healing."

Robert stared at the scar again, then at his right palm, which retained no mark at all. He quivered with the slightest of inward tremors as he noticed that some of the worshippers were still watching him. All these people had come here—were coming here—to be healed by these priests. With crystals. By magic. "Who are you waiting for?" he asked nervously.

"The Son of the Morning," said a different priest, smiling from halfway across the temple.

Robert looked from the priest to Alanna, then to Danyel, then all around. "Who is the Son of the Morning?" He felt like a child again, at catechism, asking his questions.

"The most perfect expression of all that is good in Man," the first priest answered. "The Or-dhamu incarnated as flesh."

Robert frowned. In general, he had little regard for religions. Still, he couldn't deny the magic these people seemed to command. "You said you're waiting for him. He's gone?"

The priest moved back a pace and knelt beside a pregnant woman to check the small amber bead balanced upon her swollen belly. He glanced up at Robert. "Gone?" His expression turned wry. "You would say so, Son of Paradane. He is dead."

Robert turned away, feeling as if he were in a dream. Without another word he drifted back outside, out of the temple, to the multitude of faces that waited for him to emerge. Again they reached out to touch him as he walked down the hill. He felt their hands in his hair, on his arms and back, on his shoulders, and he tried to shut his ears against their singing.

When he reached the bottom of the hill he found Alanna and Danyel were still with him. So, too, was the crowd. "Make them stop," Robert said again to Alanna, though this time there was little emotion in his words. He felt almost detached from himself, as if he were standing outside his body somehow, feeling, yet not feeling, watching it move.

She looked up at him, her brown eyes moist and large as she touched his arm. "Only you can do that, Robert," she answered. A note of sorrow floated in her voice. She had counted on him to be her Son of the Morning. "They'll do what you ask."

He drew strength from her touch and found it within himself to turn and face those who had followed him down from the House of Healing. There was such hunger in their eyes, such longing. And such joy. But he was not what they wanted him to be. His throat went dry. "Go back to your temple," he said to them. "I am not your Son of the Morning."

The singing ceased as he spoke. The air vibrated with the sudden silence. He swallowed hard. His voice was little more than a rasp when he spoke again. "I'm not the Shae'aluth," he said once more. "I'm just Robert Podlowsky."

"Your eyes!" cried an old woman beside him. "You have the eyes!"

Robert caught her hands as she reached out to touch him, yet he treated her with gentleness. "I'm just Robert Podlowsky," he repeated, releasing her.

The crowd stared for a long, empty moment. Danyel tugged on Robert's sleeve, and Alanna nodded in the direction she thought they should take. Robert cast a final glance up at the temple, then departed with his *sekournen* friends. No one followed them.

"I'm sorry, Just Robert Podlowsky," Alanna apologized after they had turned a corner and moved a block away. "A part of me truly thought you might be the Shae'aluth."

They entered a large square. Small kiosks and booths were set up, and baskets of fruits and vegetables were on display barely shaded from the heat of the sun. Wagons with wooden cages full of chicks and ducklings and young rabbits for sale were ranged about. Hard-looking farmers from the outlying communities peered over their merchandise at a handful of citizens who wandered about. They all stared slack-jawed when Robert went by.

"Tell me about your Son of the Morning," Robert said in a quiet, serious voice.

They walked silently across the market square before Alanna answered. A gaggle of laughing children ran in front of them, around them, and darted off behind a cart. An old woman rocking on a small wooden stool and stroking a somnolent cat on her lap muttered a reverent greeting. On the far side of the square a simple fountain spewed water into a wide circular pool.

Alanna led them to it, dipped her hand in the

water, and wiped it over her neck. "The Son of the Morning," she said at last. "Well, first of all, he has green eyes." She gave him a short smile and looked away. "Of course, you've figured that out by now. And hair the color of the sun, like yours."

They each cupped their hands and drank from the fountain. The water was surprisingly cool and very sweet. Robert splashed some over his face, and Danyel did the same. Refreshed, they began walking again, leaving the market behind.

"Though each nation has its own kings or councils, he is the spiritual leader of all the Domains of Light," Alanna continued.

"Wait a minute," Robert interrupted, holding up a hand. A light breeze blew down the street, ruffling his hair, bearing with it the smell of water and fish. They were approaching the ocean. "You speak of him in the present tense. But the priest . . ."

"Healer," Danyel corrected, "or Father."

"Whatever," Robert responded curtly. "The healer said he was dead."

Alanna brushed a hand over her hair as the breeze swept a lock of it into her eyes. "That's true," she answered. "He was quite old, and his strength had waned. But though his body is dead, his spirit will rise and live again in a new host. The Son of the Morning will be strong once more." She turned slightly and looked toward the west. "In the Dark Lands he will first appear, and he will harrow the Heart of Darkness. Then he will dwell once more among us in Rasoul."

"Sounds like some kind of legend to me," Robert said, with an unintentional sneer.

"No legend," Danyel said softly. He didn't look

at Robert as he spoke. He stared at his hands, which he massaged gently. "Perhaps someday you'll feel his touch, feel his power moving upon you." His young face took on a distant expression, and suddenly he seemed older than his scant years.

"He called me when Darkness might have taken my soul. My homeland, Chule, had fallen to the sorcerous onslaught of the Kingdoms of Night. My whole family was captured, but I escaped and made my way on foot across Prydeet and Trilayn to Guran and, eventually, to Rasoul. My heart was so full of pain and hatred for Shandal Karg and Keris Chaterit, but he took that from me and gave me to the dragons, who are his angels."

"Angels?" Robert said, raising one eyebrow. He found all this fascinating and totally unbelievable. Yet he kept his opinion secret and waited to hear more.

"Nothing that hates or is evil can ride the *sekoye*," Alanna told him. "Shandal Karg has no power over the creatures. When the Heart of Darkness calls, the dragons turn away."

Danyel took up the story. "She could not have the dragons, but Darkness was determined to have a beast that would serve her. No other creature of Palenoc was suitable, though, so she made the *chimorgs*."

They turned down yet another street. This one was wider. Here and there, thick fishing nets hung stretched on poles. A young boy stood upon a box, mending a hole in one such net. Nearby, an old woman sat cross-legged upon a cushion, a basket of fish at her side, a small pile of guts in the dirt before her feet. Intent on her work, she never even glanced up at Robert. In one hand she held a knife, in the other a fish. She paused long enough to shake the blade to shoo away a bothersome flock of noisy gulls, then turned back to her work. With each stroke of the sharp knife, silver scales flew.

"Made them?" Robert questioned.

"The first *chimorgs* were twelve men," Danyel continued. "Generals in the armies of Darkness. But their souls, what was left of their souls, were stripped away and their bodies tortured, twisted and shaped by foul spells until they became beasts. Then they bred, bearing others of their black kind, and they ranged throughout Palenoc as Darkness's spies and obedient servants."

"The thing we killed was no man," Robert told them.

"Nothing remains in the *chimorgs* that could ever be recognized as manlike," Alanna answered. "They are monsters in the true sense."

"Until you and Eric came along," Danyel said, brightening, "only a dragon could kill a *chimorg*. No man had ever done such a thing."

"*Sekoye* and *chimorgs* are natural enemies," Alanna explained.

"Or unnatural, as the case may be," Robert interjected with a smirk.

Straight ahead, a score of masts rose like sharp spears into the blue sky. A handful of fishermen passed up the street, carrying their catch in heavy buckets, laughing and talking among themselves. Another group moved rapidly down the street toward the sea, barely sparing a glance for Robert and the *sekournen*.

The wind blew upon Robert's face again, and he sniffed. At once he realized something was missing. Salt. There was no smell of salt in the air. They reached the wharves. The boards rose and fell ever so subtly, rocked by the water. White-winged birds played in the sky. A number of ships were tied up at docks, their bare masts swaying, but most of the fleet was out. Tiny sails dotted the horizon, barely visible in the sunglare.

Robert sniffed again. "This is fresh water?" he asked.

"Of course," Alanna answered.

Robert scratched his chin. "I expected an ocean." He walked a few paces to the very edge of the wharf and stared down into the greenish water. A huge fish swam briefly into view just below the surface, then vanished into the depths under the wharf.

"This way," Alanna said, brushing his elbow.

They walked south until they reached the end of the wharf, then jumped down onto the beach. Thick tufts of grass grew in the sand, and trees grew closer to the water's edge. Robert was mystified that Rasoul's growth simply seemed to stop at the end of the wharf. The city had spread out so much in every other direction.

A dragon swooped low overhead. The wind of its passage stirred their hair and snapped their garments. The grass bowed, and trees shook their branches. Robert turned to see where the beast had come from and found he could barely see the city. The trees had become a thick forest.

"We're almost there," Danyel told him reassuringly.

They moved inland and found a well-worn footpath. A young woman came their way, humming a little tune and bearing a stout pole upon her shoulders, from which depended two large ceramic jars. The lids of the jars were sealed with wax, Robert noticed, as they stepped off the path to let the woman by. She said nothing, nor did she stop her humming, but she smiled and nodded and went on toward Rasoul.

"She looked awfully happy," Robert commented.

"She's a groom," Alanna said. "It's special work, and a much-sought-after honor to be chosen for it."

A huge shadow passed over them. Another dragon soared above the trees and gyred suddenly upward into the sun. Or perhaps it was the same one—Robert couldn't tell. It hung there for a instant, silhouetted. Then it folded its wings and plummeted toward the sea. Robert caught his breath. At the last minute the wings opened. The trees obscured Robert's view. A moment later, the beast sailed upward into the air.

An odor touched Robert's nose, and he knew it at once. The smell of dragons. He knew it from riding Alanna's beast. It was in her hair and in her clothing too, but faint. This smell was far stronger.

The path widened. Then, of a sudden, they emerged from the trees onto a long stretch of beach. A pair of gray dragons reclined in the sand, their tails stretching into the water, their flat, horned heads lolling on the warm earth. Their bellies were swollen. Diamond eyes turned toward the humans moving out of the trees, then turned away again, disinterested.

"Females?" Robert asked, suddenly understanding. This was the nest Alanna had mentioned. "Pregnant females?"

Alanna and Danyel nodded at the same time. The *sekournen* wore huge smiles. "Have you ever milked a dragon?" Alanna asked, and Robert couldn't tell if she was serious or teasing.

Perhaps twenty women hovered around the dragons. Some of them held ceramic jars similar to the
ones the woman on the path had carried. Others
held long wooden scrapers. As he watched, one of
the women passed her scraper along the underside
of a dragon's wing. A thick milky substance flowed
down the scraper's blade. Another woman caught
the substance in a jar. The process was repeated
until the jar was full, then it was taken aside and
sealed.

"*Sekoy'melin*," Alanna told Robert, leading him
to one of the work stations where the vessels were
sealed. The groom there stepped back for the
dragonrider, and she pointed to an open jar. Robert
reached down and dipped his fingers into the contents. It reminded him of warm syrup, though it
bore an odor all its own. He wiped his fingers on
the side of the jar, then on a cloth that Danyel
handed him.

The groom leaned close to Danyel, one eye on
Robert, and whispered, "Shae'aluth?" The youth
shook his head.

"A dragon uses the glow of its wings to attract
mates," Alanna continued to explain, as the disappointed groom stepped back. "Along the underside,
just below the thin skin, are thousands of small
sacs. These sacs are filled with *sekoy'melin*."

"There's gallons of the stuff here!" Robert exclaimed as he dipped his fingers into the jar again.
The stuff really had a unique texture, like liquid
velvet.

Danyel grinned. "You know females, Robert Podlowsky," he said. "They go a little crazy when
they're pregnant." He ducked Alanna's playful
blow at his head, but he never stopped talking.

"The female *sekoye,* as she approaches her time, secretes an overabundance of *sekoy'melin.*"

"It's the grooms' job to collect it," Alanna said, seizing the thread of conversation.

Robert interrupted. "The lights," he said, recalling the small glowing bubbles of glass he'd seen in Sheren-Chad, and the larger bubble atop its roof. "The *sekoy'melin* continues to glow. You put it into glass containers and use it to light your homes and cities."

"Only the public streets and public places," Alanna corrected. "And a few very important buildings. There's never enough for private use. For that, we rely on candles and lamps."

Robert wiped his hand on his trousers and turned to watch the grooms continuing to milk the dragons. He realized then that Roderigo Diez had had some fun with him when he told him that the lights contained dragon piss. A private grin turned the corners of his mouth. He would find some way to pay Diez back for that.

A shadow raced across the beach. "I suppose," he said, pointing up at the dragon that played so energetically overhead, "that is a nervous father?"

"Hard to tell," Danyel answered with a lopsided smirk. "Dragons can be real whores."

The boy didn't duck fast enough to dodge Alanna's blow this time. Or, rather, he ducked right into it. It was only a playful little tap, but she caught him off balance. Danyel toppled over into the sand and sat up laughing.

"That's no way to talk about an angel, little boy," Robert chided with mock solemnity.

"I'm not a little boy, Robert Podlowsky," Danyel stated matter-of-factly, his grin fading as he stood up and brushed himself off. "Do you have angels on Paradane?"

"I'm afraid not," Robert answered, turning suddenly serious. He opened his left hand and regarded the white scar upon his palm. For a moment, Scott's face swam in his memories, and he allowed himself to savor his recollections before he forced them away again. He looked past Danyel and out toward the dragons, noticing how the sand was piled up around their fat bellies and how their tails trailed in the water to keep their bodies cool. Nests, Alanna had said. It had such a homey sound.

Robert looked back at Danyel and clapped the boy on the shoulder. "In our world, Darkness won a long time ago."

Chapter Nine

ERIC paced back and forth along the low wall on Sherin-Chad's rooftop. The air was cool and damp, absolutely still. Sometimes he stopped and peered over the side. A thick gray fog filled the streets and dimmed the lights below. A few passersby moved in the night through the haze, no more than shadows or ghosts.

Ghosts. He had spent the afternoon reading Blor's book. His mouth drew into a taut line, and his brow furrowed. He leaned his hands on the wall and glanced up toward the sky, where clouds hung low, like an oppressive blanket. He didn't want to think about ghosts.

He wanted a beer. He wanted several beers. It hadn't occurred to him back in Dowdsville how much he needed that stuff. He'd never thought of himself as an alcoholic. He licked his lips and wiped a hand over his face. His skin was slick from the moisture in the air. He paced some more and thought about an ice-cold cooler of Budweiser. Or Corona. Or Tsing Tao, his favorite. Anything was better than thinking about ghosts.

It was like they had a goddamn evolution of their own. Some *dandos* evolved into *ankous*. Sometimes into *leikkios*, or *poltergeists*. In time, those became screamers and banshees, chills and shades. There were worse things too. *Utburds,* which were murdered children. *Shrikers,* which were the spirits of sacrificed animals, controlled by the killer and sent out to do evil.

He thought he had stopped believing in good and evil years ago when he quietly walked away from his Catholic faith. Now he couldn't help but question. Question everything. And the answers, when he saw them at all, frightened the hell out of him.

He wanted a drink.

He slapped a hand on the stone wall, turned sharply, and left the roof, going down several flights of stairs, past the lavatorium, with its pale globes of light, past Phlogis's chamber, past the level where his own rooms were. It surprised him to find no one else in the corridors. The place had been full of people in the late afternoon.

Reaching the fourth level, he found the great doors to the dining hall and flung them back. It was dark within, but from the kitchen area a pale light shone. He wove around the low, oriental-style tables and the piles of cushions. A thin red wine had been served with dinner. He'd turned his cup upside down, not caring for wine, and taken water instead. Now, though, he was ready to give it a try.

He opened cupboards and closets, trunks and casks, checked shelves. Dishes, pots, pans, glasses, earthenware goblets. Vegetables and fruits. He seized an apple, bit into it, chewed, and cast the rest of it on the floor. Bread. Herbs. More bread. Finally, a pair of bottles turned up, each more than half full. With a grunt of satisfaction he carried them back into the dining room.

A number of windows were open, unshuttered.

He chose one with a thick ledge and curled up in it. It was a four-story drop if he fell, but so what. He rolled up his sleeves and settled himself comfortably. Then, setting one bottle within reach on the floor, he put the cork of the other to his teeth. Pop! He spat it out into the night and watched it fall as far as he could. Then he took a drink.

Even as he swallowed he felt a vague sense of guilt. He looked around the darkened dining room. His belly was full with the dinner he'd eaten here. Roderigo Diez and Blor had introduced him to a score of other dragonriders. It seemed they all lived here at Sheren-Chad unless they were on a mission or on patrol. Like monks, he'd thought at the time, and the tower was one big monastery.

He took another drink.

Robert had been in one of his moods. He'd barely spoken through the whole meal, just sat and stared out the window and occasionally lifted a bite of food to his mouth. Alanna had fawned all over him, and he'd been oblivious to it, treated her like she wasn't even there.

Damn, but she looked good with her hair all pinned up and wearing that long dress with those close sleeves and that high collar. It had startled hell out of him when she walked in. He was used to her in leathers, dammit.

Diez had leaned over and whispered in Eric's ear, "She's in love."

Bad move, Alanna, Eric thought to himself as he took another swig. He lowered the bottle and chewed on the corner of his lip. *I know my little brother.* He raised the wine again. *Better than he thinks,* he added.

It was really foul stuff, the wine, and he didn't

have any regrets at all when the first bottle was empty. Maybe the second bottle would be better. He pulled out the cork with his teeth and sent it to join the first cork. He sampled the new vintage. Nope, just as bad as the other.

He leaned back in the window and rested his head against the cool stone. He looked for the moon and the pale blue ring that he thought was so beautiful. The clouds were too thick. Down below, the whole world looked as if someone had wrapped it in a shroud.

He put the bottle between his legs and closed his eyes.

At first he thought it was the alcohol. He hadn't heard the doors open, hadn't heard anything at all. But suddenly someone else was in the room. He felt it, like an itch on the back of his neck. He opened his eyes, trying to stay calm, and looked slowly around.

No one was there. Only the lamplight from the kitchen penetrated the darkness of the dining hall, but it was enough to tell him he was still alone. He gazed across the low, polished tabletops, noted the undisturbed piles of cushions, the shadow-filled corners. The itch was gone.

Yet a face hovered uninvited in his memory. The blond guy. He knew the face because he'd seen him before in a dream. Scott Silver. He didn't know how he knew or why he was so sure. But it was Robert's friend.

The bottle slipped under Eric's left knee and fell to the floor. For a moment it teetered as if it might actually land upright without spilling. Then it toppled and rolled. Wine pumped out, forming a dark, rapidly spreading pool.

Eric's heart skipped a beat. He leaped up from the window ledge and ran across the dining room, flung back the great doors and raced through the halls. He took the first flight of stairs two at a time, slipping once and catching himself on his hands and knees. He paused long enough for the walls to turn solid again and for his head to clear a bit, and then sped on.

He dashed into his room, threw open his wardrobe doors, and grabbed his brother's khaki shorts. He dug in the pockets again, taking out the Boy Scout penknife and the newspaper clipping. He unfolded it and read it once more, cursing when his eyes focused slowly. He blinked and read it again, mouthing the words.

He crumpled the clipping in a fist and fell back against the wardrobe. The image of the wine wouldn't leave him. The wine, pumping. Pumping like blood.

He had to find Robert. Had to see his brother. Now.

He lurched toward the door, but before he got halfway across his small room it flung back. Robert stood there in the entrance, bare-chested, his hair rumpled, looking like he'd seen a ghost.

"Scott . . . !" Robert said, coming forward.

"What about Scott?" Eric demanded, raising his voice as he thrust out the clipping.

Robert's gaze locked onto the crumpled square of paper on his brother's palm, and he stopped in his tracks. "I . . . I just saw him!" he continued. "I was dozing . . ."

"Me, too, Bobby!" Eric replied sharply. "I've seen him twice now, I'll bet. He could pass for your twin, right? But his eyes are blue."

Robert nodded nervously. He reached out to take the clipping, but Eric snapped his hand closed. "Not yet, Grasshopper." His words came out laced with anger. He didn't quite understand it, or maybe he just hadn't admitted it to himself. But he *was* angry with his brother, angry that Robert had kept things from him.

With a quick, savage motion he tossed the wadded clipping at Robert. It bounced off his brother's chest and fell to the carpet. "Who got shot, Bobby?" he demanded as Robert bent to pick it up. "Was it Scott?" He leaned over his brother, shouting, his voice ringing in his own ears.

Robert squeezed the clipping in his fist and rose, his face turning to stone. Eric wasn't fooled, though. He knew his brother too well. It was only a mask; rage was seething underneath. "Is he dead, Bobby?" Eric shouted.

Robert glared, then spun and headed for the door. Eric couldn't physically get around his brother to stop him, but he threw a kick that caught the edge of the door. It slammed shut with loud force in Robert's face. Eric shouted again: "He's dead, isn't he, goddamn it?"

Robert gave an anguished cry. Hot stars exploded in Eric's head as the back of his brother's hand knocked him to the floor. It took a moment for the pain to reach him through his alcohol fog. He raised up on one elbow and wiped at a trickle of blood at the left corner of his mouth.

Robert stood over him, trembling. "Yes!" he screamed, shaking the fist that curled around the clipping. His face was purple, swollen. "No!" He shook his head and stepped away from Eric. "Goddamn you, Eric! I don't know what's happening!"

Eric sat up slowly, testing his jaw. The room swam, and he knew it was as much the wine as his brother's blow. "I'm drunk, Bobby," he said thickly, apologetically.

Robert looked down at him. His mask was gone, but what Eric had seen wasn't anger. It was pain. A lot of pain. Robert bit his lip, then his mouth drew into a thin, tight line of barely contained emotion. Eric realized suddenly, with one of those odd insights you get only when you're drunk, that he couldn't remember the last time he'd seen his brother cry.

But that wasn't going to happen now either. Bobby's walls were too strong, too high. He reached down a hand, and Eric let himself be helped up. "What happened?" Eric asked quietly, getting control of himself. He went to his bed and sat down on the edge, never taking his gaze from his brother.

Robert went to the door, but he only leaned his back against it and stared across the room toward the open window. "We were coming out of a bar," he said at last. "I'd just talked Scott into moving to New York. He'd been there a week." He squeezed his eyes shut and opened them again to look at the clipping he held. Carefully he unwadded and refolded it. "We were going in separate directions, though. I was half a block away when I heard the shouts. Then I heard the shots." He squeezed his eyes shut again and rubbed a hand over his forehead. He drew a deep breath and let it out. "He died in my arms on that damn dirty sidewalk, Eric."

Eric nodded. That explained the clipping. He felt guilty as hell for confronting his brother about it. He thought he should say something, but he didn't know what.

Robert banged his head twice lightly back against the door. "Yet I saw him in the clove," he said, quietly insistent. "I swear I did. Standing right by the tent. He looked straight at me. Then he turned and ran into the woods."

"It was his ghost," Eric answered. He no longer had any doubts about such things. They were real. As real as the sky or the air. Maybe you couldn't always touch them or see them, but like the sky and the air, they were real.

"I don't think so," Robert said stubbornly, staring at the clipping.

"It was his ghost," Eric repeated. "It lured us here, to Palenoc."

Robert pushed away from the door and paced in front of the window, his hands folded over his chest. "Why?" he snapped in irritation. "How would Scott know about this place? How would even his ghost know?"

Eric pressed a thumb against his temple, trying to clear his head, damning himself for the wine he'd consumed. "A more interesting question, little brother," he said slowly, "is how you know about this place."

Robert stopped his pacing.

"You write a book and call it *A Pale Knock*. Odd coincidence. Or is it coincidence?" Eric rose to his feet. It was his turn to pace. "It's a ghost story about twelve evil spirits. Did you know there were originally only twelve *chimorgs*?"

Robert shook his head, looking troubled. "But I knew the moon was called Thanador, and the ring around it is Mianur. The name means 'Way to Paradise.' "

Eric slumped down in one of the room's two chairs. "What else do you know?" he pushed, folding his hands across his stomach and stretching his feet out. "I mean, your novel seems like some sort of a weird, screwed-up tourist guide to this place."

Robert's mouth settled in a sharp frown. "I don't know about that," he said, resuming the pacing. "I just can't shake the feeling that Scott *isn't* dead, Eric! Not really! Could a ghost have carried that medallion into our world and left it for us to find?"

Eric shrugged. "Sumeek moved that rake," he reminded.

Robert wasn't convinced. "Alanna said that was an act of rage, and a pretty rare one at that. Leaving that medallion wasn't rage. That was planning."

Eric steepled his fingers and regarded his brother over the tips. "You yourself said Scott died in your arms."

Robert's frown deepened. His head bobbed up and down like a puppy toy in a car window. "I know," he answered, barely whispering. "It's a conundrum." He turned away from the window toward his brother. When he spoke again there was a harder edge to his voice. "But Eric, I'm not leaving here until I solve it."

Eric got up from his chair and went to stand beside his brother. Together they peered out into the gray fog and mist. Eric, though, turned his gaze surreptitiously toward his brother's face. Robert's eyes had a hard, cold cast. His mask was solidly back in place. That alone was enough to tell Eric that Robert hadn't told him everything yet.

"What the . . . !" Eric gave a jump as something

flew in the window and landed on his forearm. Tiny serrated feet took a firm grip on his skin. The candlelight from the table gleamed on veined, membranous wings and luminous green eyes. A ratchety noise issued from the ugly little creature. Eric grinned. "A cicada!"

Robert forced a patient smile, obviously a strained effort. Another cicada flew in after the first and landed on the foot of the bed. Outside the window, a dry scraping sound began to grow in volume. A third insect flew into the room and settled on the leg of Robert's leather trousers.

Suddenly Eric gave a sharp cry. "Damn!" he shouted, giving his arm a violent shake. Then, "Goddamn it!" The cicada wouldn't let go. He beat at the insect with his other hand, finally ripping it free and hurling it to the floor. It crunched under his boot heel.

Eric held up his arm. "It bit me!" A thin stream of blood ran down toward his fingers. Another insect darted into the room, and another. One buzzed around the candle flame. Robert instantly knocked away the one on his leg and crushed it. Eric pushed down his sleeves to cover his arms, then lunged for the shutters, drew them close and slammed the latch into place.

Robert gave a shout and slapped desperately at his back. Eric turned him around. One of the things was trying to chew a hole between Robert's shoulder blades. He dug his fingers under its plump carapace and ripped it free. It wriggled and sang angrily. Eric flung it against the wall with all his might. It made a satisfying *pop* as it splattered against the stone.

Eric reached into his wardrobe, snatched up one

of his hiking boots, and made short work of the remaining cicadas. "That's the last of 'em," he said, hammering a shapeless blob on the table near the candle. He whacked it twice more and stood back.

"I don't think so," Robert said grimly. He pointed toward the shutters. "Listen."

Outside, the night was full of a harsh rasping. The shutters vibrated under the impact of insect bodies striking against them. Eric tore a corner of his bedsheet and daubed at the wound on Robert's back.

"There must be thousands of them," Robert muttered. "Millions."

Then another sound rose over that of the cicadas—A strange trumpeting and trilling that both brothers recognized at once. "Dragons!" Eric cried. The two looked at each other. Eric flung down the bloodied sheet, grabbed a shirt from his wardrobe, and tossed it to his brother. They bolted for the door.

"Wait!" Eric cried suddenly, spying the Boy Scout penknife on the floor where he'd dropped it when his brother had knocked him down. He snatched it up and tossed it to Robert. "It's not much, but it's sharp."

He ran back to the pedestal by the wardrobe. His own Swiss army knife lay beside the pitcher and basin of water. He'd used the blade earlier to shave and left it there to dry. He grabbed it. "Aren't we a fearsome pair," he muttered, as he ran by Robert and into the corridor.

The hall was full of leather-clad *sekournen*, all running for the stairs that led to the upper levels. "This must be what Scott was trying warn me about!" Robert said, as he and Eric followed the dragonriders.

"Warn you?" Eric shot back, pounding up the steps. But he was thinking back to the dining room and Scott Silver, a vague shadow in a troubled dream. Had Robert's friend been trying to warn him as well?

"Sort of," Robert answered. "He was just there in my dream. And I had the feeling something was really wrong!"

They hit the next level and the next. Servants and *sekournen,* some bearing torches, candles, or glass bubbles of *sekoy'melin,* ran ahead of them. The lavatorium was crowded with everyone pushing their way to the only staircase that led to the roof.

From above came the sound of singing! Eric and Robert surged out onto the roof. The air was full of swarming cicadas. The light of the great *sekoy'melin* globe was nearly obscured by the insects that clung to it. A fat bug landed in Eric's hair. With a short curse, he grabbed it and crushed it in his fist.

"What are they doing?" Robert cried. It was almost impossible to hear over the singing of the humans and the dragons. At least a score of *sekoye* flew swift circles around the tower, their wings blazing.

More of the Sheren-Chad's residents rushed up the staircase and joined the great ring of people that encircled the rooftop. Everyone stood, hands joined and lifted, singing at the top of their lungs. Eric spied Roderigo Diez and the boy, Danyel, in the ring. He grabbed his brother's arm and ran toward the old Spaniard. Diez would be able to explain.

But Diez only grabbed Eric's hand and drew him

into the circle, and Danyel did the same with Robert. "Sing!" the physician said between breaths. But Eric didn't know the words. It was an anthem of some kind. He caught the tune though and vocalized a few notes self-consciously.

Holding to Diez and his brother, he leaned over the low wall. Far down in the fogbound streets, he saw figures moving. The citizens of Rasoul. They surged out of their houses, out of their beds into the roads or onto their rooftops. Everywhere he looked, people joined hands. Their voices soared into the night, drowning the sawlike rasp of the cicadas and the humming of uncounted wings, filling the darkness with a power of spirit that awed Eric to the core of his soul.

> *Gather, people! Stand together!*
> *Darkness has no power here!*
> *Join your hands and raise your voices!*
> *Filled with Light we have no fear!*

Eric sang, giving himself to the power, becoming one with it. Cicadas landed on his arms. On his clothing. In his hair. He felt their weight. But more, he felt Diez's and Robert's hands in his. Something stung his cheek. A strange, vibrating buzz, the rapid brush of wings on his skin. A warm trickle. Still he sang.

> *Men and women, little children!*
> *We are not afraid tonight!*
> *The smallest of us is a fortress!*
> *Stand as one against the Night!*

Farther down along the circle, Alanna rose up

onto the wall. She still wore the sweeping gold-colored dress she'd worn at dinner, its sleeves close-fitting, glittering with buttons, its collar high about her white throat. Her black hair streamed back, and the folds of her garment fluttered in the wind. For an instant, her voice soared higher and sweeter than the others. She flung out her arms and stood there on the wall as if crucified on the darkness. Then she hurled herself out into space.

Eric and Robert screamed at the same time, but Diez and Danyel held them fast. Even as she reached the apex of her dive and began to fall, a dragon plunged down out of the flock circling above the tower. Eric recognized its amber wings as Alanna caught the horn of the saddle around the beast's neck and pulled herself into the seat.

Danyel pressed Robert's hand into someone else's and climbed onto the wall. There was no trace of fear on his young face. His expression was beatific as he flung himself outward. He seemed to fall farther and faster than Alanna before his opal-winged mount folded its wings and dived to intersect his fall. The boy caught its saddle. Beast and rider turned away from the tower and swept low over the city.

Gather, people! Stand together!
Darkness has no power here!

Another half-dozen dragonriders threw themselves into space, each catching their dragons and speeding outward over Rasoul. Still they sang, and their dragons sang with them. Eric traded glances with his brother. Robert sang too! He had learned the words.

The cicadas swarmed and buzzed, but they did

not alight. A bug brushed Eric's ear, filling it with humming. But it didn't bite him. Like a brown cloud, the creatures darted above the tower and over all of Rasoul. Millions of them. Yet Eric sensed that something had changed. Diez bled from a score of small bites. But there wasn't a bug on him now. Same thing with Robert on his right.

> *Join your hands and raise your voices!*
> *Stand as one against the Night!*

Eric didn't understand it. Somehow the singing was driving the insects back. All of Rasoul, joined in one voice! It was magic, and he was part of it! At last he was part of something. Years of secret loneliness and isolation and private fears melted from him in an instant. He had hidden for so long in his own world, caged himself in the false security of safe and familiar things, never venturing out, never reaching out, never really touching anyone or anything.

He looked at his brother, seeing more clearly than he had ever seen before, and wondered if Robert felt it too. *God, let him feel it!* he prayed.

He barely finished the thought. The raw edge of a scream cut through his ears. No, not his ears. His brain! It was in his head. Then someone screamed for real. He spun around as light suddenly flooded the rooftop.

The great globe of *sekoy'melin* burned with a near-blinding intensity. Instinctively, everyone cowered in front of it, but there was no place to run. The top of the globe exploded, sending glittering fragments into the night. The liquid within rose up, bubbling and hissing. Streamers of colored fluid shot high, evaporating almost instantly, filling the darkness with a surreal, glowing mist.

And in the center of that cauldron of radiance a huge and transparent figure writhed. The light danced upon it, through it, swirled around it. The giant opened its mouth and screamed again. It seemed to pull itself up, growing with every heartbeat, like something hatching from an egg. But though it was in pain, it was also angry. A wave of psychic rage swept outward from the creature. It made a clawing motion, raking its hand across the sky. Every cicada near the tower burst into a white-hot spark of flame. A collective gasp went up as everyone threw themselves to the floor of the rooftop or crouched against the wall for shelter from the ash that rained down.

As suddenly and unexpectedly as it had appeared, the manifestation shriveled back into the broken globe and disappeared. The light, too, faded rapidly as the *sekoy'melin* diffused into the air.

"Phlogis!" Roderigo Diez cried, rising. He ran for the stairway, but someone beat him to it. The dragonrider Valis bounded down the steps at a full run. Others followed. Eric hesitated only long enough to glance over the side of the wall again. The drone of cicadas yet filled the air, and the song of Rasoul's people still swelled up, uninterrupted, from the streets to meet it. Some of the *sekournen* on the roof joined hands again and resumed the anthem.

Robert was already heading for the stairs, and Eric followed.

The old woman, Blor, lay sprawled on the floor outside the entrance to Phlogis's sanctum. A deep

bruise purpled the area above her right eye where;
her head had struck the stone tiles.

"Kaesha!" Diez shouted in dismay. He leaped
toward her.

Valis caught the physician's arm and stopped
him. "Stay back!" he ordered. Then he pointed to
a small, glimmering stone, no bigger than a pebble,
near Blor's body. "That's a diamond."

"So?" Robert said. He started forward too, but
Eric pulled him back. Valis wouldn't have stopped
Diez if there weren't some danger.

Diez licked his lips worriedly. "In the hands of
the right person a diamond can induce a powerful
trance. Someone has attacked Phlogis, but they
went through Blor first."

Eric looked at Valis. The dim light in the corridor filled the dragonrider's stern eyes with shadows. "The cicadas were some kind of diversion?"

Diez didn't answer. All of his attention was on
Blor. "If we go near that stone, its spell will affect
us too."

"The light," Valis said, pointing to the pair of
sekoy'melin globes on either side of the great doors.
"Without the light the diamond will lose its power."

Diez's frown deepened as he wrung his hands.
"Same problem," he said sharply. "We can't get
near those either!"

"You still have that bloodstone you used on
Eric?" Robert asked. "Or any other stones?"

Roderigo Diez put a hand to the small pouch on
his belt. "Of course," he answered impatiently.
"But these are healing stones. Nothing to combat
the diamond's magic."

Robert extended a hand and crooked a demanding
finger. "A rock's a rock," he shot back. "You want

to get to your lady friend, then give. Come on, two stones!"

Eric understood what his brother was up to. "Give me one," he said as the old Spaniard dug down into the pouch and came up with a small handful of stones. "Oh, great," he added, choosing a marble-size amethyst. "My birthstone."

Robert selected a piece of polished tiger's-eye and tested its weight. "I'll take the one on the left," he said. "You've got the right."

"I'm always right," Eric grumbled.

"Except when you're wrong," Robert made the stock reply. He glanced over his shoulder at Diez and Valis. "Don't worry. We did this with tin cans all the time when we were kids. Now stand back."

They let fly with their stones at the same time. The globe on the left shattered a split second before the one on the right. The *sekoy'melin* hissed and bubbled as it evaporated. A thin, glowing mist hovered for a moment; then even that was gone, leaving them in darkness.

Slippered feet scurried across the tiles. From near the great doors, Diez breathed an urgent *"Kaesha!"*

"Find the diamond!" Valis insisted. The dragonrider was on his hands and knees already, feeling for the treacherous gem. "If any light spills out when we open the sanctum . . ."

"I've got it!" Diez cried. "It's in my pouch!"

The sanctum doors groaned open. A hellish red glow lanced into the corridor. Diez kneeled on the floor, Blor's head in his lap, as he twisted to stare across the threshold after Valis.

The dragonrider stood stiffly in the entrance. *"Tchai!"* he cursed softly. "Oh, Mother-dragon!"

Eric and Robert stepped around Diez and into the sanctum. A chilling cold filled the room; their breath came out in steaming clouds. Twelve white-robed figures, men and women, lay unconscious. The fat doorman too. Valis went to them, one by one, and knelt to check for signs of life.

Eric crept toward the golden circle at the center of the room, stopping just at the edge. There was no evidence that Phlogis was within.

"Jesus Christ!"

Eric turned at his brother's exclamation and went to Robert's side. His stomach lurched. He clapped a hand to his mouth, tasting vomit. He swallowed it, but turned quickly away until he got himself under control. Finally he turned back again.

The open door and its shadow had hidden the body from view at first. Though it wasn't much of a body. Robert pushed the door closed a bit to better reveal his discovery. It was mostly pulp, a few clothes, a familiar lacquered mask. A thick black smear of blood and tissue ran down the wall. "He must have hit up there," Robert said, pointing to a spot near the ceiling.

Eric thought of the cicada he had hurled against the wall in his room. He heard the crack and pop of its carapace, the splash of bug guts and felt his stomach lurch again. "What did Phlogis hit him with?" he managed between clenched teeth.

"The fool!" Valis scowled from just behind them. He bent down in the gloom near the other door and poked a small upended box with a finger. Its contents were scattered over the floor—small gems, tools.

Eric went to see what the dragonrider had found.

Just in front of the doors were thick chalk marks, hasty scratchings that bore some resemblance to the hex signs on the doors. Something crunched softly under his foot. He stooped to see what it was. "Cremat leaves," he muttered wonderingly.

"The leaves, the tools and gems, the chalk," Valis said, waving a hand around the room as he rose. He let go a sigh and shook his head. "The fool tried to exorcise Phlogis."

"Looks like Phlogis didn't take too kindly to the idea," Robert responded. "This guy's been swatted like a fly."

Eric bit his lip as he looked around the room. He thought he knew Sheren-Chad well enough now. He'd spent part of the day exploring its levels and chambers, and Roderigo Diez had shown him around a bit. "How could he have done it, Valis?" he asked. "Gotten in, gotten this far, gotten the drop on everybody . . ." He scratched the back of his head, frowning in puzzlement. "This place seems so secure."

Valis pushed the small wooden box with his toe, then moved to the edge of the golden circle. "He couldn't have done it without help," he said with his back to them. His hands slowly clenched at his sides. "Inside help." He turned around to face them, and the red glow from the pair of cauldrons gave him a frightening appearance.

"We have a traitor in Sheren-Chad," he said.

Chapter Ten

IT was another sleepless night for Robert. Another in a long line. He'd stopped counting them. Sheren-Chad was calm again. Everyone had retired once more. The only exceptions were Valis, who had taken it upon himself to scour and purify Phlogis's sanctum, and Diez, who had taken his medical skills into the streets.

He needed air and escape from the confines of his small room, so he walked up the stairs back to the rooftop. It surprised him to find Alanna there. She'd changed into leathers again. Her back was to him as she stood by the parapet. Her hair stirred slightly in the soft breeze, and she poured a gentle song quietly into the misty night.

Three *sekoye* flew majestic circles around the tower, their wings seeming to beat in time to her music. By the glow of their wings, Robert could identify the creatures.

"You control them, don't you?" he asked in a low voice, stealing up behind her. She didn't flinch when his hand settled on her shoulder.

She shook her head, leaned close to him, and slipped an arm around his waist. Alanna seemed so relaxed, almost serene. She ended her song and smiled. Drops of mist clung to eyelashes more delicate than the veins of a leaf. "Nobody controls the *sekoye*," she answered. "I can call to them, but that's all."

Robert pointed to the amber-winged dragon as it swept past. The glow of its wings cast a fine radiance on Alanna's face and lit up her eyes. "I thought that one was yours," he said.

She gave a little laugh. "That's Mirrormist." Alanna turned a little to follow the dragon's flight. "I guess I belong to him as much as he belongs to me." She inclined her head toward Danyel's spectacular opal-winged beast as it came around the tower. "That is Shadowfire." The dragon seemed to turn its diamond-eyed gaze on them. Then it was past. Valis's dragon flashed by in a slightly higher orbit. "That's Brightstar."

Robert felt the warmth of her against him. It was an unsettling sensation. He wanted at the same time to draw her closer and to push her away. He listened to the *whoosh* of the dragons as they swept past and tried to think of something to say. "I nearly had a heart attack when you jumped off the tower," he told her finally.

Her smile returned and she stared outward. The night was still full of clouds and fog, but here and there globes of *sekoy'melin* and rooftop watch fires glimmered. "We call it 'becoming Taedra,'" she replied, her voice little more than a whisper. "In that moment when we hang in the air we become one with the Mother-dragon."

"Your goddess?" Robert murmured.

She looked up at him, and her smile became an amused smirk. "Goddess? No." She shook her head gently and leaned a little closer to him, her hand tightening on his side. "Taedra is no goddess, just a pure and perfect expression of Or-dhamu."

It was Robert's turn to shake his head. "I don't understand," he whispered.

They left it at that. For a long time they stood there, side by side, staring outward over the quiet shadows and misty glimmerings of Rasoul while Robert wrestled with feelings he didn't want and memories he couldn't set aside. He thought of Scott, alive or dead, impossibly out there somewhere, and wondered how he would ever find him.

He thought of home, too. Dowdsville in the Catskills. Manhattan. His apartment in Chelsea. He had a book due to his publishers. Strangely, he didn't care. None of that seemed real next to this.

"Excuse me."

Alanna and Robert turned together. Danyel stood on the roof at the edge of the stairs, little more than a vague shadow. With the great globe shattered, the only light was the glow that seeped through the doorway from the lavatorium below and the soft radiance of the dragons' wings where they flew past.

"Phlogis is in the chapel," he told them. "He wants us." His demeanor seemed grimmer than usual. He didn't seem such a little boy at all standing there, but a warrior, and a tired one at that. "It isn't easy for him," he added, "so hurry."

Alanna took Robert's hand and led him after Danyel. Deeper they went into the tower than Robert had ever gone. Then, passing through an arched entrance, they crossed a vast black chamber and found yet another stairway. Alanna and Danyel seemed to know the way in total darkness. Neither bore a light, and Alanna kept a tight grip on Robert's hand. Down three more flights of stairs. The air took on a different kind of dampness, and a chill lingered. The wall on his right was cool to the touch, and he guessed they were at subterranean levels now, deep under the earth.

Suddenly they stopped. There was a loud ring of metal striking metal. Robert strained to see, but he said nothing, trusting the woman at his side. Abruptly, a huge iron door creaked inward. The pale radiance of *sekoy'melin* infused the inner chamber. Robert let himself be led inside.

Eric nodded to him. Diez spared him barely a glance as he sprinkled incense upon a brazier, sending a stream of white smoke curling through the room. Blor was there too. The bruise on her head showed like a black stain of her beloved ink. She passed among twelve linen-wrapped corpses, each laid out on its own low dais. In one hand she carried a small pot of white paint. With a finger of her other hand she drew the same symbol on each of their brows: two half-arches, joined at one point. Wings.

At the far end of the chamber a huge dragon, sculpted with a master's skill from pure gold, dominated the scene. The incense smoke eddied around it, and though the *sekoy'melin* shone with a steadiness, the thin fire in the brazier lent a sharp glitter to the diamonds that made the idol's eyes.

"This is the blackest hour," Danyel muttered. "The Council of Twelve has been murdered, and Phlogis greatly weakened." There was a bitter edge to his young voice.

"Shut up!" Blor snapped, pausing in her labors. "Phlogis's weakness is only temporary." She gestured at the twelve bodies with the hand that held the paint pot. "But no one must know of this, so keep your mouth shut!"

"Easy, Blor-*kaesha*," Diez said, going to her side and putting an arm around her shoulders. "Why won't you let me take care of that bruise?" She shrugged him off angrily and bent to put the wing symbol on the next brow.

"How bad is it?" Robert asked, reverent in the presence of death as he slipped his hand free of Alanna's grip and went to his brother's side.

"Bad enough, Roberto," Diez answered wearily. "The Council of Twelve were our governors. But they were also our last line of defense, each a man or woman of considerable power. It's unthinkable that they could have been destroyed so easily."

"Or that we should almost have lost Phlogis!" Blor added, her every word as sharp as a curse. "It's my fault! How could I let a single man get past me!"

"It's worse than expected," said a voice from the iron door. Valis stepped across the threshold into the glow of the *sekoy'melin* lamps. "The insects diverted our attention from the sanctum. But they also devoured most of the outlying crops and livestock. We'll be surviving on fish for a while."

Danyel scowled at the news and paced into a corner off to himself. "Shandal Karg has never been this bold," he hissed.

Blor exploded into a rage. She pointed a paint-smeared finger at the youth. "I told you to shut your mouth! How dare you mention that hated name in here, of all places!"

"*Tchai,* old woman!" Danyel shouted back, red-faced. "You don't tell me anything!"

Robert interrupted them. "The Heart of Darkness had nothing to do with this," he stated. "You want to know why your council didn't see an attack coming?" Both Danyel and Blor glared at him. All the other eyes turned his way. "They were watching the wrong enemy." He reached under his shirt and brought out the black-lacquered mask he'd found in the sanctum. He stepped toward the closest corpse and laid it gently upon a pair of folded hands. "You want to place the blame for this, then look to the Kingdoms of Night."

"That's foolish!" Blor snapped. "Keris Chaterit hasn't got the power! He wouldn't dare attack us!"

The flame in the brazier flickered suddenly, and smoke swirled.

Our Brother of the Dragon is correct.

Robert heard the voice in his head, but he knew from their expressions that everyone else heard it too. Then, in the shadow of Taedra's great golden wings, a shape took vague form.

"Phlogis!" Blor set her paint pot down beside the last corpse. She turned toward the apparition and wrung her hands in nervous agitation. The wave of rage that usually accompanied Phlogis's presence was absent this time, and his spirit seemed greatly diminished. Blor hesitated, then started toward him.

He lifted a hand to warn her back. *This is hard for me,* Phlogis whispered. *I cannot take form enough to speak, so share my thoughts.* He paused, and his form seemed to waver and fade in the dim light before he grew stronger again. *In his vanity and arrogance, Keris Chaterit has dared what the Heart of Darkness would never have dared. His success can be measured in the bodies before us. He has grown stronger while we kept watch on the other enemy. Robert Podlowsky has seen this truly.*

Alanna spoke up suddenly. "Then it's more important than ever that we find the Chalosans," she said. Her mouth settled into a grim line as she regarded Phlogis.

Your sister. The words flowed from Phlogis like cold water lapping at Robert's brain, but he listened with even greater interest.

"Sister?" Eric said with surprise. "I thought you were staying with friends in Chalosa, but now I remember. There was a woman fighting at your side when the black-clads attacked."

"Maris," Alanna told him, lifting her head with pride.

She will head the new council, Phlogis informed them. *This was decided long ago. You must bring her here so that I might unlock the power within her.*

"You sound as though you know where she is?" Robert said.

Phlogis wavered. For a moment only an eddy of incense smoke marked the place where he had been. The flame in the brazier flickered again, and his thoughts came to them, broken and flaccid, as if from a great void. *In Terreborne. Not far. Follow the Shylamare River. But hurry.*

"We'll leave tonight," Valis answered. He crooked a finger at Danyel, and the boy went to his side. "Leave the packs to us and come to the roof when you're ready," he said to Alanna. The two turned and left.

"We're going, too," Eric called. "The black-clads were after us when they attacked Chalosa. They killed a friend of mine."

Revenge is a thing we understand well in Palenoc,

Son of Paradane, Phlogis answered, his voice a little stronger. *But you mustn't let it rule you. It was not I who killed the Terreborne wizard who attempted my exorcism, but the enraged* dandos *of the council. I barely had time to rip a few facts from his mind concerning the Chalosans.*

"It's not for revenge that I ask," Eric answered stubbornly. He glanced at his brother. "We want to help."

Alanna stepped forward until the shadow of Taedra's wings brushed her face. She could have reached out and touched Phlogis had there been anything there to touch. "I'll take them unless you object," she stated. "I've seen them fight. Aside from Danyel and Valis, there's no one I'd trust more than these two." She turned and stared straight into Robert's eyes.

Leave me alone with Robert Podlowsky, Phlogis requested after a moment's hesitation.

"Phlogis!" Blor shouted in dismay. "I should guard you . . . !"

Leave!

The *dando*'s sudden rage seared them as surely as if a hot wind had blown upon their faces. Blor staggered back, clutching at the arm of a corpse for support; Roderigo Diez caught her from behind and steadied her. She paled as the old physician led her from the chapel.

Eric stood his ground, but he turned toward his brother. "Bobby?" he asked uncertainly.

He didn't need to say anything more. Robert knew that if he asked, his big brother would have stayed on that spot despite all of Phlogis's threats. But there was no need for that. He didn't fear the *dando* any longer. Nor did he think that Phlogis meant him any harm.

"It's okay," he said to Eric. His brother still hesitated, but at last he crossed the room and went out at Alanna's side. Robert let go a breath and drew in another. He crossed to the nearest dais and leaned against it nonchalantly. Lifting his open hands, he said to Phlogis, "It's you and me."

The wispy form in Taedra's shadow had not revealed eyes before. Now two small red coals gleamed with a weak light where eyes should have been. *When you left me before,* Phlogis whispered, *you felt me probe your mind.*

"So what?" Robert answered curtly. He shrugged his shoulders. "You didn't get very far."

A ghostly nod. *That's what disturbs me, Robert Podlowsky. There is a darkness within you that I cannot fathom.*

"I'm afraid I can't help you," Robert replied, trying not to bristle. "If you don't trust me, say so. You think I'm the one who let that wizard into Sheren-Chad?"

The *dando's* amusement tickled across Robert's brain. *If I thought that, there would be two smears on my sanctum's wall.* The spectral image wavered and faded again. For a moment Robert found himself alone with the huge golden dragon and the twelve corpses. Then Phlogis returned. *It is hard for me to manifest here without my wards and circles.* The ghost shook its head and radiated weariness. *I am old.*

"Let me ask you a question," Robert said, drawing himself erect and folding his arms over his chest. "Do you know someone named Scott Silver?"

Two red eyes gleamed again. They blinked. *The name is not familiar,* Phlogis answered.

"Search for him," Robert said, surprised by his own authority. "You have power. Diez says you have contacts in the spirit world. If he's dead, I want to know."

Phlogis nodded. *We owe you much already for killing a* chimorg. *I will seek out your friend, Scott Silver. But this darkness that I sense within you, Robert Podlowsky. Beware of it, for it may lead to great harm.*

Robert frowned impatiently. "I won't kill," he muttered.

You have already killed.

"The *chimorg* doesn't count!"

The red eyes fixed him with a steadfast gaze, and a wispy finger raised to point at him. Phlogis's words cut across his brain like a shard of ice: *You have killed a man.*

Something fell to the floor with a loud crack. Robert jumped at the sound and spun about to see the black-lacquered mask rocking back and forth on its sculpted nose. A long fracture ran down the forehead and between the eyes.

His heart thundered in his chest. He spun about again, but Phlogis was gone. He was alone except for twelve shrouded bodies and the imposing figure of Taedra. Her ruby eyes seemed to burn into him. Much as Phlogis's eyes had in that final moment.

Robert bit his lower lip and waited. The *dando* did not return. "Phlogis?" he called quietly. No one, nothing, answered. He squeezed his eyes shut, drowning in the memories that came: Scott's cry, Scott's weight on his arm. Scott's last breath, the frightened contact of their eyes, Scott's blood.

He clamped down hard, pushing the images away. A bitter shout ripped from his throat. He raised a heel and smashed the lacquered mask into splinters, then sagged against the dais, gasping.

He knew how Blor felt. Responsible.

Go.

The word was a puff of wind in his thoughts. He wasn't even sure he heard it. He whirled, but there was no sign of Phlogis. He waited again. Then he ran a hand through his hair. His palm came away damp with perspiration. "Good enough," he said finally—aloud, just in case the *dando* could hear him. "You said you trust me, Phlogis. I'm going with Alanna. And so is Eric."

He waited once more, his gaze sweeping all corners of the room, every shadow, every cranny. But Phlogis did not reappear to naysay him. That in itself he considered to be his answer. He stared at the idol of Taedra once more and resisted an urge to kneel before it. With its outspread wings it reminded him suddenly of the holy crucifix and his Catholic youth. But that wasn't a pleasant memory either, and he thrust it away just as ruthlessly.

Small globes of *sekoy'melin* were mounted along the chapel walls in iron rings. He lifted one out and balanced it on his palm, extending it to light his way as he started up the dark stairs. Two flights up, he found Alanna sitting on a step with her chin in her hands.

"Did you overhear?" he asked.

"Nothing of importance," she answered cryptically, starting to go up the steps.

He caught her shoulders and turned her around to face him. "I know what Phlogis is," he told her, his gaze searching her face. She was beautiful in the globe's small light. "Tell me what he was."

"A wizard," she answered. "Perhaps the most

powerful in Palenoc's history. And once ruler of a land now called Pyre." She spoke matter-of-factly, not simplifying, not explaining, not waiting for him to accept. "Five hundred years ago, the Heart of Darkness sent her armies against his kingdom, intent on its conquest. Single-handedly, with his sorcerous might, he hurled them back. So Shandal Karg herself came and froze him in a block of black ice and killed him." She paused and swallowed, climbed one step higher, turned, and added, "Phlogis strives for a revenge he can never win, because Shandal Karg cannot die. Only by thwarting her smaller schemes can he gain any satisfaction."

She led the way back up the stairs. In the lavatorium she stopped and instructed him: "Wash yourself, Robert. Then find fresh clothes in the wardrobes for traveling. Choose leathers. Meet us on the roof when you're ready."

Left alone, Robert did as she requested. The cool water felt good on his body. He pulled out the Boy Scout knife, which he'd secreted in the waistband of his trousers, opened the blade, and scraped at his cheeks. Naked and clean, he searched the wardrobes, passing over the pale gray leathers until he found a stack of black garments. When he was dressed and refreshed, and the Boy Scout knife was safely tucked into his boot, he started up the stairs to the roof.

Halfway up, he halted. Abruptly he turned and left the lavatorium to seek the lower level and his private room. With the small globe of *sekoy'melin* to light his way, he moved quickly. He pushed open the door, closed it softly, and went inside. His room was exactly like Eric's but for one difference: hanging on the wall over his bed, in a scabbard hastily made from a leather shirtsleeve, was the *chimorg* horn. A throat lacing from the same scavenged shirt made a passable strap. He took horn and scabbard down and slung it over his shoulder.

It wasn't much of a weapon, he figured, but it was the only thing effective against the unicorn monsters.

The others were waiting for him when he emerged at last onto the rooftop. With the great globe shattered it was eerily dark. The sky was empty of dragons. Eric, Alanna, and Danyel stood beside a pair of packs. Danyel wore a smaller pack upon his back. Valis, Diez, and Blor stood a little apart, chatting in low tones. As Robert approached, his sharp ears picked up part of their conversation.

". . . find out who it is," Valis was saying sternly to Blor. "You're the only one I trust. No one else. Watch Phlogis, but discover this traitor."

Blor nodded gravely.

"There they are!" Danyel called out. The youth extended an arm over the parapet and pointed to the east. A whole flock of dragons flew out of the mountains toward the tower, their wings blazing with gemstone hues.

Robert heard a sound from the stairway. A pair of dragonriders set down their packs. They eyed Robert but kept their distance. A moment later a third joined them. A hand swept back a close-fitting hood, revealing cropped hair and striking eyes. A woman. All three were dressed in black, and around their necks hung familiar, silver medallions.

"Who are they?" Robert asked going to his brother's side.

Eric pursed his lips as he studied the trio.

"Teams of dragonriders will be scouring the countryside for others like Alanna's sister. Danyel says there are always back-up council members waiting to serve."

"But while they wait they live in poverty among the common citizenry," Danyel added over his shoulder. "So that they'll know something of the daily lives of those they may one day be called on to govern."

"He exaggerates a bit," Alanna said with a patient frown. "In Chule, Danyel's land, it was different. But here in Guran, all the council members are chosen from the general populace." She gazed toward the trio by the stairway and gave them a nod of greeting. As she did so, still another dragonrider rose to the roof and dropped his pack. "While we search for Maris and the rest of the Chalosans, other riders will search for the remaining eleven."

Roderigo Diez had moved over to join them. "Never in Guran's history has an entirely new council been summoned."

"I wanted to talk to you," Robert said abruptly, interrupting any further comment from Diez. "I know Rasoul has never been attacked before, so you can't be blamed for an oversight."

Diez seemed willing to listen, but Valis stepped defensively to the old physician's side. "What are you suggesting, Robert Podlowsky?" he demanded. "This man is a trusted friend."

"I'm suggesting," Robert went on, "that you start immediately to construct a *second* sanctum for Phlogis. Somewhere in the depths of Sheren-Chad. You have back-up council members. Give him a back-up place to retreat to should he be attacked again."

Diez raised one eyebrow, and his head bobbed slowly up and down. "We were fools not to think of it ourselves," he admitted. "I'll start on it at once."

"I've got a suggestion too," Eric added, leaning into their group and lowering his voice. He fixed Diez with a hard gaze. "If you can do the work, keep the location to yourself. We don't need to know where it is, and neither does this traitor."

Diez nodded again and dropped his voice still lower. "I swear," he answered. "Phlogis and myself. And nothing will make me reveal it."

A haze of light washed over the rooftop. The dragons were arriving. "Get back!" Alanna ordered. "Danyel, call Shadowfire."

The boy moved away from the wall. His body stiffened as he drew a deep breath. Then he sang out a series of notes. It was easy to distinguish his dragon from the others. Shadowfire folded his wings, separated from the flock, and descended. Huge claws scrabbled for purchase on the parapet. The beast stretched out its sinuous neck.

"Don't you ever remove those saddles?" Eric inquired.

"Almost never," the boy replied. "They're made of the dragon's own hide, very soft, and not uncomfortable at all."

Robert's eyes widened with a sudden realization. He ran one hand over his leather shirt. "The dragon's hide?" he said.

Alanna gave him a quick affirmative and picked up one of the packs to lash it to Danyel's saddle as he climbed into the seat. "As the young *sekoye* grow," she told Robert, "they shed their skin. Our garments are made from it. The dragons smell the scent of it on us."

"It enhances the bond between *sekoye* and *sekournen*," Valis offered.

"You may have noticed," Blor said. "Roderigo-*kaesha* and I both wear common cloth."

Eric felt his own supple black sleeve. "But we . . ." he started.

"You are Brothers of the Dragon," Diez interjected. "*Sekournen* in all but training."

"Brothers of the Dragon you may call them," Danyel called down from the saddle. "But not *sekournen*. They have no dragons of their own." He reached a hand down to Eric. "Once again, Eric Podlowsky. You and me."

Robert clapped Eric on the shoulder. "Looks like your ride," he said, unable to repress a grin. Eric had grumbled enough about his last ride with Danyel. "Don't fall off, big brother."

Eric made a face but accepted the boy's hand, put a foot in the empty stirrup, and swung up. He locked his arms tightly around Danyel's middle.

"Don't worry about your little brother, either," Alanna called up to him. "I'll take good care of him myself."

Eric grinned weakly around clenched teeth. "I'll bet."

Alanna ushered them all back again. Danyel sang, and Shadowfire leaped into the air and circled, waiting for them. Robert thought he heard a long, low moan of despair and grinned again.

"Our turn," Alanna said. She threw back her head and a high soprano note flowed with crystal purity into the night. In response, Mirrormist left the flock and took a perch on the rooftop wall. She picked up the remaining pack and tied it to her saddle, then mounted.

Diez touched Robert's arm before he could join her in the saddle. For a moment the two regarded each other. Then Diez reached out and touched the blunt end of the unicorn horn where it rose just above Robert's left shoulder. His fingers lingered upon it for a moment. "Be on your guard, Roberto," he whispered in a voice too low for anyone else to hear. "Remember, Palenoc is not the earth. I worry for Eric. But I worry more for you."

Robert looked queerly at Diez and backed up half a pace. "I'm not afraid," came his stiff answer.

Roderigo Diez nodded as he turned away. "That's why I worry for you."

Robert frowned, vaguely irritated, and climbed into the saddle behind Alanna. But as he settled himself, he noticed Diez's gaze still upon him. All the other dragonriders, too, and more of them were assembled now. They were all watching him. Without thinking about it, he reached up and stroked one blond lock of hair.

"Relax," Alanna told him, loosening his one-armed grip around her waist. "I need to breathe."

Robert mumbled an apology and locked his hands around her. She sang. Mirrormist's claws scraped on the stone. Wings full of amber light spread and lifted them into the air. Robert's stomach lurched, but he steeled himself and watched the top of the tower spiral away. A few moments later, Brightstar descended and rose up again with Valis.

The three dragons turned eastward and flew through the darkness above the city. Robert felt a thrill when the wind whipped his hair. He gripped the saddle with his thighs and hugged Alanna's body to his own. Wisps of her hair tickled his face as he rested his chin on her shoulder. He listened to her song, and the black land rolled by, and the edge of the world advanced.

Over the mountains they swept, then northward. After a while Alanna ceased her singing. She leaned back into his arms and nestled her head against his shoulder. Overhead, the clouds began to break up. Stars winked through one by one. The sky turned clear. A delicate silver moonlight dusted the peaks that curled away to the east. Thanador hung, an icy crescent, in the sky. The ring, Mianur, cut a blue swath through the firmament.

Thanador and Mianur, Robert thought dreamily. How did he know those names? It didn't matter now. All that mattered for the moment was the feel of Alanna in his arms, the warmth of her, the smell of her hair, and a timeless sense of the world passing away as they flew toward the stars.

But just as dreams end, the dragons eventually touched down to earth. Reluctantly, Robert unwrapped his arms from around Alanna, and she slid off the *sekoye*'s neck and down to the dew-slick grass. "Throw down the pack," she called to him. He twisted in the saddle and unfastened the lashes. The pack was surprisingly light. She caught it easily.

"Catch me," he said playfully, preparing to jump down.

Eric stepped out from under Mirrormist's wing. "Anything you say, dear," he answered, with a hint of mockery. He held up his arms, then gave a loud, disappointed sigh when Robert elected to dismount on the other side.

Alanna sang a single sharp note. Mirrormist folded his wings up tight against his body, leaving them in near-darkness. Shadowfire and Brightstar had already closed their wings.

"Is this Terreborne?" Robert asked, surveying the gloomy landscape.

"We're still in Guran," Valis said, coming up behind him. "We'll leave the *sekoye* here."

Alanna straightened and adjusted the shoulder straps of her pack. "The Shylamare River lies just over that way." She inclined her head to the west. "We'll follow that into Terreborne on foot. The beasts would be too easy to spot."

Danyel came along with the other pack. Since he already wore one smaller pack, Valis took it from him. He loosened the strings that held it closed and bent down to the ground. From within he drew a pair of gauntlets and a short pipe, which he gave to Alanna.

"My whip," Danyel said, extending a hand. Valis pulled it out, and the boy quickly wound it around his waist. "The rest in here is food," the big dragonrider said, drawing the strings tight again and shouldering the pack.

Robert noted that Valis seemed to be weaponless. And neither he nor Eric was armed—unless penknives counted. But they, at least, had their skills.

A steep ridge led through the darkness down to the river bed. The moon cast no light on the slope. The grass and weeds were slick with dew. Robert descended sideways, leading with his left foot, testing the ground with every step. Alanna came after him, followed by Eric, Danyel, and Valis. He waited for them at the bottom. The level ground was spongy underfoot. The smell of cool mud and

chlorophyll hovered in the air. Trees rose on all
sides. Thanador and Mianur were now hidden behind the summit. It was eerily dark.

"The river's that way," Alanna said. "The border's about a mile north. If Phlogis is correct, the
Chalosans are being held about ten miles further
in. Let's try to make that before dawn."

Danyel took the lead, and they made their way
across the floodplain, skirting thicker patches of
weeds and underbrush, fighting swarms of gnats in
the marshier areas. It was impossible to see very
far. Robert could smell the water, however.

At last they reached the river's bank. The Shylamare flowed passively, a wide and peaceful ribbon
between black shores. It lapped softly. A sprinkling
of stars reflected on its tranquil surface. Robert
bent down and dipped a finger thoughtfully in it.
It was the kind of river where young boys should
be dropping fishing lines at their fathers' sides. He
thought suddenly of campouts with his own father
and with Eric, of trout sizzling over open fires.

"Be alert," Alanna whispered in his ear. "It's not
unthinkable that the river is being watched."

Robert put away his boyhood memories and hurried after Danyel, who still led the way. A light
wind blew across the water, drying the beads of
sweat on his brow. The night was full of insect
noises.

A small creek cut suddenly across their way to
empty into the Shylamare. Its sides were muddy
and slick, but it was shallow, with a stony bottom.
They waded across one at a time.

Almost immediately, Robert felt the hairs on his
neck raise. The air took on a deep chill. Something
icy blew across his cheek. He jumped, allowing a

short gasp. His breath steamed out in a visible cloud.

He moved off the spot, backing into a tree. For a moment the air warmed, but then the cold returned. Eric felt it too. He barked a short curse through chattering teeth and hugged himself.

"Danyel?" Alanna turned questioningly toward the youngest dragonrider as she wrapped one arm protectively around Robert. Her other hand strayed toward the small pouch of cremat leaves at her belt. Her breath, too, clouded.

Danyel paused and gazed at them. Then he turned in a slow circle and stared into the darkness. "They're all around us," he answered uneasily.

"Who?" Eric asked, shivering.

A wispy figure stepped out from behind a tree not three yards away. It watched them with a vague, empty gaze, unblinking. Strands of flaxen hair blew across its eyes. It didn't bother to brush them away. It merely stood there, totally nude, neither advancing nor retreating.

"We're on haunted ground," Alanna informed him. "Even the dead know loneliness. Sometimes the older souls, the ones that can't find their way to paradise, gather together in special places, sometimes a woods like this."

Valis laid a hand on Danyel's shoulder. "What do you feel?" he asked gently. "Is there any anger?"

The boy didn't answer at once. He continued staring into the gloom. "Harmless phantoms," he replied. "Shades and chills."

"That's a shade?" Robert asked, indicating the nude figure with an incline of his head.

"Yes," Alanna answered. "And there." She nodded toward a faded old woman who watched from beneath a different tree. "And up there," she said again, indicating another in the tree above her.

Robert had the impression that when starlight or moonlight or a reflection off the water struck them just right, he could see through all three phantoms. "But why am I so cold?"

"Because of the chills," she explained, hugging him tighter. "They are the oldest of the spirits and have little mind or will left. No physical form at all. They just manifest as spots of intense cold."

"You say they're harmless?"

All three dragonriders nodded.

"Then let's move on," Robert insisted. "I'm freezing."

He pushed past Danyel, taking the lead. Puffs of cold continued to brush up against him, like unseen hands groping icily for his face and throat, for the warmth of his bare skin. His heart began to race in his chest. On all sides, ghostly shades stepped from behind trees or rose up, uncurling, from under bushes to watch him pass and to follow. He felt their lifeless gazes on him, and he quickened the pace.

"They seem to take a particular interest in you," Danyel said just behind him.

"I don't find that very comforting," Robert snapped with more harshness than he intended. "You saw these things before they showed themselves. How?"

"Keep your voices down!" Alanna reminded them sharply. "Sound will carry over the water for a long way."

"It's my gift," Danyel answered in a whisper. "I can feel when spirits are near."

"Can you talk with them?" Robert pressed.

Danyel shook his head and hurried to keep pace with Robert. "Phlogis says I might be able to, someday."

Robert glanced back over his shoulder, past his comrades. The shades were still following them, gray figures wafting among the trees, not walking but drifting, like slow-moving moths drawn by the heat of the living.

"How long will they do that?" he heard Eric ask.

"Until they lose interest in us," Valis answered, "or until we cross the next stream. They won't follow over flowing water."

Robert thought of the cremat leaves in Alanna's pouch, but he knew she wouldn't use them on these sad, harmless creatures. They hurt the spirits somehow, she'd told him. But damn it, he'd do just about anything to avoid the frigid touch of those chills!

The phantoms didn't follow much farther. When they came to the next shallow creek and stepped over it, it proved as good as a wall. The shades stopped at its grassy bank and stared wistfully, mournfully after them. Then, one by one, they faded away. The chills, too, stopped at the water's edge.

"I feel sorry for them," Eric murmured.

"That's good, Eric Podlowsky," Valis answered. There was a strangely heavy note in his deep voice. His hand settled briefly on Eric's shoulder and then withdrew. "Then at last I know that we can be friends."

Valis turned away suddenly and took the lead as they pushed onward through the woods.

Chapter Eleven

THEY stood at the confluence of two rivers. The smaller one flowed out of the distant mountains in the east and joined the Shylamare. The water was deep and swift, the rush of the currents audible.

"This is the Chohia River," Alanna whispered. "Everything north from this point is Terreborne."

With Valis leading, they turned their backs to the Shylamare and followed the Chohia upriver until they found a place where the water ran more calmly. The big dragonrider paused and looked toward the far bank as he slipped off his pack and set it down. Rummaging in it, he drew out a thin wire with iron rings secured to each end. He put his index fingers through the rings and approached a nearby sapling. With surprising speed he sawed through its base.

Eric watched him work. In little time, Valis cut five stout poles. Without speaking, both brothers pulled out their pocketknives, stripped and whittled away the smaller limbs and rough spots. No one spoke much now. With Terreborne just on the other bank, the sense of danger was too real. Alanna and Danyel kept careful watch on the far shore while they worked.

Soon everyone held a fine staff. Valis replaced the saw wire in the pack. Eric and Robert put away their knives. "You three have packs to carry," Eric said softly to his *sekournen* comrades as they took off their boots and prepared to cross the river, "so you go between us."

He led the way into the water. The staves were more than just weapons. Eric used his to probe the river bottom before him and to steady himself against a surprisingly strong subsurface current. Alanna, then Danyel and Valis, came after him. Robert brought up the rear. The water never came higher than Eric's chest. Only Danyel had any difficulty, when it rose to the tip of his chin. He refused to surrender his pack though, when Robert offered to take it from him. The boy tilted his head back without complaint, held the pack high out of the water, and completed the crossing without any help.

"Can we pause long enough to wring out?" Eric murmured, staring into the woods that surrounded them. The gloom seemed blacker, more menacing on this side of the Chohia. That was just his nerves, though.

"Better than that, Son of Paradane," Valis answered. He set his pack down again, laid his staff beside it, and peeled off his leather shirt.

"We change," Alanna whispered, bending over her pack and loosening its strings. She pulled out a soft buckskin tunic, heavily worked with elaborate beads. With a flip of her wrist she tossed it to Eric. He ran his hand in admiration over the workmanship.

"The intricacy of the patterns indicates your status in Terreborne society," Valis explained, keeping his voice low as he accepted another tunic from

Alanna. He showed them the hood that was part of each garment. "In the presence of strangers be sure to wear this up. It's an insult if you let them see your hair."

"Some of these people shave their entire bodies," Danyel added, dropping his boots.

Alanna handed Robert a tunic. "You, especially, keep your hood up," she advised him. "And both of you keep your eyes averted if we meet anybody."

"If that happens, let me talk," Valis said. "We're merchants. Merchants travel around and can pick up odd habits and mannerisms." He pulled up the hood on his own tunic and stared into the woods. "But let's not put ourselves in a position to be questioned. We don't want to run into anyone until we find the Chalosans."

There were trousers of the same beaded buckskin for them to wear. When they were all changed, they put on their boots. Alanna shoved their wet clothes into her pack. Eric leaned on his staff, waiting for her to finish. He could see the moon again. It gleamed on the Chohia's rippling surface. When they pushed into the woods they would lose its light.

"We haven't made good time," Valis stated at Eric's side as he, too, observed the moon. "It's too low in the west. At this pace we won't cover the ten miles before dawn."

Robert came to join them, slinging the sheathed *chimorg* horn over his shoulder by its makeshift strap. "We'll just have to move faster," he said matter-of-factly. He bent, cupped a handful of water from the river, and drank, wiping his mouth with the back of his hand when he finished. The others followed his example.

Ever the Boy Scout, his little brother took the lead, pushing at a good clip to make their way back to the Shylamare, then northward again along its shore. Eric discovered that the tunic actually gave him excellent protection from the limbs and bushes that tried to scratch him. He pulled the hood up over his head to protect his neck and face as he kept the swift pace.

Suddenly Alanna grabbed Robert's arm and jerked him behind a tree. Eric didn't wait to ask what the trouble was. Danyel and Valis and he hit the ground at the same time. Crouching, Alanna peered cautiously around the boll of her hiding place. With a finger to her lips, she pointed so the others could see.

Eric raised himself ever so slightly on his elbows. At first he saw nothing. Then, through the trees that grew on the far bank of the Shylamare, a pair of redly glowing spots moved in unison. He caught his breath and pressed himself flat against the ground. He'd seen eyes like those before. Biting his lip, he dared to lift his head again.

The *chimorg* strode quietly down to the water's edge. It stared about suspiciously and sniffed the air. Slowly, it dipped its head and drank from the river. Those red eyes smouldered, staining the water with their blood-red radiance. When it raised its head it turned that ruddy gaze directly at them.

Eric held perfectly still for fear that any motion might catch the beast's attention. From the corner of his eye, though, he watched his brother's hand stray toward the horn in the sheath on his back. Robert's fingers curled around the broken end, but he didn't draw it.

The *chimorg* took another drink. Glittering ripples rolled away from the tip of its horn as it struck the water. Then it turned and disappeared into the trees.

"Did you see it?" Robert whispered when Eric got to his feet.

"The question is," Eric answered tersely, "did it see us?"

"Shhhsh!" Valis's low hiss interrupted them. The big dragonrider frowned, then relented. In a barely audible murmur he informed them, "There could be more. Darkness has spies everywhere. If Keris Chaterit has taken this land, you can be sure he has turned his attention here."

They started upriver again. Robert resumed the lead, setting a grueling pace. His brother moved without making a sound, and the dragonriders were nearly as silent. Eric batted limbs away from his face and swatted at bugs. He kept one eye on the far shore, watchful for *chimorgs*. The moon was low enough that its light fell on the river. The Shyla-mare glimmered.

Up ahead, another light gleamed suddenly on the water. At first, Eric thought it was the moon's reflection, but the light moved, dashing that hope. Robert stopped and waved a hand, motioning for them to take cover. Together, they crouched in the brush and waited while the light drifted their way.

"A fisherman," Alanna whispered as the boat approached, "trawling the river."

The small boat glided by. A single lantern hung from a post in its prow. An old man labored at a pair of oars while a younger man played out a narrow net from the stern. Hooks worked into the netting shimmered wetly in the lantern's yellow glow.

The younger man baited each hook with a small chunk of meat as he fed the net into the water.

When the boat was past, they rose from hiding, not daring to speak, knowing the river would carry their voices. Only when the light was out of sight did Valis whisper to Robert, "You've done well, Robert Podlowsky, but I'll lead now. I think we're near the end of our journey."

"The end comes when the Chalosans are freed," Eric answered grimly. "We're just beginning."

A short distance further, they emerged suddenly and surprisingly into a small village. It was absolutely dark, concealed by the forest on all sides, except for the river. Alanna pushed her hair back and tugged up her hood.

"Go around or through?" Eric whispered.

"I don't like it," Alanna answered, her gaze sweeping the black buildings before them. "Listen. It's too quiet. A place like this, there would be dogs at least."

Eric thought about that and remembered the dogs in Chalosa. In the countryside a lot of people kept dogs. They could detect the presence of spirits when humans could not. He touched Danyel on the shoulder. "Do you feel anything?" he asked quietly.

The young dragonrider shook his head.

Alanna pursed her lips, then crept out of the trees and into the village. No light, no candle, no lamp shone behind any of the windows. No wisp of smoke curled from the chimneys. She pointed with the end of her staff. A door stood open. Even in the dark they could see how it hung on a twisted hinge. She stole toward it, and the others followed.

A wreath of dry leaves hung over the entrance. Eric crushed one between thumb and forefinger and sniffed. The odor was faint but unmistakable. Cremat.

"A fearful and superstitious people," Valis muttered as he followed Alanna inside.

A few moments later the two dragonriders emerged again. "The furnishings are smashed," Alanna reported. "There's food still on the table, mugs of milk half full. But everything's spoiled and clabbered."

They explored another cabin and found it empty, also. Nor did they find any livestock. Pens and barns were all empty.

"Not a single boat by the dock or along the shore," Danyel said. Eric had not realized the boy had slipped away. The kid could move as silently as Robert.

They left the village and its mystery behind and reentered the woods. But Eric found himself thinking of the fishermen and wondering where the pair had come from.

Perhaps a half an hour passed before Valis brought them to a halt again. On the far shore a score of torches were visible. A long pier extended out upon the water. A large number of longboats and other river craft were ranged along the shore. A pair of black-clad guards paced along the pier, their footsteps echoing on the old wood, their low voices carrying indistinctly through the night.

Farther back from the shore stood the stark silhouettes of houses and larger buildings. It was difficult to discern everything in the darkness. It was plainly another village, though.

"Do you think this is the place?" Eric asked.

Alanna nodded. "It must be. Those guards are the evidence."

Robert pressed forward. "It's almost morning," he noted, glancing toward the sky. Streaks of royal blue and purple were pushing against the blackness. "Let's get across while it's dark, find someplace to hole up, and do a little scouting."

The others agreed. "There'll be no wading here, though," Alanna cautioned them. "The Shylamare runs deep."

Robert slipped down into the water. Pushing his staff before him, he swam away. Eric kept one eye on the pier while Alanna, then Valis, then Danyel all began their swims. He didn't worry too much about being seen. The guards were preoccupied with their conversation, and the rows of torches on the pier would play havoc with their night vision. Besides, the shadows that stretched across the river made detection unlikely. He stepped down into the water and pushed off.

Using silent breast strokes and a strong kick, he overtook Danyel. The youth seemed to be having some problem; he held his pack high out of the water with his right hand and paddled with the other. Eric stayed beside him until they both reached the opposite bank.

Robert and Valis extended hands to help them out. "I lost my staff!" Danyel muttered in disgust.

"Into the woods and out of sight," Robert instructed with a quick glance toward the pier. "Move!"

Not far back into the trees they found a path. It ran perpendicular to the river, then turned and seemed to skirt the edge of the Terreborne village. They took it because it offered a chance to make better speed and the odds of meeting anyone at this time of night were low. Before long, the ground began to rise at a steep angle. Soon they were climbing not a path but a narrow and rocky rut in the face of a natural river bluff.

Robert reached the summit before the others. Climbing cliffs and high places was his idea of a good time, something he'd always done for fun in the cloves and mountains back home and in other places around the world. Eric envied his brother's skill. When he himself got to the top he was winded and out of breath. He leaned on his staff and stared outward.

Dawn's fire was spreading from the east. Below, he could just see the edge of the village beyond a range of tall trees. There were lights in a few of the windows.

"If we make our way along this bluff," Robert whispered to him, "we should be able to see right into their living rooms."

"Living rooms?" Alanna said with a raised eyebrow.

"It's an expression," Eric told her.

When Danyel and Valis reached the top they started off again, following the edge of the bluff. In the gloom, however, it came to an unexpected end. They found themselves on a precipice overlooking part of the village on the one hand and a sprawling valley on the other.

"I think there's something down there," Eric commented as he tried to penetrate the darkness. It was only a vague impression of something, a shape, some kind of structure. But no one could be sure. Night still held sway over the valley, and the shadows were thick.

"I vote we settle here," Robert suggested, gazing toward the village. "This is the best vantage we're going to get."

The others agreed. Alanna set down the pack containing their wet clothes and pushed back the beaded hood of her tunic. Robert stripped his off and wrung water from it. The pale light of the moon shone on his damp, muscled skin. As if accepting a challenge, Alanna also stripped off her tunic, wrung it, and hung it over a branch to dry. A shadow fell across her bare breasts.

Eric noticed how his brother and the dragonrider regarded each other for a moment before Alanna sat down with her back to a tree and wrapped one arm casually about herself. Robert's gaze lingered on her before he turned away.

"Never compete with 'em, Bobby," Eric murmured as he sidled closer to his little brother and removed his own tunic. The air was cool on his wet skin. "That's the secret of getting along with 'em."

Robert gave him a sardonic look. "How is Katy Dowd these days?" he asked pointedly, reminding Eric of his on-again-off-again romance with a girl they'd both known since childhood.

"Still trying to run Dowdsville like her old man owned it," Eric answered, nonplussed. He spread his tunic over a bush and found a soft spot to sit down. His legs ached from their long march, and that disappointed him. He'd always thought his postal carrier's job kept him in good shape.

"You guys get some rest," Robert suggested, leaning on his staff. "I'll take the first watch."

Eric came awake like a bolt when Robert touched his shoulder. "What is it?" he demanded.

"It's a goddamn Dachau!" Robert said and pointed down into the valley. The sun was over the trees now. The morning was a bright blue. "A goddamn Dachau!" Robert repeated.

Eric crawled to the edge of the cliff and peered over into the valley. His breath hissed through his teeth.

Much of the land below had been stripped of trees and the logs used to build a huge wooden stockade. It was a human holding pen. From his high point of view he could see over the walls into the structure. Men, women, and children lay curled upon the bare ground or huddled against the walls. A few shuffled listlessly about, arms limp at their sides, heads down. Every head had been shaved bare. The prisoners had no clothes, not even blankets to warm themselves.

Despite the distance, Eric could see how gaunt many of them looked, how weak and dejected. "They're being starved to death," he said to Valis, who alerted by Robert's outburst, had crawled up beside Eric. His mouth formed a grim line as he regarded the sight.

"It's a relatively safe form of murder," Valis answered disgustedly. "Slow starvation. Most of the victim's initial anger, the rage that might otherwise lead a ghost to seek revenge, turns to despair and hopelessness. Eventually, death is even welcome. The few ghosts who linger rarely have any focus." The dragonrider paused and swallowed with some difficulty. "I've seen camps like these in the Dark Lands. Prisoners go in, but they never come out. They're never beaten, and once those gates close they never see their guards or captors again. They're just left to die. It makes me sick."

"We know now what happened to the people in that other village," Alanna murmured. They were all gathered on the edge of the bluff now, on their elbows, staring at the horror. "They must have been brought here."

Danyel crawled up on Eric's other side. "My family died in such a camp when Chule fell," he whispered in a voice that was utterly devoid of emotion, and all the more frightening for that. Eric gazed sidewise at the youth and laid a reassuring hand on his head. Danyel didn't react.

"Robert and I lost our paternal grandparents in a place like this," Eric told the boy quietly.

"In Paradane?" Danyel asked with surprise.

Eric nodded. "Paradane has its wars, too," he told the boy. "There was a place once called Dachau. A terrible place where thousands of people were systematically murdered, our grandparents among them." Eric bit his lip and stopped speaking. His father had told him the tale often, always with bitterness. The Podlowskys were Catholic, not Jewish, yet many Catholics had gone to the ovens too.

"We've had our own versions of Darkness from time to time," Robert said.

"We know," Alanna told him. "Some of Palenoc's greatest thinkers have debated the nature of the forces that bind our worlds. Here, good and evil have been locked in a struggle thousands of years old. More than one philosopher has thought that the essence of our war seeps into your world, maybe through the gates, and influences much that happens on Paradane."

Robert sat up suddenly and gave Alanna a rude look. "You don't know Earth," he snapped. "It's far more likely that it's our evil that leaks into Palenoc. Only here it gets distilled to its purest forms."

Eric stared strangely at his little brother. He'd never heard such cynicism from Robert. His brother had changed. How much of that change, he wondered, was attributable to the murder of his friend, Scott Silver?

He turned his attention back to the stockade. There was nothing within it that offered shelter or the slightest convenience. The prisoners slept or wandered about in their own shit and piss, exposed to sun and rain. A dirty trough of fetid water ran along one wall. They could drink from that; it kept them from dying too quickly.

Atop each corner of the stockade was a watch-tower, manned by a pair of masked and hooded guards. It was scant security, but such was the simplicity of the prison that no more was needed. It would be impossible to approach it without being spotted.

Valis tapped Eric's shoulder and directed his attention toward the village. A squad of soldiers marched in formation across a field to the stockade, all clad in the same black-lacquered armor he'd seen on the men who had attacked Chalosa. Eric squirmed uneasily as vague traces of old Sumeek's memories stirred within him, filling him with a fury that he knew was only partly his own.

A sentry on duty there stirred himself as the soldiers reached the wall. He exchanged a few words with a captain on the ground, then abruptly bent down to retrieve something from the watch-tower floor. He rose with a coiled rope. With a shout, he threw one end down to the prisoners in the stockade.

Eric couldn't tell what was happening. The near wall eclipsed his view. But those prisoners he could see looked up weakly from their huddled postures. The shufflers ceased in midstep. A few stirred themselves to gaze around their prison or up at the watchtower with nearly vacant eyes.

A few moments later, the pair of guards began to haul together on the rope. A body flopped over onto the floor of the watchtower. The guards untied the crude knot, slipped the rope from under the corpse's armpits, and callously lofted the body over the side to the ground far below.

"Goddamn them!" Eric cursed. He glanced at his brother. Robert stared wordlessly, his face drained of color. A muscle twitched under the skin near his jaw.

Two soldiers separated themselves from the rest of the squad. They picked up the body between them, seizing it by the wrists and ankles, and carried it to a narrow trench that Eric had not previously spotted. With no more care or concern than the watch guards had shown, they swung the corpse high in the air and into the trench. Meanwhile, the watchtower guards had hauled up a second body—that of a child. Eric imagined he could hear the impact and the crack of bones as it hit the ground by the stockade wall. He squeezed his eyes shut.

A hand touched the back of his head. He opened his eyes and met Danyel's sympathetic gaze.

"Look!" Robert said, with sudden excitement. He crawled forward to the very edge of the cliff and pointed. "Isn't that the blacksmith?"

Eric squinted and blinked and finally spied the man his brother indicated—a large, naked man with a dark scowl leaning in a corner by himself near the water trough. Without his heavy beard and hair Brin was hard to recognize, but by god-damn, it *was* the blacksmith!

"That's Brin, all right!" Valis announced, abandoning his usual reserve. "We've found them!"

Eric touched the thin scar near his hairline and searched the rest of the prisoners' faces for anyone he might recognize. Pietka was dead, but what of crazy old Frona?

"We've got to get them out," Robert growled.

"We will," Eric answered, tight-lipped. "Tonight. I don't know how yet, but we'll figure something." He crawled back from the edge and sat up. His shoulder had cramped a bit, and he massaged it as he considered how to break the Chalosans free. No solution came to him right away. Certainly nothing could be done in broad daylight. They would have to wait until the sun went down. Surely in that time they could come up with a plan. "Let's try to get some rest," he said at last.

The others crawled away from the edge—all but Robert, who continued to stare down at the stockade.

"Come away, Robert-*kaesha*," Alanna called, leaning her back against a tree and wiping a hand across her eyes. But Robert didn't hear.

Eric glanced curiously at Alanna. She had slipped back into her tunic, which was dry again. There was an odd look on her face as she stared at Robert's bare back. He knew she was attracted to his brother, but she'd used the endearment *kaesha*. That surprised him.

She noticed him watching and met his gaze. Eric took that as an invitation and moved over to sit beside her. "Are you all right?" he asked with gentle concern. "You know, in our world it would probably be illegal for a woman to trudge through the woods all night and look as good as you do."

She didn't react to his compliment, except to turn her gaze back to Robert. A frown of worry curled the fine, sculpted corners of her lips. "I'm afraid for him," she confessed in a whisper meant only for Eric's ears. "There's a splinter of darkness in your brother's soul that could make Palenoc dangerous for him."

"Palenoc?" Eric said, raising one eyebrow with sarcastic humor. "Dangerous?" He pushed out his lips and shook his head. Then he turned serious again. "That's just Robert," he told her in a lower voice. "He's always been a private person. He keeps his feelings to himself and never lets anybody get too close. Hell, kiddo, I know him better than anyone, but he's got places even I can't reach."

"Dark places," Alanna murmured in a grim tone that Eric found irritating. A pause fell between them as they both watched Robert sit up long enough to slip into his tunic. He also pulled the *chimorg*'s horn close and laid it in the grass near at hand, giving it a pat, before he stretched out again at the cliff's edge. "You love him very much, don't you?" Alanna said, picking up the conversation.

A smile forced its way to Eric's lips. "You know, when he published his first book," he answered, "I hated him. I was the one who wanted to be a writer when I was younger. Poetry, in my case. Here he'd gone and realized my dream, and done it with a piece of commercial trash." He shook his head and the smile turned wry. "That attitude lasted about a minute. Mind you, it was *good* commercial trash." He gave a shrug and tilted his head. "What can I say? He's my little brother."

Alanna reached over and patted the top of his knee as she flashed him a grin. "Do you still write your poetry?"

Eric put a finger to his lips and gave a soft *shhhh*. "Nobody else knows."

She leaned back again and drew up one knee, imitating his posture. Locking her fingers together, she nodded toward Robert. "I'll bet he knows," she said. She sucked in her lower lip and looked thoughtful. "When I found the two of you, I thought he was the Son of the Morning."

"But the Son of the Morning is dead," Eric replied.

Alanna gave her attention to a pair of birds that soared unexpectedly up over the edge of the bluff. The birds climbed higher and higher in the blue morning sky, turned, and disappeared beyond the trees.

"You still don't understand, do you?" she said at last. "This is all some kind of holiday to you." A look of surprising hardness came into her eyes as she sat forward and stared out at the panorama before them. "The Shae'aluth is real. I've looked into his eyes—emerald eyes, like your's and Robert's, greener than springtime. No one else has such eyes on this world. I've felt his hand on my face. I've watched his power at work as he walked among the people of Guran and a score of other lands. I've walked those lands with him, Eric Podlowsky."

"A man doesn't die and live again!" Eric stated emphatically.

"This is not Paradane," Alanna reminded him. "Open your parochial little mind! There's a war going on here, a very real war between Darkness and Light, forces that find their ultimate personifications in Shandal Karg and the Son of the Morning. But they are not the same! They are not equal! The Son of the Morning lives a cycle, as a man lives. He grows old. His power weakens and eventually he dies. For a time, then, Shandal Karg rises to preeminence. Soulless and immortal, she reaches out to seize the world."

She leaned toward him suddenly and laid her hand upon his knee, squeezing it with earnest strength as her gaze bore into him. "This is that time, Eric Podlowsky, when common men and women have to fight or see our world perish. From the time when the Shae'aluth dies until the time he returns to us again, Shandal Karg's power pours out from the black depths of Srimourna to devour the world." She backed away from him and drew both her knees to her chest, wrapping her arms about her shins and clasping her hands. "The nations of Palenoc are like chess pieces. If, in that period when the Son of Morning is away from the board, Darkness can claim them all, then he will never return. Palenoc will be forever lost."

Alanna rocked herself slowly back and forth as she closed her eyes and laid her chin on her knees. "Tell me, Eric Podlowsky," she said softly. "With Palenoc vanquished, and the gates under Shandal Karg's control, where do you think the Heart of Darkness would turn next to satisfy her appetite?"

Eric didn't answer. He got to his feet and stared beyond the cliff toward the village. His thoughts churned. It was hard sometimes to accept the things this world asked him to accept. Some of what Alanna said skated dangerously close to beliefs he'd dismissed long ago. The *chimorgs* might be this world's demons and the *sekoye* its winged angels. But a devil and a savior? How could he deal with that? How was he supposed to deal with it?

He snatched his tunic from the bush where he'd hung it to dry and pulled it on. Then, picking up his staff, he started back down the trail away from the precipice and the others.

"Hey!" Robert called after him in a sharp hiss, half rising from where he kept watch on the village and the stockade. "What's up, big brother?"

"Nothing," Eric answered roughly, noting how the gazes of Valis and Danyel also turned his way. Alanna, however, hadn't moved. She still sat with her chin on her knees, eyes closed, almost as if she were mocking him. He looked back at his brother and grabbed his crotch. "Private business," he said. "That's all." He turned away and started down the trail.

When the others were out of sight, he stepped into the woods just off the path and took care of that private business. As he closed his garments, a dark brown nut plopped down on the ground beside him. Eric glanced up. A squirrellike rodent perched in the branches above him, its cheeks puffed, its tail swishing back and forth. It scolded him in a chittering voice, and Eric grinned.

The sun streamed down through the leaves and branches, casting spears of light all through the forest. The smells of moist earth and moss and bark wafted through the air. An old log lay half-hidden in the high grass and weeds. Fallen leaves littered the ground, almost obscuring a patch of tiny purple flowers. Everywhere in the forest life mingled with decay.

Eric was not a religious man, though his parents,

especially his father, had tried their best to make it otherwise. While Robert had actively rebelled against their teachings, he had just quietly stopped believing. He didn't even know when, exactly. Alanna's claims troubled him. On a very fundamental level her stories appeared to require his acceptance of things he had long ago rejected.

He glanced around the forest again and rubbed the furrow from his brow. Palenoc was not Earth, he reminded himself. Alanna had said that, too. He would cling to that for now. It was time, instead, to think of how he would free the Chalosans and all the rest of those poor men and women.

Curse me for a postman, he thought disgustedly as he started back toward the trail. *Roderigo Diez at least had his medical skills to bring to this world. What have I got? I'm just an ordinary guy, and nobody here looks like they need a letter delivered.*

A sharp crack caused him to freeze in midstep and look slowly around. Farther down the hill, nearly obscured by the trees, a *chimorg* paused and sniffed the air. Near it, a pair of black-armored soldiers stole through the bushes with nets over their shoulders and batons held at the ready.

Eric crouched down. They had not yet seen him. Moving silently, he reached the path at the cliff edge. Some inner voice told him to stay in the shadows of the trees. He leaned far enough out to see down the trail.

A line of ten black-clads trudged up the sharp slope.

Another branch snapped underfoot. Eric whirled, gripping his staff, heart racing. Not far away, another pair of soldiers slunk carefully through the brush. A little way to the left of those two, he spied still another pair. And another *chimorg*.

Eric cursed himself for his stupidity. It had been a mistake to make camp on such a narrow precipice, no matter how good a vantage it offered or how tired they had been. Somehow they had been discovered. Now the enemy were making their way up the hillside, fanned out in a line, determined to trap them.

It was not the soldiers that frightened Eric but the *chimorgs*. There would be no fighting such beasts on that narrow point, and there would be no place to run. It puzzled him, for the monsters had seemed to fight the black-clads in Chalosa. Now they were obviously working in concert.

As swiftly and quietly as he could, darting from tree to tree, Eric ran back up the slope, his mind racing, seeking solutions. A branch whipped his face, carving a red welt across his left cheek. He barely acknowledged the pain, concentrating instead on putting his next footfall on a safe piece of soft earth instead of the noisy twig that offered itself.

He burst out of the trees into the midst of his friends with the same sense of relief a man felt when emerging from deep water into air. It was a very temporary relief. His mind went to work at once. Soldiers could be fought, he told himself over and over. But not *chimorgs*. Not here, not on this stupid point.

Robert would try to fight though. Eric knew that as surely as he knew his own name.

The others had barely had time to acknowledge his return by glancing his way. The village and the stockade below still held Robert's attention. Eric went straight to his brother, who lay prone at the cliff's edge. Dropping his staff on the grass, he threw himself down by Robert's side. Three hundred feet down, he reckoned. "Can you climb this?"

Robert gave him a curious look. "What?"

"You're the best rock climber in the world, right?" Eric said, trying to keep his voice calm. "You've bragged to me about it dozens of times. Now's your chance to prove it, Bobby." As he spoke, he peered over the edge. The tops of the trees that grew up against the rock face rippled in the breeze. "Trust me," he insisted. "Go as quick as you can. On this side so the stockade guards can't see you. I'll meet you at the bottom."

Robert looked over the edge again and licked his lips. Then he stared straight into Eric's eyes. "What's up, Eric? Trouble?"

Eric laid a hand in the middle of his brother's back. "Just go, Bobby. Now. Trust me!"

Robert looked at him for what seemed long moments, then with a suddenness that surprised even Eric, he swung both legs out into space.

"What are you doing?" Valis shouted. He made a dive and caught Robert's hands.

"Let him go!" Eric hissed. "He can do it!" Robert's green eyes were wide with panic. Valis's unexpected lunge had nearly cost him his grip. "Look," Eric said, his voice calm again, resisting the urge to gaze over his shoulder, sure that the soldiers even now were preparing to make their charge and hurl their nets. "Look," he repeated reasonably. Inside, his heart was hammering against his ribs. "I'll bet you've found a toe purchase, already. Right?" he said.

Robert swallowed and licked his lips again. "Yeah," he answered uncertainly. Then, with greater assurance, "Yeah."

"It's not that tough a slope," Eric told him, forcing a grin. "You can do it in your sleep." He felt Alanna kneeling beside him now, though he didn't turn to look at her. *Go watch the trail*, he wanted to shout, but he didn't dare, yet. Not until he was sure Bobby was on his way. "I've got a plan," he said, and that wasn't totally untrue. "I'm going down the trail, but I need you to climb down this way. We'll meet at the bottom."

Robert shook his head, his fear turning to anger. "I'm not a fool, Eric!" he snapped. "But I'll play along. I only needed a moment. This idiot nearly knocked me off!" He glared at Valis, who still held his arms. "Let go."

"Robert!" Alanna said worriedly.

"It's all right," Robert told her. "I've got toe purchase. Eric's right. It's an easy climb." He hesitated, glancing down again. "I've done tougher ones." He shot his brother a hard look. "You'd better have one hell of an explanation when we meet at the bottom, big brother."

"I will," Eric promised him. "It'll all be clear. Now get going!" A moment later, Robert's head sank beneath the rim of the cliff.

Eric leaned as far out as he could to watch Robert make his spiderlike descent down the rock face. All the while he listened for warning sounds from the forest. When his brother was well on his way, he leaped up, clutched at Alanna and Valis, and pulled them back. He motioned for Danyel to come closer too.

"Have you gone crazy?" Alanna demanded.

"Maybe I have," Eric answered grimly. "The woods are full of soldiers and *chimorgs*. They're coming up the trail too. We're surrounded." He let go a sigh and resisted the urge to reach out and draw Danyel to him and rumple the boy's hair, sure that Danyel would object. "Robert was the only one of us who stood any chance of getting out, but if I'd told him he wouldn't have gone."

Valis turned away and picked up a staff. Danyel, also, snatched up one of the slender weapons. Alanna stood her ground, however, facing Eric. "You had to make sure he got away," she stated, folding her arms across her chest, peering into his eyes with almost painful understanding. There was no anger in her voice. "You asked him to trust you. But you're the one with all the trust."

"If they kill us, at least he's safe," he told her bluntly. "So sue me. But if they take us prisoner, then Bobby's on the outside. And if my butt's gotta be pulled out of a fire, there's nobody I trust more than him to do it. Question now is," he said, catching the staff that Danyel flung his way, "do we make it easy on 'em, or do we give 'em a few bruises?"

Alanna moved toward the tree where she'd been resting. Her pack lay there with her blowpipe and gauntlets on it. "They're soldiers," she said over her shoulder as she picked up the weapons. "Let them earn their pay."

But it was not the soldiers who emerged first from the woods. Two black *chimorgs*, horns and razored scales gleaming in the sunlight, eyes full of red fire, strode with an unnerving calm out of the trees and stood perfectly still, as if daring them to make a move.

Eric bit his lip as he regarded the monsters. Trembling inside, he willed his fingers to open, and he dropped his staff. He'd fought one of the beasts, but on open ground under better circumstances. Up here, it was a fool's fight. Alone, he might have chanced it anyway. But not with the others' lives at risk.

He glared at the *chimorgs*, and intuitively he realized something about Palenoc. These monsters, creations and servants of Darkness, *could* kill. What kind of ghost would waste its time seeking vengeance on an animal?

The dragonriders noted his action and recognized the hopelessness of their situation. Reluctantly, they dropped their weapons. An instant later, a net sailed through the air, ensnaring Valis. The soldiers of Terreborne emerged from the trees and up the trail. A second net fell over Eric. He didn't try to dodge it and threw up an arm only to protect his face as it draped over him.

The soldiers apparently didn't think a woman and a boy warranted such measures. Two of them caught Danyel by his arms. Two more flanked Alanna. She didn't resist as they seized her. When a third soldier, however, approached her and laid a hand on her breast, she brought her leg up with almost casual grace and threw the prettiest front snap-kick Eric had ever seen, catching the unsuspecting fool right under the chin. His head jerked back in its helmet, and he crashed backward into another pair of soldiers before he hit the ground. Blood poured from under his mask. Eric hoped the jerk had bitten his tongue off.

Alanna gave each of her flanking guards a big

innocent grin before they twisted her arms roughly up behind her back.

"Sekournen!" one of the soldiers shouted with disgust as he knelt over Alanna's pack. He held a handful of damp dragonskin garments up for the others to see.

Great, Eric figured. They were not only captured but identified as well. "You really don't have to do that," he said to a soldier, as the man prepared to give a yank on the rope that would gather the four corners of the net that entrapped him. An instant later, Eric's feet were jerked out from under him. He hit the ground hard without even the chance to make a breakfall as the damn thing closed tight around him. "I don't suppose the word *motherfucker* would mean anything to you people!" he muttered as his captor bent over him.

Someone spit on his face. Another kicked him in the ribs. "Then again," he groaned, trying to curl into a protective ball, "maybe some things *are* universal."

Through the net, a soldier shoved a rag into his mouth and rolled him over. His friends also had been gagged. A strange precaution, he thought. These guys ran the whole damn countryside. Who did they think would care about a little thing like a scream? Alanna and Danyel were both bound with ropes. Valis was in the same uncomfortable, netted predicament.

Suddenly one of the *chimorgs* gave a loud snort and reared. Its hooves tore divots in the grass as they struck the earth. It shook its mane. The other beast raced to the edge of the cliff, nudged something on the ground with its nose, and gave a wild, angry bellow.

A soldier hurried to where the beast stood, then froze, hesitation and fear evident in his posture. His hand shook visibly as he reached toward the ground, then stopped again. He turned a stricken expression toward his fellow soldiers. Finally, summoning courage, he bent down, picked up Robert's makeshift sheath and drew out the black unicorn horn.

"Oh, shit," Eric muttered, letting go a sigh. Robert had taken it off and laid it in the grass while he was lying there watching the stockade.

The *chimorgs* reared and stamped the ground. Their trumpeting cries echoed from the bluff and out across the entire valley. Eric closed his eyes and let his head sag wearily against the rough ropes and the grass. *Some mornings,* he thought, *it just doesn't pay to wake up.*

Chapter Twelve

ROBERT heard the trumpeting of the *chimorgs*. Halfway down the rock face, he froze, his fingers grasping small crevices, one foot resting on a tiny jut of stone as he stared upward. His heart raced, not for himself but for his brother. He remembered that sound too well.

Eric had tricked him! Damn it, he'd known the beasts were coming.

He clung to the cliff, sweat pouring down his face and inside his tunic. The *chimorgs* were quiet now. He listened. For a long moment there was no sound at all except for the strong beat of his pulse in his ear and his own rapid breathing. Then, a few muffled voices from above and a sharp command was followed by silence.

Leaning his head against the stone, Robert cursed his brother. But the curses were born of fear as much as anger. He looked up again, wondering what to do, wondering what he would find if he climbed back up. He'd heard no screaming, no sound of fighting. A few indistinct voices, he recalled, and a single shout. Now that he thought about it, none of those voices had belonged to his brother or his dragonrider friends. Soldiers, then. If Eric had spotted the *chimorgs*, he must have seen the soldiers. And if he'd chosen not to fight, then it must have been pretty hopeless.

He knew I could handle the cliff, he thought, as his anger subsided and reason began to take over. *I was the only one who could get away.*

He hung motionless for a while longer, full of uncertainty, until his finger joints began to ache from the strain. Abruptly, he realized how exposed he was on the rock face. He twisted his head over his right shoulder until he could see the village rooftops through the trees. There was the open field between the village and the stockade to his right as well. No way to tell if any of the enemy had seen him or not, but they certainly could if they bothered to look his way.

There was no point in going back up. If Eric was still alive his captors would take him to the village or the stockade. If he was dead, then Robert's business was still with the village and the stockade. But hadn't Eric said he'd meet him at the bottom? That indicated he had some hope at least of being taken alive.

Robert grasped at that hope. He would not believe Eric was dead. He forced the thought out of his head and slid one toe further down the wall, seeking his next purchase in the stone. He found it, a crack just wide enough to fit his soft-booted toe. He shifted his weight. For an instant he seemed to hang in space, but he didn't fear. He'd done this before. He enjoyed the sensation as he enjoyed the risk.

Just before he reached the bottom, he paused and gazed down into the trees immediately below. If he'd been spotted climbing it would be easy for a force to hide down there. He could be dropping right into their arms. He saw nothing, but the foliage was thick. Well, no matter, he was here now. There was nothing to do but take the chance.

He dropped the last twelve feet and landed in a crouch on a bed of old leaves. A twig snapped loudly underfoot. He didn't pause but took off at a run, putting distance between himself and the sound, until finally he ducked behind a fat black tree trunk and leaned there to catch his breath. Carefully he peeked out and spied no one.

Relaxing a bit, he licked the tips of his raw fingers and blew on them. He pulled off his tunic. The heavy beaded leather was drenched with sweat. Rivulets still poured down his chest and sides. The slight breeze felt good on his bare skin, though, and cooled him. He spread the tunic on the ground as he sagged down and sat with his back against the tree. He could afford a few minutes to rest after his descent.

He realized he was hungry and thought of Valis's pack. The dragonrider had said it contained food, but everyone had been too tired or too keyed up to eat. His thirst, at least, presented no problem. The river was close enough to take care of that.

When he was recovered, he rose, slipped into his tunic again, and got his bearings. The stockade was to the north, and the village to the northwest. The river was straight ahead. He headed for the Shylamare at an angle that took him away from the village, moving silently, using his best woods skills.

Before long he found the trail they had followed from the river to the cliff the night before. Pausing briefly, he crossed it and melted into the deep woods on the other side. The sun streamed down through the trees, and the morning was already warm. He might have discarded the tunic, but it was the closest thing he had to a disguise if he ran into anyone. With that in mind, he tugged up the hood to hide his hair as Alanna had cautioned him to do.

Robert pushed on through the woods, making for a point farther downriver where he might drink without being seen. It surprised him when he came upon a second, wider path that led back through the woods toward the bluff. It was better-traveled than the first path. The grass and weeds had been trampled away and the brown earth left packed hard. It led straight down to the river. Looking to his left, he could see a little piece of the blue Shylamare. He crossed the path quickly and concealed himself again. His throat was so dry he could almost taste the water.

Suddenly he heard voices. He pressed himself against the black trunk of a tree as they drew nearer. A squad of armored soldiers approached from the direction of the bluff. Cautiously, Robert slunk a bit farther off-trail and stretched out on the ground. He could still see the path, but only an alert and determined observer would be able to spot him through the bushes.

The soldiers—more than twenty, he estimated—passed without even glancing his way. When he saw Alanna, securely bound and escorted by two large men, his heart quickened. There was nothing he could do, though, but watch. Danyel came along just behind her, trussed like a Thanksgiving turkey. Four more soldiers passed, each carrying the corner of what looked like some kind of big sack. When a second similar team went by, Robert got a better look. They weren't sacks at all, but the netted forms of Eric and Valis. He blew a little stream of air and nodded to himself, relieved that they were all alive.

The relief he felt was short-lived, however. He peered all around the forest. Where were the *chimorgs*? He'd heard them, at least two of the beasts. One hand went to the sheath on his back. Then he uttered a silent curse and slammed a fist on the mossy earth. The horn! He'd left it on the precipice!

When the last soldier passed by, Robert debated with himself whether he should go back for it. The horn was the only weapon that could hurt the *chimorgs*. He bit his lip. There was no choice really. The wiser course was to follow the black-clads and try to learn what they did with his brother and his friends. Rising, he skirted the edge of the path, hugging the trees and shadows as he set out after the soldiers.

At the river the force turned north. Robert watched them from behind a thick bole as they headed for the village. Carefully, he slipped down to the bank, bent, and cupped a handful of water to quench his thirst. Crossing the path then, he took once more to the woods, avoiding the shore where he might be seen. He could barely see his brother's captors through the trees ahead, but he caught up quickly.

A pair of sentries stood watch on the river pier. They leaned on staves and watched as the company marched into the village with their captives. Disinterested, they resumed their own private conversation.

Robert considered just walking into the village, counting on his merchant's disguise to protect him.

An inner voice said to forget it. He saw no citizens anywhere, no merchants, no fishermen, no women, no children. Only soldiers. They had taken over the village. The real residents were probably in the stockade.

The squad carrying his brother and friends was no longer in sight. Robert chewed his lip again, his mind racing, and decided to scout the village as best he could from the woods. That plan proved futile, however. All he saw was the backs of houses and shops, with tiny glimpses of the streets beyond. And soldiers. There were more soldiers than he would have guessed from his view at the precipice.

He crouched in the bushes where he could observe through a gap between buildings. He had hoped to see where the soldiers took his brother. He didn't believe that Eric or the dragonriders would be thrown in the stockade, at least not right away. Spies would be questioned first.

Robert made up his mind to get his hands on some of that black armor. The only way he could move about the village was to blend in with the soldiers. He thought about the two sentries on the river pier and figured he could take them both out quietly and quickly. But what would he do with them then? The only way to keep them quiet was to . . .

Kill them.

He looked at his hands. He had the skill, he knew that. But he began to tremble. Was this what all his training, years of practice, travel around the world, had been for? To make him a killer? The trembling became more violent. He leaped up from behind the bushes and pressed himself against a tree, unable to breathe, his heart hammering.

He was already a killer.

He squeezed his eyes shut, and his hands curled into fists. Suddenly he was back in an alley off Sheridan Street between a florist's shop and a bar. There was no light, just trash and empty boxes and a stink that he would never get out of his nose, but he could see that punk's face as he smashed it again and again, as he systematically and efficiently broke every bone one at a time. Long after the little bastard had stopped resisting, he'd continued to beat him. Robert had waited nights to find him without his piss-ass little gang to back him up. Waited, prayed to get him alone, *prayed* that he would draw that gun, that same gun that had killed Scott.

The punk drew it, too, drew it from the same pocket in the same jacket. Robert threw one kick, a perfect crescent that sent the weapon flying. "Thank you," he muttered. Everything after that he did with his hands, raining one textbook blow after another until the kid's own mother couldn't have told that face from a piece of veal in a butcher shop window.

Scott, Robert thought, his heart full of grief as he banged his head back against the tree. He opened his eyes, trying to force the memories away. *I should have saved you. I was there. I should have moved faster!*

A few days later, he had called Eric and suggested a camping trip. He had to get out of New York, not because he feared getting caught—no one had seen him—but because he knew if he stayed he'd go looking for the rest of the gang.

He closed his eyes again and tried to force away the memory of holding Scott's body on that oily pavement, but other memories surged up, memories of their travels in Okinawa and China, of their workouts in the dojo together, of the good times they'd shared after returning to America. He'd just talked Scott into moving from Florida to the Big Apple.

Robert peered around the tree back toward the village. At least the trembling had stopped. He bit his lip as he watched through a narrow gap and saw the soldiers moving along the street. He had killed for Scott, he told himself bitterly. What was he prepared to do for Eric? And Alanna?

God help him, he feared the answer. Maybe that was why he disliked Roderigo Diez. Somehow that old Spaniard could see the evil in him. Phlogis could see it too.

Before Robert could decide on his next move, the loud bellowing of a *chimorg* filled the air. At the same time a wind blew up out of nowhere. It ripped through the trees, sweeping leaves from the branches. The old building nearest Robert swayed uncertainly on its foundation. Dust swirled around him, stinging his eyes. He tugged a corner of his beaded hood closer around his face and cowered against the sudden gale.

In the bright blue day, thunder cracked with shocking force. The very air turned electric, and he felt his hair stand on end. From the village came the deep-throated cries of fearful soldiers. Thunder blasted again, and over it all rose the trumpeting of the *chimorg*.

The wind took on a sharp chill. At first Robert thought some phantom had brushed against him.

Then the sunlight began to weaken and fade. He stared upward through the trees. Black clouds boiled across the sky, devouring the sun, drinking its light.

Lightning made a crackling lacework at the edges of the encroaching darkness. Thunder matched the shattering of limbs deep in the woods as they gave way before the wailing wind. The *chimorg* screamed. Over it all, a man's cry touched Robert's ears. Through the gap between buildings he watched a soldier fall to his knees and prostrate himself in the dirty street.

Robert could hide no longer. He had to know what was happening. He rushed out of the woods, through that gap, paused behind a corner, then ran into the street. No one paid him any attention. One end of the street opened into a huge square. The soldiers that filled it lay on their faces or knelt with their brows pressed to the earth.

Robert stood paralyzed as he digested the scene.

A black hole, a round empty *nothingness,* hung above the square, radiating wildly colored lightnings. The air crackled with heat and energy. Directly under that hole, a large, powerfully built figure stood with upraised arms, head flung back, screaming strange words. Black robes swirled about him, snapping in the violent wind. On his head sat a delicate gold circlet. In one hand he clutched the missing unicorn horn. An electric spark touched the tip of it as he stretched it toward the hole, and for an instant he burned in a nimbus of shining fire.

Behind the figure was an open, flatbed wagon. Alanna, Valis, and Danyel stood, each bound securely to the spokes of its wheels, gags shoved deep into their mouths, feet tied. Alanna struggled uselessly to free herself, the strain showing in her livid muscles and on her face as she stared wide-eyed at the black hole. Her wrists gleamed, wet with her own blood. On the other side of the wagon Danyel and Valis wrenched frantically at their ropes.

On the flatbed itself, Eric lay spread-eagled and naked. The ruins of his garments were scattered on the ground beneath him. Ropes encircled each hand and foot and passed under the wagon to the massive axles. His head was at the end nearest the figure with the unicorn horn. The lightnings that shot from the hole reflected on his bare flesh, casting shimmering, shifting patterns as he arched his back and strained to see what was happening.

The black-robed figure—priest, wizard, whatever—took a step closer to Eric and raised the horn. The point gleamed over Eric's throat.

Robert cringed inside. In a world where ghosts were real and vengeful, how could they even consider human sacrifice? He had to save his brother. But how? All his fighting skills counted for nothing against so many soldiers. As soon as they noticed him he would be lost, and his brother and the *sekournen* as well.

He had only one desperate chance. In a swift motion he whipped off his beaded Terreborne tunic and strode into the middle of the street. The wind swept through his blond hair.

A fatalistic calm descended upon him. He locked his gaze on the wizard with the unicorn horn and walked straight ahead. A soldier kneeling on the ground looked over his shoulder as Robert's shadow fell upon him. He leaped up and raised his baton to strike. Then his eyes snapped wide and his mouth gaped. His hands fell to his side, and he stepped back out of Robert's way. Another man leaped up and raised his club, but the blow never came. The weapon slipped from numbed fingers. Others rose, stared, and fell back.

From the right came a muttered "Shae'aluth!" The word spread swiftly through the ranks.

"Look at his eyes!" someone cried.

"His hair!" a warrior murmured.

The wizard turned away from the wagon. Across the distance, Robert saw the rage in his dark-eyed gaze. A black-clad arm raised the horn. Again a spark caught it, and again electric flames bathed the wizard in a fiery radiance. He pointed a finger at Robert.

Robert walked on, full of a strange serenity. It was as if this were the moment he had lived his life for. Here his fate awaited him, and for the first time in his memory he felt no fear and no anger. On the flatbed, his brother writhed and arched his back, straining to see, until his spine looked as if it would snap in two. Alanna went crazy, striving to break her bonds.

The hole above the wizard churned with a liquid energy. An evil presence lurked within it, and it watched, pouring forth a visceral hatred. The lightnings intensified, as if whatever dwelled within was trying to frighten him. Then they weakened ever so subtly.

"You!" the wizard shrieked, pointing his finger. "This is not your time or place!"

Robert lost all sense of the wind or the heat. The world and time seemed to move through him. He regarded the wizard and the horn and the hole.

There was no sense of *her*. How he knew that he couldn't say. But this was not the Heart of Darkness.

The murmurings from the soldiers rose around him like a fearful chant. *Shae'aluth! Shae'aluth!*

"You can't be here!" the wizard raged. The language of Terreborne was not so different from that of Guran. He pointed again, but with the unicorn horn, as if it were a weapon that could keep the Son of the Morning at bay. "Not yet! I'm not ready!"

"I am here," Robert answered quietly. Somehow, his voice carried across the square. The soldiers of Terreborne grew silent and gave way, pressing back against the buildings, against each other, until he had the street nearly to himself and there was nothing between him and the wizard.

The wizard raised the horn over Eric again. "His soul is for the Heart of Darkness!" he shouted. "He killed a sacred *chimorg!*"

"You lie. You're a pretender." The words flowed from Robert and stayed the wizard's hand as surely as if they had been a vice. Closer and closer Robert drew to his brother. "You are not Shandal Karg, nor her agent." It was Robert's turn to point. He raised a finger and leveled it at Eric. "You will not have him."

"Then I will have the others!" The wizard caught a handful of Alanna's hair and jerked her head back sharply, exposing her white throat as he raised the horn again. She tried uselessly to wrench free.

"No," Robert said with utter calm. "I'm the one you want." He stood only a few paces from the wagon now. His brother's eyes pleaded with him, but Robert looked away and met the wizard's hateful gaze. Slowly, he opened his hands and sank down on both knees in the street. In a gesture of submission he lowered his head until his chin rested on his chest. He slipped his fingers secretly into the top of his left boot.

The wizard glowered distrustfully at him but stayed his hand. Suspiciously, he took a step closer toward Robert and stopped, gripping the horn as if it were a dagger. Half-crouched, he crept forward again, his gold crown sparkling in the lightning, the hems of his black robes sweeping in the dust.

Robert closed his eyes. All at once fear surged up in him again. He thought of Eric, but it was Scott's face he saw, and the face of the punk. The darkness that hung over this village was the darkness of that night outside that bar on Grove Street, and the darkness of that alley, and none of it was as black as the darkness that filled his own damned soul.

An icy hand caught Robert's chin in an iron grip, and the smell of death swam sickeningly in his nostrils as he was forced to look up. Robert opened his eyes and stared, horrified, at the white, bloodless face before him. It was not human, this thing he had called a wizard.

With a despairing cry he knocked the hand away and lunged upward. The small blade of his Boy Scout knife sank to the hilt in the creature's soft throat. With a savage jerk, he ripped the blade sideways, then free again.

The wizard-thing staggered back, clutching the wound with one hand. No blood poured forth. Instead, a shimmering black energy burst out, stretching and widening the gaping rent that the blade had caused. The wizard's head teetered backward on the stump of a neck. The unicorn horn fell to the ground. With hands as pale as only long-dead flesh can be, the wizard grasped for the edge of the wagon and found Eric.

Robert gave another cry as he saw those cold fingers close on his brothers' arm. He ran, grabbed the collar of the wizard's robes, and flung the creature away from the wagon. Still, it kept its balance, teetering from leg to leg, and staggered toward the wagon again.

A cry born of all his fear and turmoil ripped from Robert. He threw a kick. The creature's head went flying through the air and splattered in the road like overripe fruit. Yet the corpse continued to stand! The black energy that poured from its neck spiraled up into the hole above the square.

Shouts of dismay went up from the soldiers of Terreborne. Robert stared uncertainly at them. Then, remembering what he had come to do, he turned and put his knife to work on Eric's ropes.

Alanna twisted around and tried to shout through her gag. He paused on the ropes long enough to reach over and rip the cloth away. She wasted no time on thanks but began to sing with a powerful, full voice.

Eric's right hand came free, and he pulled his own gag out of his mouth. "My knife!" he shouted. "It's in my boot down there!" He gestured toward the ruins of his clothing. Robert gave his own knife to his brother while he picked up first one boot, then the other, and shook it. Eric's red-handled Swiss army knife slid into his palm.

"Cut the others loose," Eric instructed as he severed the rope on his other hand and sat up. He went immediately to work on the ropes at his feet. "I'll take care of these!"

Robert raced around to Alanna's side. Her wrists were bloody messes. "My God!" he muttered. She paid him no attention. Her eyes were squeezed tightly shut, and she sang as if that were all that mattered in the world. He glanced over his shoulder as he cut through her bonds.

The headless corpse spun around and around, its arms outstretched, like some kind of broken dancer. It's life-force funneled upward in a twisting, writhing line of rapidly diminishing intensity. The hole itself seemed to be changing shape as its own lightnings turned back upon it.

The Terreborne soldiers were no longer on their knees, though. They were staring at the spectacle before them. Robert had the distinct feeling that the fearsome sight of that spinning corpse was all that kept them at bay. He worked faster, cutting Alanna's last bond. "Run!" he shouted in her ear, but she ignored him and kept on singing.

Eric leaped down from the wagon and ran to free Danyel. Robert hurried around to Valis and pulled his gag away. "What's she doing?" he cried, sawing at the first rope.

"She has the voice of Taedra," Valis answered grimly. Robert's knife was only halfway through the stout cord, but the big dragonrider gave a loud groan, flexed his arm, and snapped what was left.

Robert didn't stop to figure that one out, but started to work on Valis's other bonds. They'd left the dragons ten miles and more behind in Guran, on the far side of the Shylamare River. Could Mirrormist hear her that far away? He sliced through the second bond, and Valis's hands were free. He left the *sekournen* to untie his own feet.

An all-too-familiar trumpeting caused him to turn. A *chimorg* charged into the square, crushing a soldier as it turned a corner between two buildings. It seemed smaller than the first creature he had faced, the fire in its eyes less bright. It was no less deadly for that. It screamed a challenge, lowered its horned head, and ran at the wagon.

"Look out!" Danyel cried, as he swept the severed ropes from his wrists.

Robert looked frantically around for the horn, but the damned corpse must have kicked it somewhere during its crazy spinning. Let the wizard be his weapon then! Rushing forward, he caught the thing by one arm and jerked it off its feet. With one hand in the small of its back, he lifted it high. It weighed almost nothing, a mere husk. The *chimorg* screamed again as Robert heaved the body through the air and impaled it upon the monster's spike. He leaped out of its path. The momentum of its charge carried it forward, and it smashed into the now-empty wagon. The impact did not dislodge the corpse.

"Robert!" Danyel called suddenly.

He looked around in time to see the young dragonrider make an arching dive-roll and come up with the original horn in his hand. In one smooth motion, he tossed it. The *chimorg* spun, reared, and bucked, trying to shake free of its burden. Robert caught the horn and hurled himself at the monster, plunging the weapon into his chest with all his might. The beast screamed in pain, and black fluid spurted from the wound. Robert danced away, but not quickly enough; its flank brushed against him and knocked him to the ground.

The *chimorg* gave a vicious snap of its head, and the corpse went sailing. Voicing its triumph, the beast reared above Robert, and those hooves came crashing down. Barely in time, Robert rolled under the wagon, while off to the right, Valis shouted and waved his arms to attract the *chimorg*'s attention. Danyel, not to be left out of the action, flung a handful of dirt at its eyes.

"Bobby, you okay under there?" Eric shouted. He was standing on top of the flatbed.

"Well, my heart rate's up a little!" Robert answered, clutching the bloody horn.

"Untie a rope from the axle!"

Robert understood his brother's intention and quickly estimated which knot might belong to the longest piece of rope. He worked with desperate speed to unfasten it and threw the end out. "Take it!" he called, and the rope zipped away. Robert scrambled out again.

Eric already had his lasso fashioned and a large loop swirling above his head. "Lure it over here!" his brother shouted. Then, "Danyel, watch out!"

The *chimorg* charged the boy. Danyel's hands worked furiously at his waist as he turned and ran. The monster lowered its head, but Danyel skipped sideways, avoiding the deadly spike. At the same moment, his whip cracked through the air. The creature dug in its hooves and whirled about. Twice more Danyel laid leather across its nose.

"That kid's crazier than you are!" Eric muttered.

The unicorn ignored the lashes, lowered its head, and charged again. Again Danyel ran away. The monster turned on the speed. The youth cast a fearful glance over his shoulder, but let go no cry.

Brandishing the horn, Robert ran to intercept the monster. Before he had taken more than a few steps, though, a loud *whoosh* filled his ears. A wind ripped at him and smashed him flat on his face. The *chimorg* screamed.

Massive talons reached down out of the sky and closed around the terrified *chimorg*. An opalescent radiance lit up the ground. Shadowfire climbed in a steep arc above the village, wings beating furiously. Then, it seemed to pause, to hover for a moment. The dragon twitched its forelegs and ripped the *chimorg* in half like a piece of onionskin. Shadowfire sang with vengeful trilling as it let the pieces fall. Half the *chimorg* crashed through a rooftop; the rear quarters splattered sickeningly in the street.

Suddenly the sky was full of dragons. Robert shot a glance around to find Alanna, but there was no sign of her. A score of the creatures attacked the village. Terreborne's soldiers screamed in panic and ran. Black-clads were swept into the air and dropped, or treated as the *chimorg* had been treated. Some were flattened by the winds and buried under collapsing houses and shops. Hundreds ran for the woods or the river.

Robert saw a dragon turn his way and felt angry diamond eyes lock on him. His heart lurched when he realized the creatures didn't know friend from foe. He rose to a crouch as the *sekoye* dove at him, and raised the unicorn horn, his only weapon.

But before those claws could seize him, Valis appeared from out of nowhere, flung his arms around Robert, opened his mouth and sang. Instantly the dragon swooped away and instead found a house to vent its fury upon.

Robert whirled, searching for Eric. There was no need to worry. Danyel stood with his brother, arms outspread protectively, singing.

"Look," Valis said in Robert's ear, turning him around. The street that ran through the square led straight out into the field beyond the village. The stockade rose like an evil monument.

It was a shattered monument, though. The entire front wall had been ripped away. Alanna, a small but valiant figure at such a distance, stood on the shattered timbers, singing. The prisoners streamed out, the stronger helping the weaker. A familiar trio of dragons flashed through the air. As Robert watched, Mirrormist struck the west wall, smashing it to fragments with a sound like thunder.

"They need help!" Robert called to Valis over the tumult. He caught the dragonrider's arm and pulled him along. Valis shrugged free, but ran at his side down the street and out into the field. Eric and Danyel chased after them.

They met the first line of escaping prisoners and gathered them together. "Wait!" Eric cried at the top of his voice. "Wait! It's safe here!" He caught an old man, who toppled from sudden weakness, and eased him to the ground.

"Stop!" Robert shouted, catching a woman as she tried to run off toward the woods. She struggled, shrieking with terror, and broke free. Two more followed her toward the trees below the bluff. "We're safe from the dragons if we stay together!" he called to the rest. "Safe from the soldiers, too!" He pointed to Valis, whose voice suddenly soared. "He's a *sekournen*! He sings to the dragons!"

Valis's song calmed the frightened prisoners. A few of them nodded with understanding and huddled together to watch the destruction of the village and the stockade. Robert spied the blacksmith, Brin, among the gaunt faces, and motioned to Eric. His brother waded through the crowd and clapped the big, burly man around the shoulders.

Alanna came walking across the field. Another woman, whose features closely resembled hers, strode proudly at her side. Alanna had found her sister, Maris. Her eyes gleamed. She was plainer than Alanna but still possessed a hard, settled beauty. The soldiers had shaved her head, but they had not broken this woman.

Robert continued to search the faces, seeking one in particular, but there was no sign of crazy old Frona. His heart sank a little, and his mouth settled in a tight line.

Alanna came to him, put her arms around his neck, and leaned her head on his chest. He planted a kiss on the top of her head and smoothed her hair. Then he drew her hands down. Her wrists were raw and red with sticky blood. He raised them to his mouth and kissed them too. Emotions he didn't understand and didn't want to deal with churned inside him, but he embraced her again while Maris stood by and watched.

Another explosive crash made him glance up momentarily. The last wall of the stockade went up in an impressive shower of fragments and splinters as Brightstar sailed through it.

"How could they hear you from so far away?" he whispered in Alanna's ear.

Alanna shrugged wearily. "They hear," she answered simply. "It's my gift."

"Gift?" Robert raised her chin and looked into her eyes. "You mean like Danyel's gift?"

"Different," she said.

"She can call the dragons," Danyel explained. Robert had not heard him come up, nor Eric right behind him. "I can call Shadowfire, and Valis can call Brightstar. But Alanna can call them all." He pointed toward the village, which was now a flattened ruin. There were fewer dragons in the air, but still a good half-score. "Even the wild ones," Danyel added. "She has the mother-dragon's voice."

Robert drew Alanna close and stroked the back of her hair. She didn't resist, but gave a little sigh. All her energy seemed drained.

"If Danyel sees spirits, and you call dragons," Eric said, turning his gaze toward Valis, "what can he do?"

Alanna didn't look up when she answered, "I'm afraid you'll find out shortly."

Danyel reached out and entwined his fingers in Eric's as he looked toward the wreckage that had been the village. Robert followed the boy's gaze. There was no remaining trace of the black hole or its foul lightnings. Even the clouds were beginning to break apart, and the sun fought its way through.

He thought suddenly of Pietka and felt some small part of the little man's spirit stir inside him. He wondered if Eric felt Sumeek the same way. The Chalosans were free, and these other Terreborne prisoners were too. Pietka and Sumeek could rest easy. As he glanced at Maris, who stood with quiet dignity beside him, he felt a fierce pride in that accomplishment.

"Let's get these people to the boats," he said. "It's time to go home."

Chapter Thirteen

BUT they couldn't go home. Not yet.

"Valis says old Frona is dead," Danyel remarked as he dug through the ruins of yet another building. With strength that belied his youth, he picked up one end of a wooden beam that blocked a doorway. Eric moved quickly to help him. "I liked her."

Eric only nodded. Brin had already told him. The crazy old woman had slipped her bonds on the long ride up the river and jumped overboard. Apparently, Pietka's death had unhinged her mind completely. The guards hadn't made a move to save her, and the currents had proved too much.

"There they are!" Danyel exclaimed suddenly. He pointed to three familiar packs half-buried in the rubble of a collapsed roof. Eric breathed a small sigh of relief. His leathers should be in one of those packs, still damp maybe but better than the rag he had tied around his waist right now. He reached for the nearest pack, but Danyel snatched it first and shrugged into the shoulder straps. "I thought I saw a soldier bring them in here."

"What in the world have you got in there?" Eric asked curiously. Except for their brief captivity, the kid hadn't let that pack out of his sight since they left Rasoul. But Danyel kept a nervous silence and stepped back outside, leaving Eric to shrug as he opened one of the others and found his old garments. He wrinkled his nose. Wet leather had its own pungence. On the other hand, loincloths weren't really his style. He dressed as fast as he could.

Danyel was waiting for him outside, his thumbs hooked in the pack straps, gazing around at the wreckage that had once been a village. "This is all my fault," he said with a grim shake of his head. His brows pinched together, and his mouth drew into a taut line. For a moment Eric thought Danyel was going to cry, but no tears fell from those large brown eyes.

"Don't be silly," Eric told him, rumpling his hair.

But the look of pain in his young friend's face did not ease. "If I hadn't lost my staff in the river . . ." he started. He bit his lip and swallowed. "That soldier we carried to the trench—" he continued, "you recognized him too. It was the fisherman we passed last night. He was a spy, set to watch the river. My staff probably alerted him. It would have been easy to find our footprints in the muddy bank."

Eric winced as he glanced far out beyond the field. Fire and smoke and ash rose up like a curtain from the trench near the stockade. They had placed the bodies of the soldiers with the bodies of their victims and burned them all, according to the customs of the Domains of Light. "You can't be sure that that soldier and the fisherman were one and the same." He tried to sound reassuring, but even he had his doubts. Still, he wasn't going to let the kid carry around that kind of guilt. "It was dark on the river. There could've been a dozen ways we betrayed ourselves. Hell, the *chimorgs* may have just sniffed us out."

Danyel gave a sigh and hung his head briefly. His hands tightened on the shoulder straps of his precious pack.

Eric stared at the fire again. Valis and Brin were still out there tending it, feeding the flames with logs from the shattered stockade, making sure the bodies were consumed. The smell of smoke and burning flesh drifted on the wind.

"You get used to it," Danyel said, following his gaze across the field.

Eric looked sharply at the boy, studying his face. Danyel's expression was dispassionate once more. Sometimes he seemed soft as cotton candy, other times harder than steel. He had that look now. Eric had been calling him "kid," but he forced himself to remember that Danyel was no kid at all. He had seen his parents killed, his country conquered. He had marched alone across three nations to reach Guran. Whatever his age, he was now a soldier in a thousand-year-old war.

"Sometimes, Danyel," Eric said in a little more than a whisper, "you scare me more than anything else I've seen in this damned world." He waited for some response. When the young *sekournen* made no answer, he clapped him on the shoulder. "You come from Chule, is that right?"

Danyel nodded.

Eric pursed his lips. "What's the Chule word for 'little brother'?"

Danyel glanced up at him strangely. "*Mew*," he answered suspiciously.

"*Mew*," Eric repeated. He reached out and rumpled Danyel's hair once more. *"Mew,"* he said again, grinning when a smile finally cracked the boy's rigid expression.

Alanna walked wearily up the street from the direction of the river. Someone had bandaged her wrists with strips of soft cloth. Under her belt she wore a unicorn's horn, nearly identical to the one Robert carried. She'd wasted no time finding the remains of the monster Shadowfire had killed and smashing off its spike with a heavy rock.

"Let's see what progress we're making toward getting out of here," Eric suggested to Danyel, and they went to join her.

"Maris has most of the Chalosans ready to board the boats," she reported, laying one hand on the haft of the horn and brushing back a stray lock of hair with the other hand. Her face was sweat-stained and streaked with dirt. "Most of the locals have taken off into the woods. The weakest ones are on their way downstream to the empty village we found, along with most of the food we could dig out of the rubble."

"They'll spread the word that their king is dead," Danyel said approvingly. "Terreborne never went over to the Dark Lands. Keris Chaterit must have slain him and used his body as a revenant to make it seem so."

Eric had already discussed that with Valis. He understood now about animated corpses and why the Domains were so intent on burning their dead. What he was less clear about was why Keris Chaterit was here in any guise, waiting so close to the border with Guran.

"That's not the only word that will spread, I

think," Alanna added. "A lot of them think they've seen the Son of the Morning."

"Where is Robert?" Eric asked abruptly. He hadn't seen his brother since they'd carried the last body to the trench and lit the fire.

Alanna hesitated. "Danyel," she said, turning one eye toward the fire that burned beyond the field. "You'd better find Valis. He might have need of your gift shortly."

The boy made a face. He knew he was being sent away, but he said nothing, just turned and left them.

"He's down on the pier," she continued when they were alone. She bit her lip and looked away nervously, unable or unwilling to meet Eric's gaze. "He said he wanted to be alone for a while."

Eric scoffed and headed toward the river. "He always says he wants to be alone," he answered impatiently. "That doesn't mean he does." He walked around a pile of rubble, part of a house that had collapsed into the street. He paid it little attention, though. His thoughts were on his brother. Robert had hardly said a word since the smashing of the stockade.

Alanna hurried along with him. Her boots made a squishing sound as she slipped in a muddy patch where blood had mingled with the street dust. The grim look on her face had nothing to do with that unpleasantness. He thought he knew her well enough to tell that by now.

"You might as well get it out," he told her. "You've wanted to say something all afternoon. You're pissed off because Bobby knifed that monstrosity."

"Pissed off?" She caught his arm, her face clouding with sudden anger, and jerked him to a stop.

"Neither of us is a fool, Eric Podlowsky, so don't play me for one, and I'll extend you the same courtesy." The sharpness of her voice was matched by the hard glint in her eyes. Her fingers tightened around his wrist. "I'm in love with Robert."

"I'm not blind," he shot back uncomfortably.

"But you are," she answered, "to the ways of Palenoc." Finally she let go of his arm. The anger also drained from her face, and the look of weariness returned. She paused long enough to squeeze her temples with the thumb and forefinger of one hand. "He put his knife right through its throat," she continued, and her voice gave a small quaver of barely checked emotion. "He didn't know it wasn't human. It might have been a man, and that wouldn't have mattered to him, even though Diez warned him not to kill!"

Eric's own rage welled up within him. "How do you know what went through his mind?" he hissed, making the effort to keep his voice down. They weren't that far from the river, and there were still others about. "That thing you call a revenant had me laid out ready to carve like a Sunday roast beef. And you might have been next!" He turned and started down the street again, shaking his head.

Alanna came right after him. "He's seen what some *dandos* can do!" she shouted. "He risked a terrible revenge!"

Eric stopped and thrust a finger at her. "To save our fucking lives!" he reminded her. "This whole Son of the Morning look-alike business has him freaked. But he used that to walk right in through all those soldiers." His eyes narrowed to slits as he glared at her. "Give him a break, Alanna. If you love him so much, give him a break."

Her entire body tensed for a moment as if she wanted to hit him. Then her shoulders sagged ever so slightly, and she turned her palms outward in a gesture of helplessness. "What am I supposed to do?"

"I don't have an answer for that," he said with a mixture of impatience and regret. But he reached out and laid a hand on her arm and squeezed it. She covered his hand with one of her own and forced a worried smile. They finished the walk to the river in silence.

Robert sat at the end of the pier in the classic lotus position, his hands curled on his knees as he stared up at the sky where a pair of red-winged birds dipped and gyred playfully. The afternoon sun shimmered in his golden hair and gleamed on his bare shoulders. The old planks creaked and groaned as Eric and Alanna walked toward him, but he didn't move.

"All they have to be is birds," Robert said when they stopped behind him, his gaze still on the sky. "All they have to worry about is being birds." He paused. Crimson plumage spread suddenly. The birds skimmed the river, rose again, and disappeared into the trees.

Eric and Alanna exchanged troubled looks.

Robert lowered his gaze finally, and his left hand dipped into his lap. When he opened his hand his Boy Scout knife gleamed on his palm. The sunlight seemed to dance on the clean, open blade and on the small silver emblem set in the worn plastic handle. Robert held it out over the water and balanced it on the tip of his right index finger. The knife teetered for a moment, briefly finding equilibrium, before it fell with a small splash into the river.

"That's what I feel like," he told them with chilling calm. "Out of balance."

Eric knelt down and slipped his arms around his brother. "It wasn't human, Bobby," he said, his voice straining with emotion. "It was already dead. You didn't kill anyone."

A shiver ran through Robert's body, so violent that it startled Eric.

Alanna bent down. Eric moved aside so she could take his place. Her hand stroked the back of Robert's neck as she whispered in his ear, "You did nothing wrong, *Kaesha*," she said, hugging him with all her might.

Robert freed himself from her embrace and stood up. For a long moment he stared down into the Shylamare's crystal depths, then he turned. "I knew that thing was not the Heart of Darkness," he told them. There was a look of fear and determination on his face. "I *knew* it as surely as I know your names! I *felt* it!" He flung his hands up, then braced them on his hips as he turned and stared back at the river. "I don't know how or when or why . . ." He shook his head and faced them again. "But I've been here before."

"But how, Bobby . . ."

Robert exploded. "I said I don't know how!" Then he got control of himself. He rubbed a hand over the back of his head and down his neck. "So many things are familiar, yet I don't remember any of it. But I'm going to." His voice turned grim, his hands curled into tight fists. "I'm going to remember it all."

"We've never really thought it was an accident that brought us here," Eric reminded him.

"No, not an accident," Robert agreed. "There's a plan at work. But whose plan?"

Eric scratched his chin and frowned. Eight long canoelike boats were waiting on the shore just down the bank from the pier. Some vessels had already shoved off and started their journeys downriver back to Guran. But a lot of Chalosans were still there. Most of them had at least found clothing among the ruins or taken it from the soldiers' bodies. Alanna's sister, Maris, moved among them, encouraging them, chatting, tending to hurts and wounds.

"I don't know," he said finally, letting go a long sigh. "But we should get these people out of here. After dark, some of those soldiers might come back. And there were two *chimorgs* on the bluff. We don't know where the second one is."

Robert looked down at the group on the shore. Without looking at Alanna, he slipped his hand into hers, and their fingers interlocked. "Some of us are missing," he observed.

"They're out by the trench," Eric answered. "I'll go round them up."

"I don't think Valis will come," Alanna told him as they walked back down the pier together.

Eric gave her a curt glance, then increased his pace and walked on ahead. "He'll come," he called back over his shoulder, "if I have to drop-kick his ass into the boat myself."

He strode up the street alone. When he reached the square he saw Brin, Danyel, and Valis coming toward him across the field. The blacksmith had dressed himself in the clothes and armor of one of the soldiers. The sun gleamed on the black lacquer and on his newly bald head. He seemed little the worse physically for his experience, but there was a harder look in his eyes.

"We should get out of here," Eric said as he met the trio at the edge of the village. "There's still that second *chimorg*."

Valis dismissed his fear with a wave. "It won't attack us now," he answered. "It's the eyes and ears of Darkness. It will observe from a distance, and Srimourna will know what it knows."

Eric glanced past the big dragonrider. In the distance, the flames crackled and soared above the trench. A thick veil of smoke drifted southward. "Now why doesn't that comfort me?" he asked sarcastically. Then he grew serious again. "Besides, I think these *chimorgs* were loyal to Keris Chaterit."

"That's not possible," Brin interrupted with a shake of his head. "The Heart of Darkness spawned those creatures. They belong to her."

Valis laid a hand on the blacksmith's shoulder. "I'm not so sure Eric isn't right," he said in a low voice. "Keris Chaterit seems to have grown in power and ambition. The Kingdoms of Night may represent as big a threat to us now as the Dark Lands."

"We should get a report on this back to Rasoul as quickly as we can," Danyel said reasonably. A single blade of grass hung from the corner of his mouth, and he chewed thoughtfully on it.

Eric pursed his lips. "I thought we should ride down with the boats. Some of those people are pretty weak."

Brin scoffed. "My people can take care of themselves. We were born handling boats. From what

I've heard you say, you need to get Maris back to Sheren-Chad. She's your biggest responsibility now."

Valis agreed. "Brin can guide the boats down the Shylamare all the way to the Great Lake and into Rasoul. Brightstar will carry Maris, but the rest of you must go with her."

Eric arched an eyebrow. "What about you?"

"I can't leave," the *sekournen* answered dourly. He looked back toward the fire and made a sweeping gesture. "There's too much anger here. Too much death. I can ease some of it." He turned an intense, black-eyed gaze on Eric and clutched at the small silver medallion he wore around his neck. "The living aren't our only concern, Eric Podlowsky."

Eric was unable to keep the disdain from his voice. "You're worried about the ghosts of the soldiers?"

Valis nodded. "Yes, but also those unfortunate prisoners whose souls found no welcome release in a slow death. I can ease the passage for some and point the way to paradise."

"That's your gift?" Eric frowned. "You're some kind of exorcist?"

Valis looked at him for a long moment, and Eric realized he had gone too far. "I'm a priest, Eric," the dragonrider answered calmly. "Just as Roderigo Diez heals the living, I minister to the suffering of the dead. I don't call it a gift in the same way Danyel or Alanna might, but it is my responsibility."

Eric faced the fire again, an uneasy feeling squeezing his gut. "There are a lot of dead people here."

Valis shrugged, and the gesture betrayed a weariness Eric hadn't noticed before. "I can help only a few," he replied, "but I have to do what I can."

The dragonrider's hand fell on Eric's arm. "You and your brother are good men," he said earnestly. "You get Maris back to Rasoul. Brin will leave me one boat, and I'll be along when I can."

Eric saw no chance of changing Valis's mind. Cursing inwardly, he started back toward the river with Danyel and Brin. Funny, he reflected, he'd never really had friends back in his own world. Acquaintances, students, co-workers. But not really friends. He didn't like leaving Valis behind.

At least Robert seemed his old self again. Most of the boats were in the water. He stood hip-deep, steadying one craft while a group of Chalosans settled themselves and took up the oars. Maris handed him a small, quiet boy-child. He passed it over the side and into its mother's arms.

"Leave one boat on the shore," Eric called to his brother as Brin waded down to take his place. "Valis will need it. We're taking Alanna's sister back on the dragons."

When the last Chalosan was aboard, Maris waded down into the water to say good-bye to them and to whisper something in Brin's ear before she gave the old blacksmith a little kiss on his cheek. Then she trudged back to shore, straight to Eric and Robert. She was older than Alanna, though not by much, and slighter. Her voice was small and low as she touched her palms to each of theirs in turn. Yet there was strength and dignity in her bearing.

"I didn't have the chance to meet you when you stayed in my village," she said with a tiny smile, "but Alanna speaks well of you both." Her gaze went to Robert and lingered on him with barely concealed awe. "Thank you for saving my people," she said simply.

"We were the ones who put them in danger," Robert answered.

Her smile wavered, then returned as she looked toward Alanna. "You're right, sister," she said. "They still don't understand." She reached out and took both Eric's and Robert's hand and squeezed them with a grip that was nearly the equal of her sister's. "None of us has ever known a moment when we were not in danger," she told them. "Whoever stands against Darkness—be it Shandal Karg or Keris Chaterit—gives over any notion of safety."

She turned away from them and waved to the last waiting boat. Then Brin climbed over the side and into the prow. At a word from him, two pairs of oars amidships dipped into the water. The vessel made its way into the center of the river, and no one aboard glanced back.

"Where'd Alanna go?" Eric asked as he turned back to his comrades. She had been with them just moments before.

"To call down the dragons," Robert answered, his eyes still on the departing boat.

Maris wasted no more words, but led the way back through the shattered village, her arms pumping as she set a brisk pace, water streaming from the legs of her oversized black trousers, which had formerly belonged to some luckless soldier. Her poor shaved head gleamed dully in the sunlight.

Shadowfire, Mirrormist, and Brightstar settled down in the field beyond the village. Eric had no idea where the three dragons had gone after they'd destroyed the stockade or where they had just come from. The wild dragons had simply scattered. Alanna waited for them at the edge of the field. In the far distance, near the flames and smoke that rose up from the trench, he could see Valis.

"I don't like leaving him," Eric repeated again.

Alanna helped Maris into Brightstar's saddle, taking pains to tie her legs to the stirrups. It was plain that Maris was no dragonrider. Still, she showed no fear of the creature as she clung to the small saddle horn. "He'll carry you straight to Rasoul," Alanna said in soothing tones to her sister. "We'll be beside you all the way."

Maris nodded and turned her eyes skyward expectantly. Alanna backed away and sang a high-pitched note and Brightstar sprang upward. Eric saw Maris's head snap back and her eyes widen suddenly. Her grip on the horn tightened. Yet she kept her balance admirably without giving so much as a squawk. In moments, she and Brightstar were beyond the rim of the trees, flying southward toward Guran.

Alanna and Robert, on Mirrormist, followed swiftly after. Danyel took off his pack and put it on backward, so that it hung on his chest. Eric said nothing about it. He was growing used to the boy's secrecy. There was something else on his mind anyway. As Eric settled behind Danyel, he whispered in his ear. "Once we're in the air, can you circle?"

"Why?" Danyel asked, surprised.

"I want to see."

Danyel knew what he meant. The boy hesitated, frowning. Then he sang the command that sent Shadowfire aloft. Higher and higher they climbed, gyring over the field. Smoke blew into Eric's eyes, and the heat of the fire momentarily enfolded them. But they circled. Eric leaned as far out as he dared and gazed toward the ground.

Thinking himself alone, Valis walked slowly into the center of the field. For what seemed like long moments, he just stood there. Then he flung out his arms and spun drunkenly. Eric and Danyel were too far up to see his face, but Eric thought he heard a long wail. Valis seized the neck of his tunic in both hands and ripped it. Another wail, then he stumbled to his knees and drummed his fists on the earth.

Eric sat erect, his arms tightening around Danyel as a shiver ran down his spine. "What's happening to him?" he muttered.

Shadowfire spread his wings and glided in a tight circle. Danyel called back to Eric. "He draws the angry spirit into his body," he said, his voice barely audible over the rush of the wind, "and lets it express its rage at dying through him until that anger is exhausted. Only then will it seek the peace of paradise."

Eric leaned out again to see. "No wonder he wouldn't call it a gift," he told Danyel, remembering Valis's words.

"It takes a terrible toll on him," the boy continued. "He'll keep at it, though, as long as one spirit will let him help. Then he'll find someplace to sleep for days before he makes his way home."

Far below, Valis ripped away the last of his clothing and flung up dust before he rolled on the ground. Bloody scratch marks showed even at a distance on his broad chest. "He's hurt himself!" Eric cried.

Danyel shook his head. "That's nothing," he answered. "The greater danger is that he'll lose himself in all the personalities that he touches."

Eric bit his lip, admitting to himself how

strongly Sumeek's memories yet stirred within him after their brief contact. It was Sumeek's language he spoke, not his own, and even now he wasn't absolutely sure if he had come to rescue the Chalosans out of his own desire or at Sumeek's bidding.

"We should leave," Danyel said abruptly. He sang a sharp note, and Shadowfire turned southward. "Valis doesn't like to be watched. It's too private for him."

Eric understood. But he was still curious about one more thing. "What do you see down there, Mew?" he asked, gazing back over his shoulder. "With your gift, I mean?"

Danyel twisted in his saddle, clinging to the horn with one hand, bracing the other on Eric's thigh as he bent outward at a dangerous angle. When he sat upright again, his voice was grim. "It's awful," he answered. "So much unfocused anger and grief. Ghosts everywhere." He swallowed and shook his head. "That will be an evil place for a long time to come."

For a while neither of them said more. Eric listened to the rush of the wind and the steady beating of Shadowfire's great wings and tried to empty his mind of all thought. Then they crossed the Chohia River, and Danyel began a song. In response, Shadowfire flew faster and faster until the ground blurred and fear started to chew at Eric's heart. But when he listened again to the words of the song, the fear left him. It was Rasoul's anthem the boy was singing:

> *Gather, people! Stand together!*
> *Darkness has no power here!*

"That's just a song!" Eric called, knowing even as he said it that it wasn't quite true. "How can Shadowfire understand that?"

Danyel stopped singing long enough to answer. "It doesn't matter what you sing," he said. "Music is just a vehicle. It opens the mind and lets us communicate. In Guran and Chylas we sing to our dragons. But it's different in other parts of the Domain. In Wysotoweem and Pylanthim, the *sekournen* play flutes. In Pylanthim, they use drums and percussion."

"But if you don't make music," Eric said, "the dragons are deaf?"

Danyel's body quivered with laughter. "The dragons are not deaf," he corrected. "It's the human who is mute."

In no time they overtook the others. Danyel didn't slow down but swept past Mirrormist and Brightstar with a challenging wave. Eric barely caught the frown on Alanna's face, but in only moments she moved up on Shadowfire's left wing and Brightstar surged up on the right. Eric glanced over. There was no fear on Maris's face. She seemed to be thoroughly enjoying herself.

And why not? he thought, realizing suddenly that his own fear of flying had completely disappeared. He threw back his head and laughed as the silver ribbon that was the Shylamare, glimmering below them, pointed the way home.

The return trip was made with far greater speed. The mountains reared up in the east. In the distance ahead, the vast blue expanse of the Great Lake rolled to the horizon. But on the eastern shore of the lake, where Rasoul should have been, hung a thick cloud of darkness.

"Shit!" Eric cried, slamming his palm against his thigh. "Danyel, look!" He pointed over the boy's shoulder, but Danyel had already seen. A dim red lightning flickered throughout the cloud. The women saw it too. Alanna leaned down close to the neck of her dragon and pulled Robert tight against her as Mirrormist raced ahead. "Go, Danyel!" Eric urged, his heart thundering. Danyel sang. Shadowfire swept past Mirrormist, leaving Alanna and Robert behind. Eric didn't even glance toward Brightstar and Maris. He kept his eyes on the darkness.

As if they'd crossed some border, the sun disappeared. Shadowfire's wings ignited with opalescent fury as they sped toward Sheren-Chad. In the streets below, people stood with torches and small globes and bottles of *sekoy'melin*. Joining hands, they hurled their song against the unnatural darkness, fighting it with only the nobility of their spirits.

A scarlet bolt lit up the top of Sherin-Chad. Unexpectedly, Shadowfire opened his great mouth and emitted a harsh scream. The beast did not slow, however. Eric shot a look back over his shoulder. Mirrormist and Brightstar raced close behind, wings burning with light.

Danyel aimed Shadowfire for the tower and sang a note to slow him down. "Don't land!" Eric directed. "We'll jump!"

The boy didn't question. As they approached the rooftop, he sang a single sharp note. The dragon slowed to an angled glide. At almost the same time, Eric and Danyel leaped. The roof came up fast. Eric pumped his arms for balance, hit on both feet, and rolled. But it was not a perfect landing. Stone scraped flesh from his cheek, and when he got to his feet his right ankle failed to support him. "Damn it!" he muttered. But he forced himself to get up again and willed the ankle to work.

Danyel was already at the tripod, activating the mechanism that opened the door. Eric ran, limping, toward his young friend. At the same time Mirrormist's cry sounded behind him. The dragon's claws barely connected with the parapet before Alanna and Robert flung themselves off.

"What about Maris?" he called to them.

The door creaked upward. A line of light appeared under the edge and widened. "Brightstar will circle until I call," Alanna answered breathlessly.

Danyel kicked the door impatiently and slipped under the edge as soon as it was wide enough for his small frame. "Wait!" Eric called after him. "We don't know what we're up against!"

"It's Keris Chaterit!" Danyel shouted back with startling bitterness. "Valis said we have a traitor in Sheren-Chad. Somehow he must know that Phlogis is unguarded!"

Alanna nodded as the door finally ground open. They bounded down the stairs and across the lavatorium, only to find Danyel beating on the inner door with his fists. "He may be right," she agreed. "All the other *sekournen* are out scouring the countryside for the new council members. There's only Diez and Blor to protect Phlogis. It's a perfect time for him to strike."

"It's locked!" Danyel cried, striking the door another blow.

"It's not Shandal Karg," Robert muttered. "I think I'd feel her."

"Maybe you're sensitive," Alanna said cryptically. "That may be your gift."

Robert caught Danyel by the shoulder and pulled the boy away. "My gift, lady," he said with a determined frown, "is smashing things!" His front thrust-kick split the wooden door frame. His second kick shattered it completely, and the door flew open.

"Take a globe!" Eric shouted, but he seized one of the glowing vessels before anyone else could and led the way down the stairs into darkness, ignoring the increasing pain in his ankle. Straight to Phlogis's sanctum he went. There was no doubt in his mind: whatever was going down was happening there.

Diez lay face down outside the great doors, which stood partially open. Within, a wild scarlet flickering lit the usual gloom. Smoke drifted out into the hall. Something not quite human screamed.

Alanna bent down by the old Spaniard as Eric and Robert flung back the doors. Danyel sped between them into the sanctum. "Look out!" he heard the boy cry suddenly.

Too late. A fat hand, jangling with bracelets, shot out from the shadows just inside the doorway and knocked the globe of *sekoy'melin* from his hand. It shattered on the stone tile. The radiant liquid hissed as it swiftly evaporated.

Eric had little time to orient himself to the new darkness. Blor hurled herself at him, leaping, wrapping her huge legs around him as they crashed to the floor inside the chamber. Eric felt the crunch of glass under his leather-shirted back and Blor's fingers dug for his eyes. "Get off!" he shrieked. "Get off me!"

"Phlogis!" Robert's shout accompanied another long scream and a familiar wave of rage.

Suddenly Blor's head snapped back. Eric stared up to see Alanna standing above him with a handful of the fat librarian's hair. Her fist crashed downward, sending Blor sprawling sideways, and she pulled Eric to his feet.

"Help me, Master!" Blor screamed, rising to her knees.

To one side of the room, near the two great copper cauldrons, a black hole exactly like the one he'd seen in Terreborne crackled with inner lightnings. The fat woman scrambled on her hands and knees to a box of tools, seized a piece of chalk, and tried to add a line to the scratchings already drawn on the floor. Phlogis screamed again.

"She's trying to exorcise him!" Alanna shouted. Again she grabbed Blor's hair, dealt her a savage backhand blow, and smeared the marking with the sole of her boot.

Robert strode to the center of the chamber and stared into the flickering hole. "Stop!" he commanded. "You know who I am!"

A snaking bolt of electricity struck Robert's chest, flinging him backward. For the first time a voice issued from that blackness.

Yes, now I know who you are, Son of Paradane. My slave has told me all. A wave of mirth radiated around the room. Eric felt it as he limped to Robert's side in much the same way as he felt Phlogis's rage. Then the mirth faded, and there was anger. But it was not the *dando*'s anger. It, too, came from Keris Chaterit.

From a distance I sensed only your brother when you killed the chimorg. *Even now, I can sense his thoughts, but not yours. There is a shield, a darkness in your mind, blacker than I can penetrate. I do not know who or what you brothers are, but if one can kill a chimorg and the other can resist my powers, then it is best I forget this pathetic, bothersome thing in its silly golden circle and kill you both. There will be time then to take Phlogis and Rasoul. Then I will have accomplished what not even the Heart of Darkness has dared!*

A raw red spot showed lividly on his brother's chest, and Eric felt for a heartbeat. But Robert's eyes fluttered open. He gave a groan and sat stiffly up.

"Because Shandal Karg knows we will not fall!" Danyel shouted. Unseen, the boy had crept dangerously close to the black hole where Keris Chaterit lurked. In his arms he clutched the pack that he had kept like a secret treasure for so long. "I know you, too, Monster!" he screamed. "You killed my family and raped my nation!"

You are an insect, said the voice from the hole. A flicker of lightning lanced outward. Danyel flew backward and slid on the tiles through Blor's chalk marks until he struck the opposite wall. The voice laughed. *An insect to be swatted.*

Surprisingly, the boy sat up. Pain flashed across his eyes, but also hatred. He rose shakily to his feet and strode toward Keris Chaterit, physically pushing Alanna away when she tried to stop him. "I said I know you, Monster!" he shrieked again, shoving one hand into his pack. "I know why you strike at night, or only when you conjure darkness to shield yourself. I know why Blor shattered the globe of *sekoy'melin*. The light makes you burn! Well, I'm going to burn you, Monster! Burn you until you die!"

Danyel flung the pack away. In his hands he held the Coleman camping lantern that Eric and Robert had brought with them through the gateway. Eric had completely forgotten it. The boy hit the switch. An intense white light flooded the sanctum.

A psychic wave of terror and agony swept out from the hole as Keris Chaterit screamed. Lightnings shot wildly around the chamber, crackling and hissing. A bolt danced across Eric's arm. It seemed weaker than the bolt that had struck his brother, yet still it left a red scorch on his flesh.

Blor scrambled up from the floor. "Nooooo!" she wailed. She ran at Danyel, her hands grasping for the lantern. But Alanna intercepted her, locking one arm viciously around the fat woman's throat and dragging her down to the floor again.

"Burn, damn you!" Danyel shouted as he advanced toward the hole. The lightnings zeroed in on him, striking him again and again until he glowed with scarlet fire. Still he refused to fall. He drew back his arm and threw the shining lantern. Straight into the hole it sailed.

Keris Chaterit screamed again, and his despair filled the chamber. The lightnings seized immediately, and for an instant, the hole shone with the brilliance of a sun gone nova. Eric screamed and flung up an arm to shield his eyes as he hurled himself protectively across his brother.

He wasn't sure how long he lay there before Robert whispered, "It's all right, big brother. It's over."

Eric sat up. The only source of light was the dim red glow that emitted from within the two cauldrons. That poor radiance was enough to show them Danyel's smoking form stretched on the floor nearby.

A familiar smell hung thick in the air, a smell that reminded him of the trench.

He scrambled over to the boy and stopped without touching him. His hair and brows were singed away. The skin on the right side of his face had melted to reveal the cheekbone. His right eye was gone. All that remained of his clothes was ashes and charred strips. "Mew?" he said helplessly, one hand hovering. He wanted to gather the kid in his arms, but he knew the pain it would cause. "Mew?"

Mew gave no answer. Nor would he ever.

A snarl came from behind him, then Blor screamed twice. Astride the fat woman, Alanna filled her hands with hair and slammed Blor's head against the stone tiles three times before Robert dragged her off. After the third impact, the librarian screamed no more. A pool of blood spread under her.

Eric held his breath. Alanna stood up and shoved Robert away from her as she glared at Blor's body. "Come on!" she shouted, her face contorted with rage, her hands curled into fists. "Come on!"

Blor's soul, made visible somehow, rose up out of her body into the air and turned toward Alanna. Its hands opened, clawlike, and its eyes gleamed with a vengeful fury. But before it could harm the dragonrider, another *dando* appeared between them. Phlogis, swollen in size and stature, seized the smaller soul and ripped it in half before it could even utter a cry. He cast the pieces into the cauldrons, which flared briefly and dimmed.

Alanna seemed enraged by the interference. She glanced at Blor. Then at Phlogis again. Slowly she seemed to realize what she had done. Robert, on his feet again, reached out for her, but she batted his arms away, turned, and fled into the outer darkness.

Eric watched her go, then glanced at his brother before he bent over Danyel again. Was this what it was like for Robert, bending over his friend Scott Silver this way? He raised his fists and slammed them down on the stone. "My God!" he screamed helplessly. "My God!"

Robert came, slumped down, and wrapped his arms around him. Phlogis was gone too. Alone, in the darkness, they cried together.

Chapter Fourteen

DRESSED only in soft trousers of loose white leather, Robert flowed through the movements of the Gankaku kata with slow precision, every gesture fluid, like quiet water. His skin glowed with a fine sheen of sweat in the red light cast by a pair of braziers that stood on either side of the great sculpture of Taedra.

Alanna moved at his side like a shadow. Her technique lacked power, but that would come. She was learning rapidly. Blor's death had left a subtle mark on her though. In a moment of anger she had violated her own code and killed. He could see it in her eyes between the lessons as her thoughts returned to that moment, replayed it over and over. It would haunt her for a long time. He knew.

A muffled wail broke the silence of the chapel and caused them both to pause before the kata was complete. Robert looked at Alanna as she stared toward the ceiling. "Shadowfire," she said needlessly.

The dragon's cry sounded again, reaching even this deep level of Sheren-Chad. For days and nights it had flown circles around the tower, disappearing toward the mountains sometimes but always returning to call and call for Danyel. Its cry could be heard throughout the city.

Robert picked up his shirt, wadded it and wiped his chest and armpits. "That's enough," he told Alanna. He wasn't in the mood to work out anymore. His thoughts kept turning toward home, toward the Catskills and Dowdsville.

Draping the shirt over one shoulder, he left the chapel and sought his room in the upper levels. The window by his bed was unshuttered. He sprawled on his back on the mattress, folded his arms under his head, and stared out. The day was balmy, the sky bright blue.

He got up a few minutes later. A shadow eclipsed the light beyond the shutters, and Shadowfire let go another wail. The dragon's voice sounded clearer, louder up here with fewer walls to muffle it. Its pain cut Robert like a knife. There was nothing he could do, though. The bond between rider and *sekoye* was a strong one, Alanna had told him. When it was broken the beast either starved itself, refusing to eat from grief, or turned wild again.

He paced to the washbasin in the corner of his room and splashed a little water on his face. A quick toweling, and he turned. The unicorn horn hung on the nail on the opposite wall in its makeshift scabbard. But something else hung there too. A silver chain with a small silver medallion. Hesitant at first, he took it down and placed it around his neck. The metal felt cool against his skin.

He and Eric each had one, gifts from Phlogis. With the medallions they could travel the gateways between Paradane and Palenoc. Home was not so far away now. He could go if he wished. The

thought turned over and over in his head as he
tried to decide.

Pulling on a fresh shirt from his wardrobe, he
left his room, walked down the hall, and knocked
on his brother's door. No answer. Of course not.
Eric would be on the roof. He walked up a couple
of levels instead to Phlogis's sanctum. In the two
weeks since Danyel's death, he had spent quite a
bit of time with the *dando* seeking with him answers to some of his questions. The answers were
few and far between though. Still, he couldn't
shake the certain feeling that, somehow, he had
been to Palenoc before.

He knocked on the sanctum doors. A moment
later, one creaked back, and Roderigo Diez greeted
him with a smile. "Roberto!" he said pleasantly.

Maris appeared just behind the old Spaniard.
"Come in, Robert." She spoke in a small, soft voice
that nevertheless commanded authority. "We poor
students have just finished with our lessons today."

He entered the sanctum and Diez pulled the door
closed again. Eleven white-robed figures filed out
through the small door in the opposite wall. Only
Maris remained. "I see Guran has a complete council again," he commented.

Maris nodded. The stubble showed on her head
in the crimson light from the cauldrons. Her hair
was beginning to grow back. "The final two came
in last night," she told him.

He looked around the chamber and toward the
mysterious circle. "I was hoping to see Phlogis," he
said.

"I know he wants to see you," Diez replied. "It
is daylight, though. He won't take corporeal form."

Nonsense.

Robert steeled himself for the psychic rush of anger he knew would come. The wispy figure of an old man regarded him with baleful eyes from the center of the circle. Phlogis hovered a few feet above the floor, the hem of his robe stirring lightly in some draft, his hands folded into voluminous sleeves.

"Have you any news at all?" Robert asked with a greater sense of urgency than he had felt in days.

Go to the cauldrons, Phlogis instructed. *Gaze within.*

Robert had long since lost his dread of Phlogis's magic. He walked to one of the two copper cauldrons, leaned on the edge, and stared. His face lit up with a red glow, and he felt the strange light like waves of warmth on his skin. But all he saw in the cauldron was a deep and bottomless blackness.

> *Sing Woe! Remember*
> *And pity us our plight!*
> *The dead dwell in the Dark Lands*
> *And the Kingdoms of Night!*

Robert shot a harsh look toward the circle again. "How do you know those words?" he demanded. "I wrote them! They're from my novel!"

The dead dwell in the Dark Lands, Phlogis repeated thoughtfully, offering no other explanation. *Your friend is there, Robert.* The *dando* sorcerer pointed at the cauldron. The darkness within began to swirl, and an image of Scott's face regarded him placidly from the stygian depths, his blond hair floating on the black currents as if they were water. *Alive or dead, I cannot say. But Scott Silver is in the Dark Lands.*

"She has him?" He didn't need to say more.

Phlogis nodded. *That is my belief.*

Maris came and touched his arm, her concern clouding her features. "I'm sorry, Robert," she said, "for both you and your friend."

Robert leaned on the side of the cauldron and stared at Scott's face until the darkness stilled and the image faded away. He tasted his own anger like salt on the back of his tongue as he straightened.

We will find him, Robert Podlowsky, the *dando* promised. *The new council agrees. We owe you this for the service you have done Guran. We will free either his body or his spirit from her thrall.*

Robert pressed two fingers to his lips and thought, *Scott in her hands!* The idea chilled him to the bone. Body or spirit, Phlogis had said. He was still no closer to solving that mystery. There was one way to solve it, though. Illegal. Possibly dangerous. But certain.

"I'm going home," he announced, moving away from the cauldrons and going to the edge of the gilt circle. "I've got to know what, if anything, lies in Scott's grave."

"Use the gateway near Chalosa," Maris suggested, touching his arm again. "A guardian will always be there, one of my own people, to assist you, as there was long ago before that gate was forgotten."

Robert remembered the crumbling old shack above the cave and nodded. He and Phlogis had talked some about the gates. There were many, some known, some forgotten, others not yet discovered, scattered across Palenoc. They could no longer be used easily, though. Something to do with the shattering of the moon, Mianur, which now made the pale blue ring in the Palenoc night. Now the gates required a key. He touched the small medallion at his neck again.

When will you leave us, Son of Paradane? Phlogis asked with a surprising hint of sorrow in his mind-voice.

"I don't know," Robert answered. "Soon. I'll need to talk it over with Eric."

Roderigo Diez came closer. "He's on the rooftop."

Robert blew a little stream of air and chewed the corner of his lower lip. "I know. He's been up there for days. I'd better go see how he's doing." He thanked Phlogis, knowing the energy the *dando* had expended to generate a form and deliver his news personally. Then he said his good-byes to Maris.

"I'll come with you, if you don't mind," Diez suggested as Robert turned to him. "I have something for your brother."

They walked from the sanctum together and up the stairs to the lavatorium and the rooftop. At one point Robert frowned, but he decided to speak his mind. "Roderigo," he said, pausing on a stair. "We've had our disagreements, you and I. But I want to thank you for the friendship you've given Eric."

Diez stared at him wide-eyed. "I hope I am your friend, too, Roberto."

Robert pursed his lips, then bobbed his head up and down. "Are you . . ." He hesitated again, then changed his approach. "Blor meant a lot to you, didn't she?"

Sadness clouded the old physician's features, and Robert wished he hadn't mentioned it. But Diez looked up suddenly and shook his head. "She took me in completely," he answered with a voice full of regret. "But when she attacked me outside the chamber there was such hatred in her eyes. I thought she meant to kill me."

"She didn't," Robert reminded him gently. Blor had, in fact, rendered Diez unconscious with a dart like the ones Alanna sometimes used. "Could she have been possessed by Keris Chaterit? Like Terre-borne's king?"

Diez put on a small, weary smile. "No, Roberto." Diez gave a sigh and started up the stairs again. "I've lived in Palenoc a long time now, and I've seen it happen before. Every person has their private motives for serving good or evil. I thought I knew Blor. But I didn't."

Robert touched the mechanism at the top of the stairs that opened the outer door and then stepped out onto the rooftop. The sudden sunlight made him blink and shield his eyes. A new globe of *sek-oy'melin* rested atop the tripod that straddled the doorway. Three days ago he had watched as a pair of dragonriders and their mounts carried it, suspended in massive ropes, up from the shores of the Great Lake and lowered it into place. It had been an awesome operation.

Eric hadn't noticed him yet. He stood leaning on the parapet, singing an old Appalachian folk song in a less-than-impressive baritone, watching Shadowfire fly around and around the tower. He looked thin and weary as he slumped against the stone. He'd slept little since Danyel's death and eaten next to nothing.

Shadowfire swept past again, his huge mouth opening to emit a mournful trill.

Robert and Diez exchanged looks, then went to stand on either side of Eric. His brother hadn't shaved in days. A dark, patchy stubble colored his pale cheeks. He needed a bath and a change of leathers.

"What was that you were singing?" Robert said conversationally. " 'Wagoner's Lad'? I haven't heard that in years."

Eric gave the barest shrug. "I've tried everything," he said. "Every song I know. Valis says he'll die."

Robert could think of nothing to say. He'd never seen his brother in such a bleak mood. The loss of Danyel had affected them all, but none as much as Eric. Not even Valis's return had been able to lure him down from his watch on the rooftop.

Roderigo Diez reached into the purse on his belt and drew out a cloth-wrapped object. "*Sekoye* never bond a second time," he replied quietly. "But I've brought you something. Robert told me you could play this." He pushed the object within reach of Eric's hand.

Eric looked at him strangely, then unwrapped the Spaniard's gift and held it up. It was a small Hohner harmonica, silver and wood, crafted with fine scrolling lines. The sun gleamed on the newly polished metal.

"I brought it with me when I left Paradane for the final time," Diez explained. "I used to blow a little when I was younger, and my little Paloma would laugh and dance." He forced a smile and clapped Eric on the shoulder. "I've lost the skill, but maybe you can do something with it."

Eric tapped it on his palm and nodded wordlessly. Diez clapped his shoulder once more before he turned away and strolled to the far side of the tower, where he peered over the side toward the Great Lake.

"I won't let him die, Bobby," Eric murmured when they were alone. He lifted the harmonica and blew a short riff. The sound quality was still quite good after so many years.

It was not despair that drove his brother, Robert realized suddenly, hearing those words, but determination. He watched as Shadowfire flashed by again, cutting the air with the majestic sweep of his wings. Even in the daylight, without the shimmering radiance that filled those pinions, the dragon was a beautiful beast. It would be a shame to lose him.

But Robert didn't want to lose Eric either. "Why don't you come down and eat something?" Robert urged. "Shadowfire isn't served by your starving too."

Eric shook his head firmly. "He can hear me," he answered through clenched teeth. "The damn stubborn beast! I know he can. He knows I'm here."

Robert made a vague attempt at humor. "Maybe he doesn't like your singing. No one else ever did."

Eric balanced the harmonica between his hands. "I don't have to sing anymore," he said. A sweet tune flowed out, a sad and wistful melody. Robert recognized the strains of an old blues song, "Gloomy Sunday." Eric played it straight through, pouring his heart into the music, and when it was done, he began it again.

Shadowfire cried but flew by without even glancing at Eric. Still Eric played.

Robert saw Roderigo Diez watching them from the far side of the rooftop, and he went to join the old man. Together they leaned back against the parapet and folded their arms. "It's sad," Diez said heavily, "but there's nothing he can do." He closed his eyes briefly and listened to the harmonica. "It's good that he plays so well, though. Maybe the music will heal his own heart."

"You have him wrong," Robert responded in a whisper as he regarded his brother with pride. "That's not grief you see over there. That's steel."

The dragon screamed again. The harmonica sang.

"Tchai!" Roderigo Diez shouted suddenly. Fear filled his face, and he started forward. "What's he doing?"

Robert caught his small arm in a firm grip. "Leave him alone," he said, watching his brother climb up on the wall. Eric stood tall, his head back as he blew the harmonica. The wind whipped his dirty leathers and ripped through his hair. Suddenly the music stopped. Eric tensed and took a step toward the edge as Shadowfire swept around the tower.

"What's he doing?" Diez shrieked again. With a ferocious effort he wrenched his arm free and ran across the roof. But he was far too late.

Becoming Taedra, Robert said to himself.

Eric spread his arms and sprang into space. For a moment he hung there, limned with sunlight, like a glorious sculpture of a beautiful angel. The harmonica, too, clutched to his fist, caught a ray of light and bent it fantastically so that it blazed like a sword of fire as he started to fall.

When Eric disappeared below the rim of the tower, Robert at last dashed forward, not from fear but with a heart full of certainty at what he would see. Shadowfire screamed but was nowhere in sight.

An instant later the great beast rose. Eric dangled precariously, both hands locked around Danyel's saddle horn. As Robert reached the wall and leaned outward, his brother pulled himself up, found the stirrup and climbed into the saddle.

"He's always complaining about the crazy risks I take," Robert said with a bemused smirk. Eric raised one triumphant fist, then put the harmonica to his mouth again. Only the dimmest strains of the music reached the tower as Shadowfire turned away and flew over Rasoul toward the blue peaks in the east.

"This is amazing!" Diez shouted, dancing up and down. "*Sekoye* never bond twice!" He stared after the rapidly shrinking forms of dragon and dragonrider, and after a moment he grew quiet. "Where will he go?"

"To the mountains," Robert answered, grinning. "It's where he always goes when he's happy or sad." He slapped his palms down on the stone wall and bit his lip to keep from laughing. He felt good! For himself and for Eric. "He's not going to need me for a while, so I can't think of a better time for that trip back home." He turned and started for the stairway, then paused there long enough to cast one more glance toward Eric and Shadowfire. The two were small figures in the vast blue of the Palenoc sky, and growing smaller.

"You shouldn't go without him," Diez cautioned. "You're a team. Brothers of the Dragon."

Robert gave him a sardonic smile and remembered how Eric used to treat Danyel. He reached out and rumpled the nonexistent hair on Diez's bald head. "We're all Brothers of the Dragon, old sod," he said. "All of us who fight together. Be-

sides, Eric belongs here now. And I'll be back."
He clapped his hands together, brightening, as he
continued. "But you know what? Right now I'm
starved, and nobody should ever be sent off without a farewell feast."

Diez gave a small sigh, and his gaze took on a
mischievous twinkle. "I think I can arrange something," he said. He put his arm around Robert, and
they went down together.

As the door slowly closed, a dragon's cry and the
faint strains of a silver harmonica echoed across
the distance.

THE world of Palenoc was once closely connected to our own Earth (or Paradane, as they call it on Palenoc), but most of the gates between the worlds were destroyed in one of the magical battles between the Dominions of Light and the Heart of Darkness.

Although both worlds are related, Palenoc has gone in a different direction than Earth; where we developed technology, they developed spiritual awareness. Ghosts are real, and a part of everyday life. Crystals are used to channel inner energies for healing or—more darkly—destruction. Dragons and unicorns serve the faces of good and evil, both of which are more open and clear than in our own world.

Palenoc remains connected to Earth, even if travel between them is no longer easy. If the Heart of Darkness is successful in wiping out the last strongholds of the Dominions of Light, our own world will fall just as surely as Palenoc.

The Dragon: Its immense wings, glowing with some strange bioluminescence, gracefully pinion the air. The light from its wings washes the land below with a pale yellowish illumination.

Sekoye: These giant winged creatures bond for life with a single human, communicating through song or music. The dragons are characterized by their beautiful luminescence. No two *sekoye* glow in exactly the same shade and pattern.

Chimorg: These evil unicorns were once men, but have mutated beyond recognition. They retain human intelligence, and act as the eyes and ears of Darkness on Palenoc. Tough and vicious, *chimorg* are nearly immortal.

The Battle at Chalosa: Eric struck with his best punch. The warrior screamed as he flew through the air.

After the Battle: For the first time, Eric noticed the still figure that lay on the ground at the rear of the alley . . .

Rasoul: Most of the buildings in this city are low and dark, seldom more than two stories tall. Here and there, a single minaret or tower thrusts up against the night.

The Key to the Gate: The ornament sparkled in the Coleman's light. One side had been polished to mirror brilliance. The lettering caught the Coleman's glow and shot back rays of silver.

Snared! A face floated out there in the night. Her hair drifted like a mist about her face, and her lips were the color of a rose with bloody thorns.

Evil Speaks: A priest of Darkness prepares his sacrifice.

You are invited to preview the next book in the exciting saga of *Brothers of the Dragon: Hands of a Dragon,* coming to you from ROC in early 1994.

The smell of burnt timber wafted in the air. Plumes and wisps of gray smoke curled up from the fire-ravaged ruins of homes and shops. Smoldering posts and planks jutted at awkward angles, some yet flickering with tongues of blue flame.

A dog wandered up and down the only street, sniffing the ground and whining forlornly, its eyes round and empty, its tail between its legs. In a blackened front yard, a pair of fat chickens pecked at the scorched grass. A red-crowned rooster perched imperiously on the shoulder of a dead little girl.

Bodies lay everywhere.

"What could have done this?" Alanna spoke softly, her eyes full of horror and anger. Her fingers curled tightly around her blowpipe, the knuckles straining at the fabric of her leather gloves. "The fire alone couldn't be responsible."

Eric shook his head and stopped as they reached the center of the town. Alanna continued to the end of the road until she stood by the charred ruins of a pier that had once reached out into the wide river. The afternoon sun glinted on her smooth leather garments as she gazed down into the water. The wind stirred her black hair.

Evander and Doe stopped beside Eric. Tall and

slender, the two men could have passed for brothers. They leaned on the staves they carried, adopt-
ing almost identical postures as they stared about
with grim expressions. Neither seemed inclined to
speak. Doe had been the first to spot the cloud of
smoke from the air and suggest they delay their
mission to Wysotoweem and investigate, but none
of them had expected to find this.

A young woman lay beside the road in the
shadow of a crude picket fence that the flames had
not touched. Eric knelt beside her, rolled her gently onto her back, and pushed the strands of black
hair from her face. Wide brown eyes stared blankly
up at him. He eased them closed with his left
thumb and forefinger. Maybe seventeen, he
guessed. Quite pretty, too.

A shadow fell over him, and he glanced up as
Evander bent closer.

"Not a mark on her," Eric commented in a
muted voice.

"Maybe she inhaled too much smoke before she
managed to get outside," Evander suggested.

Eric frowned. "No," he answered, tight-lipped.
"Look how she's lying here." He pointed from the
fence gate to a pair of smoking doorposts and the
collapsed structure of which they were a part.
"Her head is toward the house, not away from it.
And from the look on her face, she was scared.
Terrified. I think she was running inside."

"From something she saw in the street?" Evander
suggested.

Doe crept up to join them. "The fire must have
started later," he said. In his right hand he held a
child's doll. He set it down in the crook of the dead
woman's arm. "If there was some panic, somebody

could have bumped a lantern or dropped a candle. That's all it would take to destroy a village like this."

Eric moved through the gate into the yard. The rooster squawked and ran behind the ruins, wings aflutter. The hens scuttled the other way. A random breeze blew a tendril of smoke that swirled around the dead girl and evaporated.

Like the woman in the street, there was no visible mark on her. Eric bent down and began to loosen her clothes.

"What are you doing?" Alanna called over the fence as she pressed between Evander and Doe to get through the gate.

Eric tore open the neck of the child's frock. "Looking for darts," he answered matter-of-factly.

Alanna put on a disdainful look as she leaned over him. "Are you suggesting these people were murdered?" She shook her head, glancing to Evander and Doe for support. It was plain enough the idea appalled her. "Not a whole village! Who would dare?"

Out-and-out murder was rare on Palenoc, and for reasons Eric knew well. In this world so different from his own Earth, ghosts were real, and the victim's spirit almost always sought revenge on the murderer. That didn't mean Palenoc was free from killing, though. Subtle men found subtle means, and something or someone had ended these villagers' lives.

"The fire didn't kill that little one," Doe said stonily from the gate as he regarded the child's body. "Nor this one here." He looked down at the woman by his feet.

"A fire by itself would have left survivors,"

Evander added as he leaned on his staff and let go a soft sigh. His watchful gaze swept the village and the edge of the thick forest that surrounded it.

Alanna bit her lip as she knelt down by the child. "Let me do it," she insisted. With gentler hands she began to remove the little girl's clothes, shifting her position so that she blocked the men's view.

Eric rose and walked back into the street. Perplexed, he rubbed one hand over the crown of his head as he stared around. He hated puzzles. Particularly in Palenoc where the answers so often were deadly.

He strode down by the river. The Kultari, he remembered from the maps he had studied before beginning this journey. In his own world it would have been the Missouri. The pier at the end of the road was burned away. Some of the boats, however, had escaped the flames. Yet, the villagers hadn't used them. Whatever struck them down had done it swiftly.

The dog gave a low whine and brushed against his leg, looking up at him with moist, begging eyes. He reached down and patted its head. Its tail lifted a bit, and after that it stayed right by his side.

Evander came up behind him. "Alanna didn't find any mark."

Eric hadn't thought she would. One man with a blowpipe couldn't have taken out the entire village, and a band of raiders would have left some evidence. Same with an army. Damn.

"That's Markmor, isn't it?" Eric said as he pointed to the land across the river. Markmor was one of the largest nations in the Dark Lands, an alliance of kingdoms under the sway of the mysterious Shandal Karg.

Evander nodded. "The Kultari forms the border between Markmor and Shad."

Eric pursed his lips. Shad was but one of the Gray Kingdoms, a group of ostensibly independent buffer states positioned uncomfortably between the warring Dark Lands and the Domains of Light. Their allegiances were ever shifting as they sought to steer clear of the conflict.

Evander laid a gloved hand lightly on Eric's arm. "I know that look, my friend," he said in a near whisper. He, too, turned his gaze across the water toward Markmor. "Do you still dream of Her?"

The moisture suddenly left Eric's throat and his tongue felt too thick in his mouth. For a moment the world seemed to vanish, and an ivory face floated before him, framed by the night and by a swirl of shimmering black hair. He had never tasted those ruby lips, though he knew their honeyed flavor. He had never met those coldly laughing eyes, though they threatened to draw the soul from his body.

She was Shandal Karg, though few dared to speak her name aloud. Most called her the Heart of Darkness.

Eric had never been this close to the Dark Lands before. Suddenly every tree and bush on the other side of the Kultari seemed to hide a pair of spying eyes.

"They're only dreams," Evander reminded him as he sought to draw him away from the river.

Eric knew his friend was wrong. They were more than dreams. There was no point in arguing about it, though. Not now. They had a mission. And now, they also had a mystery.

By his knee, the dog suddenly stiffened and gave

a low growl. Eric became instantly alert. "What is it, boy?" he said, stroking the pooch's head, peering around, himself. "Hmmm? You smell something?"

The dog gave a sharp bark and shied away from Eric. It barked again and bared its teeth. Then, it let go with a howl and disappeared across one of the yards and behind the still-smouldering wreckage of a barn.

Alanna and Doe ran down the street toward them. "Magoths!" Alanna cried as she waved a hand in the direction from which they had come. "At least three. Probably more!"

Before she could explain, a huge shaggy shape lumbered on two powerful legs around the remains of a smoking wall. Arms thick as tree trunks hung down to its knees. Its dull brown fur was tangled and matted with bits of leaves and twigs. The magoth was not a man, but neither was it an ape. It stood too easily erect and moved with a startling grace for a monster its size. It hesitated, sniffing the air.

A second magoth moved around the corner. Small dark eyes peered intensely through a mask of fur at the four humans. The beast snarled, showing teeth and four-inch fangs. The first one ignored its foul-tempered mate. It bent over the body of the woman by the fence, picked up the doll Doe had placed in her arms, and regarded it curiously before casting it aside with a disinterested flip of its wrist. It crouched lower, then, arms between its legs, and sniffed the body.

"Stay absolutely still. Magoths are scavengers." Just then Eric heard a loud, nauseating crunch.